"I know you don't like fighting, but do you ever at least fight yourself?"

Greg inched forward.

"Wh-what do you mean?" Shannon asked.

"I mean, say there's something you want that you know you shouldn't have. Say, cheese and pepperoni pizza. You know it's all wrong for you. It's never going to work. But you want it. It looks delicious." He planted his palms on the wall on either side of her head, then leaned in, nuzzled her shoulder and inhaled deeply as he skimmed the curve of her neck. "It smells fantastic. Do you fight with yourself over tasting it? Or do you just take a bite?"

"I–" She lowered her gaze to his mouth. The tip of her tongue darted out, moistening her lips, and Greg's hormones jumped to attention like a superhero to a beacon light in the night sky. "Fighting's wrong," she murmured. "Don't fight it. Taste it."

He bent his elbows, letting his body weight ease against her.

"Is that your utility belt," she muttered, "or are you happy to see me?"

Dear Reader,

It's so good to be back! I've missed sharing stories with you.

Isn't it interesting how our past influences the people we become? The good, the bad, the ugly… all the things that happen to us color the way we look at life.

I'd like to introduce you to Shannon Vanderhoff, a woman whose past has made her who she is at the start of this story—and to Ryan, her six-year-old nephew, who's going to change her. With some help from comic-book artist/art therapist Greg Hawkins and his enormous family, it's Ryan who's going to rescue Shannon, not the other way around.

I've had a lot of fun with this book. I mean, what's more fun than superheroes, comic books and impish kids who love the story *The Ransom of Red Chief*?

I hope you enjoy it.

I'd love to hear from you! Please visit my Web site, www.susangable.com, e-mail me at Susan@susangable.com or send me a letter at P.O. Box 9313, Erie, PA 16505.

Susan Gable

A KID TO THE RESCUE
Susan Gable

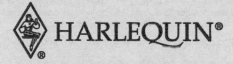

HARLEQUIN®

TORONTO • NEW YORK • LONDON
AMSTERDAM • PARIS • SYDNEY • HAMBURG
STOCKHOLM • ATHENS • TOKYO • MILAN • MADRID
PRAGUE • WARSAW • BUDAPEST • AUCKLAND

Recycling programs
for this product may
not exist in your area.

ISBN-13: 978-0-373-71545-9
ISBN-10:   0-373-71545-5

A KID TO THE RESCUE

www.eHarlequin.com

Printed in U.S.A.

ABOUT THE AUTHOR

Susan Gable's love of reading goes back to her preschool days, when books arrived at her house through the Weekly Readers Book Club. Both her parents are voracious readers, and they passed that on to their daughter. Susan shared her love of books (and Weekly Reader!) as an elementary teacher for ten years, then turned to writing after a year of homeschooling her son caused her to nearly lose what was left of her mind. Writing, it turns out, is cheaper than therapy, and homeschooling is way harder than teaching other people's kids. Susan is a Waldenbooks bestselling author. Her books have been Golden Heart and RITA® Award finalists, and twice nominated by *Romantic Times BOOKreviews* for Best Superromance of the Year. In addition, she's won numerous awards, including the National Readers' Choice Award. She has been praised by readers and reviewers alike for her ability to tell emotionally compelling stories that make them laugh and cry.

Books by Susan Gable

HARLEQUIN SUPERROMANCE
1103—THE BABY PLAN
1150—THE MOMMY PLAN
1204—WHOSE CHILD?
1285—THE PREGNANCY TEST

Don't miss any of our special offers. Write to us at the following address for information on our newest releases.

Harlequin Reader Service
U.S.: 3010 Walden Ave., P.O. Box 1325, Buffalo, NY 14269
Canadian: P.O. Box 609, Fort Erie, Ont. L2A 5X3

Dedicated in loving memory:

Of Susan Harmon, who always believed
there'd be another book.
Sus, you're missed so very much.
Storytelling's not the same without you.

And of Deandra Francis May,
who left her family way too young.
Dee, we're never letting go.
You'll stay in our hearts forever.

Special thanks to:

Stacey Konkel, Esquire, for answering
my numerous family law questions.

Jack Daneri, Esquire, for answering a million
criminal law questions and being a good sport
that a romance author, not a thriller writer,
consulted him with legal questions.

Holly, for always encouraging me to keep fighting.

Jen and Diana, tireless CPs, always there to lend
encouragement and tell me where I'd gone off track.
Di, thanks for making me laugh.

Victoria and Wanda, for bringing me back into the
Superromance lineup and making this book so much
stronger.

Tom and TJ. Living with a writer is never easy. Thanks
for understanding when I disappeared into the office
and appeared to have forgotten your existence in favor
of my imaginary friends. Do we have any clean socks?

CHAPTER ONE

FOR THE UMPTEENTH TIME, Greg Hawkins glanced at the observation window—the one that reflected into the room he used at Erie University's Children's Center—and wished he had superpowers.

Nothing spectacular, mind you. Just the ability to see and hear through walls. To know who was staring at him this time.

At least a goldfish in a bowl could stare back.

"*Kerpow! Kerpow!*" At the far end of the table, one of Greg's kids wiggled in his chair, banging his fist on the cluttered surface and sending colored pencils rolling in all directions. "Mr. Hawkins, how do you spell kerpow? I want to write it big."

"Kerpow, huh?" He jotted it on a scrap of paper and passed it down the table, sneaking a covert look at his watch as he did. They were more than halfway through the session and Julie still wasn't here. It wasn't usually a good sign when one of his kids was late. Especially this late. Without a parent calling him.

Just three weeks earlier they'd lost Scotty, a member of the group, and Greg didn't think any of them—not him, not the kids, nor their parents—were ready to deal with another setback. Hopefully there was another explanation.

"Okay, guys, quick five-minute break. Take a stretch,

look at what everyone else has been doing." While the kids got up from their chairs, he pulled out his cell, checking for messages.

"I need a drink of water," Cheryl announced as she headed for the door.

"And I have to go to the can," Michael said, following on her heels.

"Hold it. Earlier I let you get a drink—" he pointed at Michael "—and you—" he moved his finger to Cheryl "—go to the bathroom. What's going on?"

Cheryl turned in the doorway, hands behind her back. She shrugged her shoulders, but her face had gone white. That concerned him. Guilt, or not feeling well? Michael, meanwhile, danced in place, attempting, no doubt, to convince Greg of the urgency of the situation. "Got a drink before, now I have to take a leak. In one end and out the other, right?"

"Thanks for the biology lesson, professor. Be back in five. We have work to finish." Greg flipped his phone closed. No messages.

While the other three kids milled around the room, and the unseen eyes on the other side of the observation window watched, he doodled a clock, hands racing around the face, springs exploding from the side. Time. The enemy of all.

The enemy of his program.

The new university dean was on a mad cost-cutting rampage, and had made it clear that Greg's art therapy program was near the top of the chopping block. She believed his program would be better run through one of the local hospitals, or cancer centers, or even one of the social services organizations.

And being that the university provided him with

space he'd otherwise have to purchase or rent, utilities, an umbrella of insurance, grad students to do the grunt work... A serious amount of money would be needed to fill the gap if he couldn't find someone else to take on his program.

He was funded through the end of the summer semester. Unless he convinced Dean Auld otherwise, time was up in August.

"All right, you guys, back to it." The kids didn't need much encouragement and returned to their places and drawings.

Except the two who'd left the room and were still missing in action.

It was the action part that had him worried. Michael and his sidekick Cheryl, ever faithful though of late slow moving, were undoubtedly up to trouble.

He didn't need superhero powers to sense it. Being the uncle to almost a baker's-dozen kids—one of his sisters was due in two months with nephew thirteen— and having been a boy himself, he just knew it. He had a soft spot for Michael, in part because the boy shared his name with Greg's dad. But soft didn't mean he'd give the kid a free pass.

Sticking his head out the therapy-room door, he scanned the hallway. Big surprise, Cheryl wasn't at the water fountain on the corner. He couldn't see Michael, either. "You guys keep working. I'll be right back."

Greg turned toward the mirrored window, crossing his fingers Dean Auld wasn't behind it. "Watch them," he said, exaggerating the words in case the observers didn't have the speaker turned on. At the very least, they could make themselves useful.

At the men's room, a quick search revealed Michael

wasn't there. He rapped on the women's door next. "Cheryl? Are you in there?"

"Yeah, Mr. Hawkins. Sorry, but after I got a drink, I had to go to the bathroom again. I'll be right out." Suppressed giggling followed her confession.

Crap. "Do you know where Michael is?"

"Uh, no. Didn't he come back to the classroom yet?"

"If he had, would I be asking you?"

"Oh, right. I guess not."

"You have two more minutes. If you're not back by then, I'm coming in there after you."

"You wouldn't!" she shrieked. "This is the girls' room."

"Try me. You could be sick in there. It would be my duty to be sure you're okay."

"I'll be back to the classroom." Cheryl's voice was more subdued this time.

"If you see Michael on your way, tell him he's pushing it if he wants to keep working with me. I don't tolerate nonsense like this."

A loud gasp echoed in the bathroom. He didn't often threaten to kick kids out his program.

Satisfied she'd roust Michael, Greg hustled to the classroom, resisting the temptation to open the observation-room door and find out exactly who was in there. Low voices reached him as he passed.

Back inside, he walked around, praising the other children. Stopping at Cheryl's empty chair, he studied her four-panel page. An honest-to-goodness strip in the making, it had real potential. There was definitely art talent there, not that this was about talent. Still, he loved to nurture it when he found it.

The Dastardly Duo skittered in the door and into their seats next to each other, both out of breath. "Sorry,

Mr. H.," Michael said. "Didn't mean to take so long. I went for a stroll. Needed to stretch my legs, you know?"

Greg narrowed his eyes, but opted to let it go. No fire alarms had gone off; there hadn't been a flood coming out of the bathroom. "Cheryl, this looks great. I love your use of color here." He pointed to the first panel, where a flying dog carried a basket of treats toward a building labeled Cleveland Clinic—where Cheryl had had her tumor removed three months earlier.

She looked smugly at Michael, then beamed up at Greg. "Thank you." She elbowed the boy. "Come on. Show him."

"Are you crazy? No way."

"But it's great. I want him to see."

"No."

"Yes." Cheryl grabbed Michael's Penn State baseball cap and yanked it off his chemo-bald head.

"Cheryl! You know we don't touch people's caps in here," Greg scolded, reaching for the hat, then stopped, staring at the crown of Michael's head.

"See? Now if someone at school steals his hat, it won't matter. Because they'll think it's cool. Isn't it cool? Don't you love it?"

He had to admit, the superhero about to kick the snot out of a cancer-cell bad guy drawn in black Magic Marker actually looked good. Maybe Cheryl had a future as a tattoo artist. "Not bad, Cheryl. Still, I don't think Michael's mother is going to be happy when she sees this. What's wrong with working on paper like everyone else?"

"Michelangelo painted the Sistine Chapel ceiling," offered one of the others from the end of the table. "That's not paper."

"He didn't paint someone's head and besides, that was a commissioned work," Greg said.

"Does 'commissioned' mean someone asked for it?" Cheryl said. "'Cause Michael asked me to do this. And he paid me." She yanked a rumpled five-dollar bill from her pocket and displayed it proudly. "Now I'm a professional artist, Mr. Hawkins, just like you."

Greg swallowed his chuckle, turning it into a cough. Then, recalling that he was being watched, he pasted a stern look on his face. "Go to the bathroom, Michael, wet some paper towels and clean that off. With soap." Thank God they only used water-based art supplies, nothing permanent.

"Awwww, come on. At least let my mom see it first. Maybe it will make her laugh. She hasn't laughed in a long time." Michael made sad, puppy-dog eyes at him, a technique the ten-year-old had perfected with hospital nurses.

"You can't pull that face on another guy, kid. It only works on women."

"Damn. Well, it was worth a shot."

"Language, mister."

"Leapin' lizards, Batboy, it was worth a shot."

Greg struggled to keep a straight face at that one. Then the idea of what Michael's mom would say chased the fleeting humor away. "You seriously think your mother is going to laugh when she sees your head?"

The boy shrugged. "Like I said, it's worth a shot, don't you think?"

"Put your hat back on. Save the surprise for after you're out in the car, okay?"

The boy's grin returned as he crammed the cap back on his head. "You're cool, Mr. H. Thanks."

Greg wasn't sure Michael's mother would thank him.

If nothing else, it would remind her that despite her child's illness, he was still a kid. All boy and then some, despite his second bout of cancer. "Now, all of you, finish your work. On the *paper*. We've got ten minutes left."

The door flew open, crashing into the wall as Julie came barreling into the room, causing the drawings taped nearby to flutter upward, then slowly fall back into place. The group stared at her, pencils, crayons, markers, poised midstroke.

"Woo-hoo! Guess what, everybody? I did it." She waved a piece of paper in the air. "I kicked cancer's butt! I'm in remission."

"All right!" Greg caught the girl as she launched herself into his arms, lifting her up in a celebratory hug as a wave of relief washed over him. A win. Not a loss, but a win. Exactly what they needed right now. He glanced over her now-curly-haired head at her mom, who leaned against the door frame. He smiled.

Happy tears glistened in the woman's eyes, but didn't spill over. "Thank you," she said.

He just nodded, then set Julie back on her feet. "That means I owe you a special certificate, doesn't it?"

"Yes, you do. And you hafta make me a character in your next comic book, too."

While the rest of the kids hugged her—no more work was getting done today, that much was obvious—Greg thumbed through a folder he kept in his briefcase, looking for her certificate. He kept one prepared for each kid, showing it to them when they were down and needed some extra motivation. A lump filled his throat as he flipped past Scotty's to find the right one. It featured Julie in a flowing purple cape, one fist raised victoriously, booted foot on the "head" of a cancer-cell villain with black X's for eyes—because he was dead. Using a calligraphy marker, he inked in the date, then blew on it before presenting it to the girl with a flourish.

"There you are. I knew you could do it. And so can the rest of you. Say it with me…"

Voices blended together as they all shouted, "Captain Chemo kicks cancer's butt!"

"KICKS CANCER'S BUTT?" Shannon Vanderhoff raised a skeptical eyebrow at the social worker as they watched the commotion from the dimly lit observation room. "See? That proves my point. This man, this *comic-book artist*—" she let the phrase drip with as much scorn as she could muster "—encourages violence in children. Ryan hardly needs more violence around him. Besides, my nephew doesn't have cancer. I'm not sure why you wanted me to see this."

"Greg Hawkins isn't *just* a comic-book artist, Ms. Vanderhoff. He's got a master's degree in art therapy. And he doesn't only work with cancer kids. He's had amazing results with children who need empowering. Children like Ryan."

Shannon turned to the opposite window, moving closer and leaning her forehead against the glass. In this other room, set up like a mini preschool with a wide variety of toys and books on short shelves, Ryan sat at a low, kidney-shaped table. A social-work grad student was vainly trying to coax the boy into helping her assemble a wooden puzzle. "Really? Children like Ryan? So, he's worked with kids who've watched their father kill their mother? How many?"

"Well, I don't know if Greg's worked with kids exactly like Ryan. I just meant emotionally traumatized kids."

In the room, Ryan shook his head at the young blond woman, pushing the puzzle to the far end of the table. He rose from his chair and wandered to the bookshelves. Without being choosy, he pulled out a picture book and plunked down in a beanbag. He held the open book close to his face, effectively shutting out the student who'd followed him.

Shannon closed her eyes and drew in a deep breath. Breathe in, take what life hands you; hold it, accept it; breathe out, let it go.

The mantra had worked well for her up until almost two and a half months ago, in early February, when six-year-old Ryan had come to live with her. Neither one of them quite knew how to deal with what life had handed them this time.

His mother, her sister, dead.

His father, her brother-in-law, sitting in jail, awaiting trial.

Ryan, the nephew she'd only had personal contact with twice in his six years, living in Shannon's computer room, both of them struggling to come to grips with it all.

The social worker gently laid her hand on Shannon's shoulder. "You look completely exhausted."

Exhausted didn't begin to cover it. Shannon worked nights as a hotel auditor, doing bookkeeping. Finding a reliable babysitter hadn't been easy. And she wasn't getting much sleep during the day, since she had to take care of the boy. Single parenthood wasn't for the weak of body or spirit.

"I'm worried about you as well as Ryan. Please, speak to Greg. I think he can help. What have you got to lose by talking to him?"

Lose? "Absolutely nothing." Shannon straightened

up, moving from beneath the woman's palm and returning her attention to the scene in the art room. Parents who had come to claim their children had joined in the celebration and were exchanging hugs and high fives.

"Great. I'll go tell Greg you want to speak with him." The door to the observation room closed before Shannon could get another word out.

She took the opportunity to get a better look at Greg Hawkins, who'd spent most of the time in the classroom with his profile to her. Now he faced the window full on, talking animatedly to one of the parents.

She'd expected a geek—scrawny, thick glasses, pants hiked halfway to his armpits. What else would a comic-book artist look like?

Not like this. He was gorgeous, with features that could accurately be described as chiseled, high cheekbones that gave his face an angular appearance, a strong chin and a wide smile that put an extra spark in his—blue? green?—hard to say with the distance and window between them—eyes. Dark brown hair. He looked fit, too, in a blue striped shirt with its sleeves rolled up to his elbows and a pair of khakis.

He probably made superheroes jealous. And geeky alter-ego personas would sell out their identities for half the charm and confidence this guy oozed.

The social worker had reached his side, and after a few murmured words, Greg looked up at the window. Shannon almost took a step back, convinced he was gazing through the mirrored glass and actually seeing her. He nodded, to her or the young woman standing next to him? After a quick glance at his watch, he made his way through the throng, offering more nods and comments as he went. Several of the children were tugging on his arms, looking up at him with pleading expressions on their faces. The positive response— "Yes" was easy enough to lip-read—made the kids jump up and down, then he disentangled himself and headed out of the room.

Only a few moments later, he entered the narrow observation room. "Hi," he said, hand outthrust. "I'm Greg Hawkins. I understand you wanted to speak to me about...?"

"Shannon Vanderhoff. About my nephew." She briefly shook his hand, then gestured in Ryan's direction. "Miss Anderson seems convinced you can help him."

"But you're not so sure?"

She sighed, looking over at Ryan, who once again sat in a chair at the table, face propped in his palms so that only his sandy-blond hair showed. "Mr. Hawkins, no offense to you, but your specialty—"

"Comic books?"

"Yes, comic books. Superheroes. Big-busted women in tight clothes, weird creatures and people fighting. I don't think that's what my nephew needs. He's seen enough violence, thank you."

"Abused?" he asked. "Because I've worked with a number of abused kids. My program, which doesn't focus exclusively on using comic-book formats, gives kids back some sense of control in their lives."

"I don't know if I'd classify Ryan as abused. No one ever hit him, at least, not that we know of. I don't think his father meant him to see what he saw."

"Which is?"

"No one knows exactly what happened, except maybe Ryan. But in the end, my sister was dead. The police believe Ryan saw his father beat and strangle his mother."

Greg whistled softly. "Poor kid. That's hard to swallow. Watching your mom die, and not being able to do anything about it, that's got to make you feel kinda helpless."

"That's how I feel right now, too." Shannon splayed her hand across the glass. "I haven't been able to help him so far. I'm taking him to a therapist twice a week, but it doesn't matter because he won't speak. He won't play for play therapy. He barely sleeps, barely eats."

"And what about you?"

She turned to him, moved by the compassion in his eyes. Which she could now see were blue. "Me?"

"Yes. Have you talked to anyone? Are you eating? Sleeping?"

"As much as can be expected, I suppose."

Greg snapped his fingers. "I remember now. I saw this on the news. Philadelphia, right?"

"Yes. The media turned my sister's death into a circus. I was glad to get Ryan away from there. Here in Erie he's not so much a news story. I detest the idea of hauling him back there when the trial starts."

The man appeared pensive for a moment. "Listen, the parents and kids from my group are all going out for lunch to celebrate Julie's remission. Why don't you and Ryan come with us? Maybe you can both eat, we can talk, and you can check out some of my references. Let them tell you if they think I've made their kids more prone to violence or if they suddenly want to wear skin-tight outfits and try to fly off the garage roof." He smiled at her. "I'll even spring for the pizza and pop. So what have you got to lose?"

What was it with these people and their asking her what she had to lose? Most of the time she stood to lose nothing. Because Shannon didn't believe in keeping things, holding on to things. You couldn't lose what you didn't try to keep.

But Ryan...

Ryan was different. If she didn't do something, it was Ryan who stood to lose himself. Someone had to reach him.

"Pizza, huh?" She shrugged. "Sure, why not?"

"Your enthusiasm underwhelms me."

"Try not to take it personally, Mr. Hawkins. Look, I never had much use for superheroes. I don't believe in heroes or white knights of any sort. I believe in not expecting too much out of life, and being content with what you have." She pointed to Ryan, waited for the art therapist's gaze to follow. "But for that little boy in there, for him, I want more. So I'm willing to entertain the notion that superheroes and comic-book artists *might* just offer him some hope. Convince me."

CHAPTER TWO

PAULA'S PARLORS was actually two restaurants connected by an open archway between the pizza parlor and the ice-cream parlor. It was a big hit with Erie-area kids, as Greg knew quite well. They'd bumped three tables together, which though they now held sixteen people, still weren't as large as the dining-room table at his parents' house. That could accommodate twenty.

Greg watched the boy seated next to him. The kid wrinkled his nose at the slice of pizza on his plate.

"Looks weird, doesn't it?"

Ryan darted a glance at his aunt, who'd ordered the small artichoke hearts and goat cheese pie. She was currently at the far end of the table with her own food, talking to Cheryl's mother.

Julie, on Greg's other side, piped up, mouth full of half-chewed pepperoni pizza. "What the heck is an artichoke heart? Eeewww. Sounds gross."

"I'll bet you'd rather have this, huh?" Greg leaned across the table and grabbed another slice from the closest "normal" pie.

At a slight nod from the boy, Greg slipped the pizza on his plate, exchanging it for the gourmet slice that no six-year-old in his right mind would eat. Hell, Greg wouldn't eat it, either. Not even if it was served by his brother Finn, who was an accomplished chef. Come to think of it, it sounded exactly like something Finn would concoct.

"Aunt" Shannon certainly had odd taste in pizza.

If you discounted the puffy bags beneath her eyes that she'd tried, in vain, to cover with some kind of makeup, she was attractive enough. Not in the super-heroine sense, but more the girl next door. The kind the superheroes always fell for. Shoulder-length burnt-sienna hair. Milk-chocolate eyes. If he had to guess he'd estimate her to be around his own age, somewhere in the early to mid-thirties.

She carried herself with quiet, easygoing grace, someone comfortable with herself and her life.

Except when it came to her nephew.

She glanced up and caught Greg studying her. With a nod to Cheryl's mother, she picked up her plate and headed back to their end of the table. She did a double take as she slid into her chair. "Ryan, you ate that whole slice of pizza already? Wonderful. Do you want anther one?"

The kid ducked his head, pleading with Greg from beneath his lowered eyes.

"Wait a minute," Shannon said, hand hovering over the artichoke pie. "There were only two slices of this left. How come there are three here?"

Ryan's expression turned beseeching.

"He, uh, decided he wanted the pepperoni instead. We traded it in," Greg explained. "Artichoke's sort of an acquired taste."

"And how will he acquire the taste if he never tries it?"

Greg shrugged. "You've got a point."

"There are so many wonderful, interesting foods. It's a pity more people don't try to expand their horizons." With a sly grin that animated her face for the first time since they'd met, she lifted the metal pan and offered it to him. "How about you, Mr. Hawkins? Ever tried artichoke pizza before?"

"N-oo. Can't say that I have."

"Well, I think you should set a good example for the children. Try it. Just a taste. If you don't like it, you don't have to eat it."

Julie giggled, then covered her mouth with her hands. Her mom also chuckled. Ryan's eyes widened. The challenge was passed from kid to kid around the table, like a lightning-fire version of the telephone game, until all conversation stopped and everyone turned to look at him.

She'd thrown down the gauntlet.

With a wink at Ryan, Greg took a slice. He slowly lifted it to his mouth, pausing to dart a quick glance with raised eyebrows at each of the kids, who all shook their heads, several of them calling out, "Don't do it!"

Like a connoisseur checking a fine wine, he inhaled deeply. "Smells okay," he reported. Not as tasty as pepperoni, or sausage. But he wasn't about to admit that.

He chomped a third of the piece, chewing with an exaggerated motion, rocking his head back and forth as if considering the flavor. He swallowed. It was edible, better than some things he'd had—Finn's frog leg gumbo experiment, for example—but not something he'd go out of his way to order in the future. "Not *baaarrg!*" He clutched his throat, gurgling, thrashing in his chair, the wooden frame creaking as he sagged back.

Julie giggled.

"It's like kryptonite," he gasped. "I'm getting weak. Weak." His shoulders dropped, his head lolled to the side and he let his tongue hang out.

As laughter rang in all directions, he heard a cluck of disapproval. Opening his eyes, he found Shannon shaking her head. "Great example. Thanks. Very helpful."

He would have laughed himself if he hadn't noticed Ryan covering his face. *Stupid move, Hawkins*. The kid had watched his mother die. He hurriedly straightened up. "Okay, okay, I'm just kidding. You knew that, right, Ryan? Really. It's not bad." To prove his point, when the boy lowered his hands and warily peeked at him again, he took another bite.

Shannon leaned closer, bringing with her a scent of flowers that should have clashed with the smell of garlic sauce and Parmesan in the air, but strangely didn't. "To quote you," she whispered, "your enthusiasm underwhelms me, Mr. Hawkins. How about it, Ryan?" she asked louder, moving away from Greg. "You want to try this?"

The child clamped his palm over his mouth.

She pursed her lips and shot Greg a dirty look.

He just shrugged, finishing up his slice.

You could lead a kid to an artichoke pizza, but you couldn't make him eat it.

Shannon Vanderhoff appeared to have a lot to learn about six-year-old boys.

LATER THAT AFTERNOON, on the other side of Paula's, the Old-Fashioned Ice-Cream Parlor part, Shannon watched as Greg, in true Pied Piper fashion, led a parade of kids around the black-flecked Formica tables to the make-it-yourself sundae bar along the far wall. No wonder he got along so well with children.

He *was* one. Only taller.

Still, Ryan eagerly held a bowl aloft, letting the man

scoop ice cream into it. Her nephew had eaten more in one afternoon than he usually did three days put together. That scored points for Greg Hawkins.

One of the moms at the table sighed, prompting Shannon to look at her. "If only I weren't married," the woman mused, watching Greg with the children. "That is one yummy man."

Nods of agreement went around the table, then all eyes turned to Shannon. The silence stretched uncomfortably, a quiet bubble in the clamor around them. She shrugged. "He's not the comic-book geek I expected, that's for sure. But he's not what I'm interested in. I want to know how you feel about him as a therapist working with your kids. Do you think the whole superhero thing is too much? Does it make your children more prone to fighting with other kids, or jumping on the furniture? Stuff like that?"

"I wish Cheryl had the energy right now to jump on the sofa."

"She had the energy to decorate Michael's head," the boy's mother retorted, unsuccessfully trying to stifle a chuckle. "Honestly. I just never know what they'll come up with next."

The women all chimed in with their opinions of Greg Hawkins. None of them had anything even slightly negative to say about him.

"He really helped Julie fight. It's hard to teach kids visualization. The comic-book drawings are a concrete first step. At the cancer center, they say visualization and positive attitude can make the difference in beating the disease. I think Greg has had just as much to do with Julie's remission as the medical doctors." The mother's eyes got shiny as they welled with tears. "I've been so scared. Now I'm just really relieved."

One of the other women wrapped an arm around her, giving her a squeeze. When one of the kids shouted "Mom, look at my sundae," they broke apart and Julie's mom wiped the back of her hand across the corner of her eye.

Ryan cradled his bowl, walking carefully back to the chair at Shannon's side. Gobs of whipped cream and chocolate syrup topped the small mounds of vanilla ice cream. Rainbow sprinkles turned it into a party in a bowl.

Shannon's throat tightened. The whole thing seemed normal. Average. Which made it feel surreal, because nothing had been average or normal for Ryan—or her—in months.

The boy dug into the creation, drizzling syrup from the end of his spoon before cramming it into his mouth. He licked dark smudges from his lips, then dipped back into the sundae.

"It's yummy, huh, sport?" Greg was busy with his own chocolate ice cream with…chocolate sprinkles, syrup, chips…and even chocolate whipped cream.

"Like chocolate much, Mr. Hawkins?" Shannon asked. "I thought chocoholism was an exclusively female disorder."

His grin lit up his eyes and revealed tiny dimples at either end of his mouth. "There is no other flavor for ice cream. And when presented with such a spread of chocolate accoutrements, well, why not take advantage of them?" From beneath the pile of napkins he'd brought with him, he pulled out another spoon. "Want some? I'm excellent at sharing."

Shannon hesitated.

"They don't have any artichoke ice cream. I checked. Please, don't tell me you don't like chocolate. I have a deeply held distrust of people who don't like chocolate. Allergic, I can excuse. But to not like chocolate…" He shook his head. "Suspect behavior."

"I like chocolate."

"Phew. That's a relief."

She accepted the spoon from him, then hesitated. There was something…intimate…about eating from the same dish, and it felt odd.

He shoved the bowl closer to her. "Go on. Have some. Or else I won't believe that you really like chocolate. After the artichoke pizza, that's a second strike, so to speak."

"I thought *I* was interviewing *you*, Mr. Hawkins."

"Greg. And you are. You now know that I am a discriminating person when it comes to new clients."

"And you accept them based on their ice-cream preferences?"

The smile faded from his face. "All kidding aside, Ms. Vanderhoff—"

"Shannon."

"Shannon. I take art therapy very seriously. Even if, at moments, it appears I don't. It's not a game. It's not frivolous, even if we use crayons or pudding finger paint."

Ryan made a gurgling noise, and Shannon glanced over at him. He had his spoon poised at his mouth but was staring at Greg with wide eyes.

"You like the idea of finger painting on the tables with pudding, huh, sport?"

The boy nodded.

"Well, maybe we'll have to try that sometime." He returned his attention to Shannon. "So? Are we going to work together?"

She dipped her spoon into his sundae, savoring the

various textures against her tongue and the roof of her mouth. "Mmm. This is very good."

"You didn't answer my question."

"Because I don't have an answer yet, Mr. Hawkins."

"Greg."

"I'm going to have to think about it."

"Fine." He leaned forward in his chair, pulling a black leather wallet out of his back pocket. "Here's my card. Call me when you decide." He stole a peek at his watch, then snatched the bill from the table as he stood. "Sorry, everybody, but I have to leave. My sister's wedding is this summer, and I have to get measured for a tux."

The table clamored with good-byes and best wishes for his sister. He made his way around to everyone, butting fists with each of the kids, admonishing them all to "fight the good fight."

Fight the good fight.

Another reference to violence. And while it might be appropriate for sick kids struggling to survive, Shannon didn't think it was appropriate for Ryan.

Maybe there was another art therapist in Erie. One that didn't come with Greg Hawkins's other "specialties."

GREG FORCED HIMSELF to stand still on the platform while the woman from the tux shop ran a tape measure up the inside of his thigh. It wasn't so much her actions that were making him uncomfortable, or that two of his brothers, Finn and Hayden, were snickering at his obvious unease. No, he was uncomfortable and on his way to being pissed off because his sister Elke, who insisted on supervising every last detail of this wedding right down to the tux measurements, had brought her best friend and maid of honor with her.

His ex-girlfriend, Denise.

The one he'd broken up with a month ago.

Hayden came behind him and leaned in. "She's eyeing you like a Doberman eyes a T-bone. She's hungry, and you're the main course."

"What are you whispering about, Hayden?" Elke demanded. "Is there a problem?"

Her groom, Jeremy Kristoff, who'd been doing his best Invisible Man act over in the corner since his measurements had been completed, looked heavenward. Something told Greg the man regretted not whisking Elke off to Vegas or anywhere else for an elopement. Not that any of his sisters would ever agree to anything less than the traditional church wedding. In his family, tradition ran deep.

"Absolutely not, Elke," Hayden assured her. "Nothing to sweat. Everything's cool. Don't go all Bridezilla on us, okay?" He walked over to prop himself against the counter, raising his eyebrows at Greg, gesturing with small jerks of his head at Denise.

Greg ignored him. And her.

When the attendant pronounced him finished, jotting down the final measurements on a slip of paper, he stepped off the platform, pulling on his mocs, and headed for the door. "Hate to measure and run, but—"

"Wait. You can't leave yet. We haven't decided what you're going to wear." Elke grabbed him by the arm.

"Whatever you decide is fine with me. It's your wedding, I'll wear what you want." He planted a kiss on her cheek.

Beaming, Elke glanced around at the rest of the

men in the wedding party. "Thank you, Greg. That's very refreshing."

"Traitor," Finn hissed.

"You can't go by him. He draws guys in tights all day long. He doesn't have any fashion sense at all," Hayden said, now taking his own place up on the platform. "Have you seen the Captain Chemo costume he had made?"

"Come on, Greg," chimed in the best man, Jeremy's brother. "You can't actually mean that. So, if she decides we're wearing purple cummerbunds and frilly shirts—and pink bow ties—you're cool with that?"

"You're not going to pick something like that, are you, Elke?"

"Of course not. I want this wedding to be amazing, not tacky."

Greg shrugged. "See? No problem."

"You still have to put down a deposit," Denise piped up.

"I can come back next week. Or even take care of it by phone now that they have my measurements. It's not like they're going to run out of order forms." Greg untangled the grip his sister had on his bicep and headed for the door again, shrugging into his denim jacket. "Sorry, but duty calls."

On the sidewalk of the strip mall that hosted Erie Bridals and Tuxedos, the April sunshine glinted off cars' windshields and into his eyes. Greg heaved a sigh of relief, a feeling that was short-lived as a voice called from behind him, "Greg, please. Give me a minute."

Great.

He turned to face her. "What is it, Denise? Really, I've got a lot to do. Deadline next Friday." Not to mention he had to figure out a way to convince Shannon Vanderhoff that he should work with her nephew. Ryan was just the kid to get his program some media attention and make Dean Auld sit up and take notice. Reconsider keeping him at the university.

Besides, he really could help the boy, despite what Ryan's skeptical aunt thought. It was a win-win situation.

"We're going to be able to get through this wedding okay, right?"

"Of course. We're both adults. We both care about Elke. This wedding means a lot to her, and I'll be damned if I'll do anything to mess it up."

"Of course not. I don't know why I even asked that." She waited a beat. "So, how's everything going?"

"Fine." He could see in her face idle chitchat wasn't what Denise had in mind. "Spill it. What is it you really want?"

"I—I just miss you, that's all." She stepped in, grabbed the edge of his jacket with one hand and used the other to smooth his tie against his chest. "Don't you miss me?"

No. Greg swallowed a groan. If he told her the truth, she'd end up back in the store in tears, upsetting Elke. "Denise, sweetie." He took her hand and eased it off his body. "It's over. It didn't work. We gave it a good shot. We had some fun. But now you have to let it go. Let *me* go."

"Let go? Excuse me, aren't you the guy who advocates fighting for what you want? Isn't that what you told me about getting that promotion? Isn't that what you tell those kids you work with?"

"Uh…" Nothing like having his own words, his own philosophy, bite him in the ass. "Well, you've got me there." Sweat beaded on the back of his neck. "But this is different."

"Why? Because you say so?"

"Yes. Because we're just not right together. And somewhere out there is a terrific guy for you."

Her lower lip quivered, taking on that little pout he'd once found cute, but that had quickly grown old. The persistence he'd admired so much was also wearing thin.

"But, Greg, *you're* a terrific guy. I love you."

The *L* word. In his opinion, it was a word women—particularly this woman—tossed around altogether too easily. He'd seen real love in action. His parents had been married for forty-six years and survived raising twelve kids and losing one of them. The love they'd shared had seen them through all sorts of trials.

And so far, he hadn't found a woman he could love like that. Or one who could love him that way, either.

Just as he opened his mouth to wiggle his way out of this jam, a car screeched to halt behind his Tracker. The passenger's door opened, and a man burst out. The driver aimed a camera out his window over the vehicle as his companion raced toward Greg.

"I am Trash Man, evil polluter of the earth!" The guy's costume consisted of a black garbage bag with a slot for his head and arms. Stuck all over his body was a wide variety of junk—Starbucks coffee cups, Oreo packages, a pizza box, an open diaper that Greg hoped was unused. The bitter scent of stale coffee competed with the overwhelming smell of apple and cinnamon emanating from the round air freshener stuck to the center of the man's chest. He wore a black Zorro-like mask across his face. "I am the world's next supervillain. Draw me or suffer the wrath of trash!"

Greg struggled to contain his laughter but couldn't. "Forget it. Even supervillains shouldn't smell quite like that."

"All right, then will you at least sign my comic book?" Trash Man reached into a brown paper bag stapled at his hip and pulled out a comic book in a plastic sleeve.

Greg recognized it immediately. *Y-Men,* issue 23. "Hey, that's my virgin issue."

"I know." The young man's hands trembled as he passed it and a pen over.

"You sure you want me to do this?" Greg asked. "I mean, this is in great condition."

"Yes, sign it."

"To Trash Man?"

The kid flushed around the edges of his mask. "And devalue it? Are you kidding? Just sign it, please."

"You're putting this on eBay tomorrow, aren't you?"

His mouth dropped open and he gawked at Greg. "No way, dude."

"Okay. Just checking." Greg scrawled his name on the cover and handed it back. "Now, do me a favor. How the hell did you know I'd be here?" This was the third "ambush" by overzealous comic-book fans in the same number of weeks.

Trash Man grinned as he tucked his treasure away. "*Bwa-ha-ha!* A supervillain never reveals his secrets." He turned and ran back to the car, leaping inside. The driver, who'd caught the entire episode on his small video camera, slid back into place. No doubt the scene would be on YouTube before the end of the day. Tires squealing, the car peeled out of the parking lot, leaving a black patch of tread on the pavement.

Beside him, Denise stared. "You live the oddest life, Greg."

He turned, and discovered the entire bridal party, along with the employees, clustered around the store's front door, watching through the glass. "Yeah. And I wouldn't have it any other way."

SHANNON HEARD the gurgle of water leaving the tub in the bathroom. A few minutes later, the boy came out, cotton pajamas plastered to the spots on his chest he'd forgotten to dry, and his sandy-blond hair sticking out in twenty different directions. "Hey, buddy, you forgot to comb your hair."

He smoothed it down with his hands.

"That's not enough." Shannon went into the bathroom, tossing Ryan's discarded clothes in the hamper before grabbing the comb. The boy was nowhere to be seen when she came back out. "Ryan? Come on, I'm just going to comb your hair. I'll be careful, I promise."

A rustling noise from his bedroom gave him away.

Shannon walked into the room that had formerly been her home office, and actually, still was. She'd put a futon against the far wall, and that served as Ryan's bed. He had a two-drawer unit inside the closet for his dresser.

Ryan had tucked himself into the corner of the futon, arms tight across his dawn-up knees. A couple of the books they'd borrowed from the library lay beside him. He shook his head as she approached with the plastic comb.

"I'll make you a deal. You tell me not to comb your hair, and I won't do it tonight."

The boy's counselors had assured Shannon that Ryan

would most likely speak again, in his own time. They'd urged her to be patient. Still, she couldn't resist coaxing him on occasion.

He turned his head toward the wall.

"Okay. Your choice." Shannon moved the books out of the way and sat beside him, then very gently began to tame his wavy hair.

The doorbell rang.

"That's weird. Did you order takeout?"

The boy rolled his eyes at her attempt at humor.

"Well, I'm not expecting anyone." Shannon handed Ryan the comb. "Why don't you finish it yourself. Maybe it won't bother you so much that way."

Shannon descended the stairs, brushing against the jackets hung on a rack in the entryway. She peered through the peephole—and drew back as if the door was on fire.

Hell's bells and Lucifer's toenails.

Patty Schaffer. Which meant Lloyd had to be out there, too.

Ryan's paternal grandparents. The ones whose calls Shannon had been avoiding.

Patty pounded on the door, and the voice that reminded Shannon of a canary on steroids called, "Shannon? Open up. We're here to see Ryan, and we're not leaving until we do. Even if we have to camp out on this doorstep until you run out of groceries."

She left the safety chain on the door, but cracked it open. "Ryan's just getting ready for bed. He's in the process of settling down. I don't think seeing you right now is a good idea. He has trouble sleeping, and—"

"And that's why he needs to see us. We're his family. We can help him. We've been driving for hours from

Philly. The least you can do is allow us a few minutes with our grandson before we have to find a hotel." Patty sniffed. "Hopefully we'll find someplace better than the last hotel. It's been over a month, Shannon. You have no right to keep that boy from us."

"The last time you visited, Ryan shut down for almost a week. Since I'm trying to get him to come out of his shell, I'd like to avoid a repeat performance. And technically, as his legal guardian, I do have the right." But morally, ethically, how could she? Shannon eased the door shut and slipped off the safety chain, opening the door wide.

"Don't get too used to it." Patty, a huge wrapped box in her arms, pushed past Shannon and began up the stairs. "I don't think you're going to be guardian much longer. You should be hearing from our lawyers soon."

A tiny dart of pain pierced Shannon's chest. They were going to apply for Ryan's custody? She heard the familiar whisper of emptiness and struggled to draw a deep breath as Lloyd followed his wife without a word.

Breathe in, take what life hands you; hold it, accept it; breathe out, let it go.

Was she going to have to let Ryan go? Already?

Another voice clamored in her head, drowning out her mantra. Greg Hawkins. And he was exhorting her, fight the good fight.

She'd never fought for anything, always doing as her daddy taught her and not holding on to things. Or people.

But Ryan was just a fragile little boy. He needed her right now.

She shoved her hand in her back pocket and fingered

the card the art therapist had given her, and which she'd carried like a talisman for some unfathomable reason.

Maybe it was time to call in a superhero.

CHAPTER THREE

PATTY SCHAFFER entered into the jail's visitation room, head held high enough to balance a book on it without mussing a strand of her recently dyed auburn hair. She strode to the space indicated by the guard, second from the end.

She eased into the stiff chair and waited. Moments later her son, Trevor, in his bright orange inmate jumpsuit, appeared on the other side of the Plexiglas. He'd lost weight; she could see it in his face. He perched on the edge of his seat, then picked up the phone. "Mom."

"Trevor. You're not eating enough. I've left you a check for the commissary. Don't use it all on nasty cigarettes, okay?"

"Thanks. Dad didn't come?"

The *again* was unspoken but plain in his eyes. Trevor, their only child, had always sought his daddy's approval. The fact that Lloyd wouldn't visit him while he awaited trial was a point of contention between Patty and her husband. Lloyd's resumption of the duties he'd passed to Trevor several years ago at Schaffer Furniture, their regional furniture-store chain, added to his resentment toward their son. "You know how stubborn he can be."

Trevor nodded. "I do."

"Maybe if you'd tell him what happened that night—"

"Mom, you know better than to even ask me about that. Especially here." He jerked his head to indicate the confines of the space, then at the guard behind him.

"But if he just knew you didn't mean to—"

"Did you see Ryan?"

"We did." Patty shook her head. "If you could only see that woman's apartment. Cold. Practically empty if you ask me."

"Is he talking yet?"

"No." The child had barely looked at her. Though she hadn't been highly involved as a grandmother to this point—she had a very full life of her own, what with all her volunteering for various charity groups, the traveling she and Lloyd did and all her friends—she'd expected more from her only grandson. Some sign of affection. She'd even bought him a remote-controlled car the salesclerk had assured her would be a hit with a six-year-old boy.

Trevor leaned onto the table, slumping. With disappointment, Patty presumed. "I did what you asked me to."

"Oh?" He shifted closer to the glass. "Did he react when you reminded him about the promise he made me?"

Patty waved the ruby fingernail of her free hand. "Not really. But don't worry. I could see in his eyes he remembered. He's your son. Of course he wants to make his daddy happy. He misses you."

"I know all about sons wanting to make their fathers proud, Mom."

"Your father is sensitive, Trevor, but he hides it well. This isn't easy on us, either. Some of your father's golf buddies have snubbed him since your arrest."

"Maybe if he'd called in a few more favors from

some of the golf buddies, I'd be out on bond and with my son." Trevor leaned closer to the clear barrier, laid his palm against it. "Mom, I want Ryan back here. I want him with you. I still can't believe Willow did this. Her damn sister saw Ryan even less than you and Dad did." Censure flooded Trevor's blue eyes, then they narrowed, turned demanding. "Get my son back."

Patty's hand appeared delicate, tiny, against Trevor's on the other side of the glass. Her baby might be full-grown and way bigger than she was, but he needed her. If she and Lloyd hadn't been out of the country at the time of their daughter-in-law's death and Trevor's arrest, if only she'd been more of a hands-on grandparent, things might have happened differently. "We're working on it," she promised.

GREG DIDN'T MIND being observed when he knew who was in the other room.

He'd been thrilled to get the call from the woman who once again stood behind the mirror. He *needed* to work with her nephew, but there was also something about Shannon Vanderhoff…something about the small boy in her awkward care…that spoke to him.

A thin layer of chocolate pudding now coated the yellow worktable. Ryan, wearing an old Y-Men T-shirt that had holes in the armpits and splotches of pudding where the child had leaned against the table, drew squiggly lines in it.

"That's great, Ryan." Greg made the same design as the child had, dragging his finger through the sludge.

The boy giggled.

Greg heard a very faint sound from the other side of the window.

Ryan reached out, tracing more shapes, then wiping the "slate" smooth, he did it again.

Greg, his shirtsleeves rolled up to his elbows, began to sketch funny faces in the pudding. After a few more minutes—this was the warm-up activity, not the main event—he announced, "Okay, sport, it's time to clean up. I've got some other stuff I want to do with you today. We can do this again another time, okay?"

Ryan nodded. Together they proceeded to scrape the pudding off with paper towels, then sprayed the table down with blue fluid. Once everything was clean, he spread out an assortment of paper, colored pencils and a new sixty-four-count box of crayons. "I'm going to make a picture of my family," he told the child. "My family is really big, so I'm going to use a big piece of paper. What paper would you use to draw your family?"

The kid leaned back in his chair, turning away from the table.

"Okay, you think about it. No rush."

Greg's pencil began to flash across the paper. While he sketched, Ryan pulled a brick-red crayon from the box, holding one end in each hand. With a twist of his wrists, he snapped the crayon in half.

Greg ignored it, and kept drawing even as Ryan broke a few more crayons. Eventually, getting no response, he picked up another and began to actually work on a picture.

Great. Now the silent boy was communicating with him, which, in his case, was the major point of art therapy.

Minutes crept by. Greg tossed out occasional words of praise and encouragement, but mostly the only sounds in the room came from the scratch of his pencil on the paper, the soft taps of the crayons touching the page or being dropped on the table. Greg kept moving after his piece was finished until the boy pushed his paper forward and set down his final crayon.

"Are you done?"

Ryan nodded.

"Me, too." Greg lifted his paper. "See all the people in my family? This is my mom and dad, and these are all my brothers and sisters. This is Alan, Bethany, Cathy, Derek, Elke, Finn, me, Hayden, Judy, and Kyle and Kara. These last two are twins. That means they were born together on the same day. This isn't even my whole family, if you can believe it. Some of my brothers and sisters are married and have children of their own. And I had another brother, Ian, but he's in heaven now." Greg laid his drawing down as Ryan grew somber. The child pointed to something in his own drawing. Someone up in the right corner, near the sun and clouds.

A female, judging by the long yellow hair. "Is that your mom?"

Ryan nodded.

Greg scanned the rest of the picture. On the left side was another figure—basically a head with arms and legs sticking out of it—with lines drawn across it. Bars. Easy enough to guess who that was. Near his jail-celled father were two other people holding hands.

In the middle of the page, the boy had drawn himself, contained inside a lopsided circle.

And way off in the bottom corner, a final figure had brown hair and, sprouting from its arm, a tiny triangle with green specks. Greg pointed to it. "Is this Aunt Shannon?"

Another nod.

A wave of sorrow for the child flooded Greg as the

symbolism sank in. Still, he forced a chuckle. "This is the artichoke pizza from the other day, isn't it?"

The edges of the boy's mouth pulled up slightly.

"That's funny. This is a terrific drawing, Ryan. You did a great job. So great that I'd like you to work on another picture for me, okay? And while you do, I'm going to take this and have a chat with Aunt Shannon, okay? I know she's going to love this. Why don't you draw something cool for Aunt Shannon's refrigerator?"

At Ryan's gesture of consent, Greg headed out the door and barreled into the observation room.

Shannon turned from the window. So far, she was impressed with the man's results. "You got him to crack. That's the first time he's almost smiled since he's come to live with me." She paused. "I'm really sorry about the broken crayons. He's not usually destructive."

"I'm not worried about a couple of broken crayons. The kid has emotions that are stuck inside him. Breaking the crayons said he's mad. He didn't want to draw his family. But he did. And I am way more concerned about this—" he thrust the drawing at her "—than I am about broken crayons."

She took it, turning the paper around to examine it. The hard edge to his voice surprised her. He'd been nothing but soft-spoken with Ryan.

The art therapist reached over the paper, pointing. "This is his mother, in heaven. Notice that she's the only person on this paper who's smiling. This is his father, in jail. That's positive. Shows that Ryan understands where his father is, and hopefully isn't afraid that his father is going to come after him next."

"We've talked about that. Well, I have. I've tried to assure him that he's safe."

"Who are these two people, holding hands outside the jail?"

"Ryan's paternal grandparents. Patty and Lloyd."

"Interesting how he kept them close to his father." Greg pointed again. "This figure in the middle, this is Ryan. Notice that he's inside a circle? Isolated?" He reached farther over. "See this, way down here? That's you, Aunt Shannon. Far away from this little boy who feels like he's all alone in the world. The kid just narced on you. He's complaining. You're not bonding with him, and I'd like to know why not."

"That's absurd. I've taken him into my home. I've spent the last three months with him damn near Velcroed to my side. I've damn near lost my job because of missing work to take care of him. Of course I'm bonding with him."

"That's not what Ryan says in this picture."

"I read to him every night. We watch TV together." Shannon's stomach felt heavy, as though she'd eaten a fast-food meal instead of something decent. "How is that not enough?"

"Well, despite all that, he's not getting the message that you want him." Greg narrowed his eyes. "You do want him, right?"

"Of—of course I want him. What kind of question is that?"

"Ryan's not feeling it."

"Do you have any suggestions?" Shannon turned back toward the window, watching Ryan work. Her nose started to tingle, and she fought against the tears welling in her eyes. Basically, she sucked as a guardian. That's what the art therapist was saying. Ryan wasn't progressing because of her.

Maybe he would be better off with Lloyd and Patty.

Maybe his time with her was already over, and she should just let him go with his grandparents.

"Yes. I suggest we move our sessions to your home, where I can observe Ryan in his own setting."

"Okay. We can do that. Just let me know what supplies I should have on hand."

"Don't worry about supplies. However, I have one more request." The man moved to stand beside her.

"Oh?"

"Yes. That you draw right alongside him."

"But—"

He held up his hand. "No buts. It will let him know you value this therapy, and him. Look, Ms. Vanderhoff—"

"I thought we'd gotten to first names? I mean, if you're telling a woman she sucks as the caregiver to a six-year-old, I think you can at least call her by her first name."

The lines in his face softened, and he lowered his hand. "Shannon. I'm not saying you suck as Ryan's caregiver. I'm saying for whatever reason, this child feels like he's all alone in the world. We have to fix that. If he can't bond with you, who can he? He needs you. He won't start talking again if he feels isolated. Getting him back in school next year won't happen, at least not in regular classes. And I don't think you want that for him, do you?"

"No." She sighed. "All right. If it's that important, I'll sit and I'll draw. But I'm not drawing any superheroes."

Greg's dimples appeared with his smile. "No superheroes. I think I can live with that. Let's compare calendars and see when we can start at your house."

OUTSIDE THE ROW of garden-apartment buildings, Greg pulled his Tracker into one of the spots labeled Visitor Parking Only. "Elke," he said into his Bluetooth earpiece, "I'm here. I have to go. Tails, no tails, whatever you decide, really, it will be fine. Just make sure I have something to cover my ass—uh—assets, and I'll be happy. Really. You're making yourself crazy for nothing."

"Denise said the same thing," Elke murmured.

Greg groaned. "Elke, come on. You promised me when I started dating her that if it crashed and burned, you'd be okay with it. Actually, I think you said you'd support me. I'm not seeing that support when you bring up her name every time we talk and drag her along for wedding stuff when she shouldn't be there."

"I know, but she's been so sad since you guys broke up. She's my best friend, and I'm the one who's had to pick up the pieces."

"That's usually how it works when a couple breaks up, Elke. The woman's best friend has to pick up the pieces."

"And the guy sails off, trauma free. End of story."

Trauma free? No, not completely. One more attempt at love that fizzled. It had been a loss for him. And if there was one thing Greg hated, it was losing. Anything. "Gotta go, sis. Love ya." Greg pressed the button on the earpiece, effectively cutting off the conversation, then he removed it, leaving it next to the empty Baby Ruth wrapper in the cup holder. From the backseat, he gathered up his supplies.

At apartment 7A's front stoop, he used his elbow to stab the doorbell. He heard footsteps on stairs inside, then the lock was released.

"Mr.—Greg," Shannon said as she opened the door. "You're very prompt. Thank you. Come in."

There was a short corridor, a private foyer, inside the

doorway. Several coats hung on a rack on the wall, with two pairs of sneakers on a rug below them. Greg toed out of his mocs, set the supplies down and tossed his jean jacket—demanded by the unseasonably cool early-May weather—on one of the hooks. Then he followed Shannon up the stairs to her second-floor apartment.

Ryan already waited at the table in the dining area. He offered Greg a half smile in greeting.

"Hey, sport. How you doing today? You ready to draw some more with me?"

The child nodded.

"Did you hear Aunt Shannon's going to draw with us this time?"

Affirmation.

"Can I get you something to drink before we start?" Shannon asked.

"No, thanks. I never drink and draw."

Her eyebrows scrunched together.

Greg laughed. "I don't like to risk spilling on the work. I learned that lesson early on the hard way. I was inking my third issue, and spilled some juice. Bad news. At least now if I do it, I'm the illustrator, too, but back then, it was someone else's hard work on the panels I'd wrecked. That nearly cost me my career in comics." As he spoke, Greg spread the supplies across the oval tabletop. "So grab a seat, Shannon, and let's get busy."

As they settled in, Greg checked out the apartment's partially open-floor layout. The living room, which flowed into the dining area, contained a black sofa and one slightly battered black recliner. A low table against the wall supported a nineteen-inch television. Aside from a clock, the walls were bare.

She made the Amish look materialistic.

The kitchen counters were likewise pristine, except for a hand-grinder salt-and-pepper shaker next to the stove and a silver toaster that seemed like something his parents might have received for a wedding gift—forty-six years ago.

The disconnect came from the set of gleaming copper pans that dangled from a rack over the breakfast bar, a set like Finn owned. Made some sense. A woman who enjoyed artichoke pizza would probably enjoy other foods that required more serious cookware than a paper plate in the microwave. Maybe he should introduce her to his brother.

A quiet tingle—a Spidey sense—told him maybe not. Actually, it screamed *no damn way.*

Kind of weird to feel that possessive of a woman he barely knew. But then, there was something intriguing about her. Too intriguing to consider introducing her to Finn.

The drawing Ryan had made at their last session was held up on the pale green refrigerator by a magnet.

"Okay, Shannon, since you didn't draw last time, I'd like you to do a family picture for me."

"Fine." She took a sheet of paper and a pencil.

Greg inched his chair closer to the boy's. "Ryan, today you and I are going to have some real fun. We're going to draw superheroes."

Shannon made a small noise, a cross between a growl and a groan, in the back of her throat. Then, catching his raised eyebrows, she studiously bent over her picture, flicking away nonexistent bits of dust from the surface.

"I love superheroes. They're so much fun. Do you have a favorite superhero?"

Eyes wide, Ryan nodded slowly.

"Great. Why don't you draw him for me." Greg flipped to a blank page in his sketchbook. "And while you do that, I'm going to draw some pictures of my favorites, too." While they worked, Greg kept up a running monologue, chattering away about superheroes, drawing techniques, whatever came to mind.

"I'm done," Shannon announced a short time later. "Here's my family picture." She held it out to him.

For a quick pencil sketch, she'd actually done a hell of a job. Ryan's face, right down to the smattering of freckles across the lower bridge of his nose, filled the right side of the paper, and on the other side, cheek almost pressed to the boy's, was a fairly accurate self-likeness of Shannon, including her perky nose.

"This is well done." He showed it to Ryan. "Check this out. Isn't this great?"

The boy flicked a quick thumbs-up to his aunt.

"You've got some talent there you didn't tell me about."

The woman shrugged. "No big deal."

"But, this is just you and Ryan. I wanted you to draw your whole family."

Pain flickered in her eyes, today more the color of dark chocolate. Then she blinked and it was gone. "That is my whole family now."

Ouch. Okay, *that* could be why she was keeping the boy at such an emotional distance. "Sorry. My bad. My family is so ginormous, it's hard for me to even imagine a family of only two people."

"Yes, how many brothers and sisters did you name last time? You mentioned a pair of twins, too?"

"I'm one of an even-dozen kids. The last two are a set of fraternal twins, a boy and a girl."

"Wow. Your mother must be either a saint or insane."

"Just a woman who loves kids and considers each one a blessing." Greg shoved another piece of paper at her. "All right, while we finish up our stuff, I'd like to see a picture of your family from when you were Ryan's age. Not just faces this time. Whole bodies. And draw your people doing something. Something your family liked to do together back when you were six."

For several minutes she just let the pencil tip hover over the paper. Then, she leaned over, forearm shielding her work like an elementary-school kid afraid her neighbor was going to copy her spelling test.

Shannon didn't want him to see what she was up to. She might have agreed to draw with Ryan, but she'd never agreed to actually let the man inside her head through her artwork.

Meticulous gray shapes took form on the paper. Precise. She used the eraser to fix any errors. Once she had the people complete, all she had to figure out was the setting. What innocuous activity could she have her "family" doing?

The image of the old beige car, Betsy, flashed into her mind, and just as quickly Shannon dismissed it. That was hardly an innocuous memory, and she didn't feel like explaining the night when her seven-year-old self had wept for hours after her father had given away their car to "someone who needed it more."

That had always been Daddy's response. Someone else always needed it worse than they did.

Clothes, food, dolls, even pets, it didn't matter what it was. The only thing that mattered was that Daddy placated his demons by giving it away.

There'd been moments as a child when she'd wondered if he'd go so far as to give her or her older sister, Willow, away. But she'd been equally certain that her mother, who always supported Dad in his donations, would have drawn the line there. Shannon had only been eight when that certainty had died with her mother.

So Shannon sketched in a lake behind her people, and a few trees, some clouds. Made it into an idyllic summer day.

They'd never gone to a lake.

Adding a few details here and there, she watched the man at her table, working with her nephew. His pencil flew across the page with an ease she both envied and despised. A flying superhero was taking shape, rescuing a cat from a tree. Superguy's cape flapped in the breeze, and a crowd of people stared adoringly at the kitty's savior.

Uh-huh. Why not just draw a fireman with a ladder? A real hero who might actually rescue a stranded pet?

Still, at least the guy wasn't bashing anyone. There were no kerpows or whammos.

It was some time later when she realized Greg was talking to her, holding up Ryan's picture. The entire top part of the paper featured Ryan's version of a flying superhero—a roundish head with long legs that grew from it, with an almost-triangle sticking out from the back of the skull—the cape, obviously. Straight stick arms poked out in the front of the hero's head.

And down in the corner, waving its arms, was another figure, this one tiny.

"It's—it's terrific, Ryan. I love the blue cape. Good job."

Greg beamed at her. "See, we agree on the color. Excellent choice, sport. Now, Aunt Shannon, let's see yours. You've been acting like it's a national-security secret over there. We want to see. Right, Ryan?"

The boy nodded emphatically, his hair askew.

"Well, all right. Ta-da!" Shannon held up her drawing. Ryan clapped his hands.

The art therapist studied it carefully, but joined in the applause. "Very nice. The scenery is an especially nice touch." Greg picked up Ryan's drawing, then hers, tucking them into his sketchbook. "Let's get cleaned up, then Aunt Shannon can walk me to my car."

With no observation room for them to chat in, Shannon presumed that was the man's subtle way of giving them some privacy to talk about Ryan.

Greg got down on one knee to say goodbye to the boy. "I'll see you again soon, okay? But I'm leaving you your own sketchbook. That way if you want to draw more before I come back, you can."

Ryan threw himself against Greg, wrapping his arms so tightly around the man's neck that Greg swayed off balance. His strong forearms went around the small torso, and he enveloped the child in a return hug.

Shannon swallowed the bitter taste in her mouth. Ryan had never hugged her like that.

Greg rose to his feet, giving Ryan a final pat on the head. Shannon followed Greg down the stairs, holding his stuff as he slipped his shoes and jacket on.

Outside, he stopped on the concrete porch, leaning against the black metal railing. He pulled Ryan's picture from the sketchbook. "See this?" He pointed to the figure at the bottom corner. "That's Ryan. This picture illustrates how inadequate he feels. The superhero is huge, and yet he doesn't see the boy who needs help. So, Ryan's still feeling overlooked. The kid is starved for some physical affection. That wasn't a hug he was giving me, it was a near strangulation. Do you have a counselor, Shannon? *For yourself?* If not, I'd suggest you get one."

She snorted. "Yeah. Right. With all my spare money. My savings are rapidly dwindling because of all the time I've taken off from work. If it weren't for your discounted fee to help Ryan, we wouldn't be able to afford you, either. I can't tell you how much I appreciate that." She nudged the sketchbook. "What did you learn about me from my drawing?"

He exchanged the papers. "You made every figure the same size. Length of hair is the only thing that varies. That's despite the fact that two of these are your parents, and the other two are you at six and your sister. So, you should have been smaller.

"What does this tell me about you? It tells me that you thought you could scam me. I'll bet this lake doesn't even exist, does it?"

She smiled. "No."

He shook his head. "You, Shannon Vanderhoff, are a control freak. And that's affecting your nephew."

"A control freak? I'm not a control freak. I'm totally Zen. I take what life hands me, I accept it, hold it, embrace it, then let it go. Nothing is ours to keep."

He arched one eyebrow. "Would you repeat that?"

"Breathe in, take what life hands you, accept it, hold it, embrace it for a moment, then breathe out and let it go. Nothing is ours to keep."

"Oh, Shannon." He stared at her with his soulful eyes. "And you wonder why you're not bonding with him?" His fingers caressed her cheek. When he let them skim along her jawline, then linger beneath her chin, she had a fleeting moment of wondering what his mouth would feel like on hers—strong and assertive, like him? Gentle and caring, also like him? Would he be as playful, as skillful, in his lovemaking as he was with his drawings?

"Ahem." Shannon glanced down at the new arrival on the bottom of the porch steps.

"I'm looking for Shenandoah Vanderhoff?"

"Yes? I'm Shannon Vanderhoff."

The young man in dark pants and a collared polo shirt passed her an envelope. "Shannon Vanderhoff, you are served." He turned and strode down the sidewalk.

"Served?" Shannon opened it, skimmed the first page. Her knees began to tremble, and she swallowed hard. "Well, my lack of bonding with Ryan may not be an issue for much longer. Like I said, nothing is ours to keep."

She passed the documents to Greg, letting him read them.

Lloyd and Patty had done it. They'd filed for custody.

CHAPTER FOUR

SHANNON DROPPED DOWN to the top porch step, the concrete cool through the seat of her jeans. Closing her eyes, she dragged in air until her lungs could hold no more, battling the pain.

Let it go, let it go, let it go, she silently chanted as she exhaled. But her chest remained tight, the pain unrelenting. She sucked in another long breath.

"Oh, no you're not," Greg said, his voice stern.

A hand closed on her elbow and he hauled her to her feet.

Her eyes flew open. "Hey! Not what?"

"Quitting. Just like that. Without even a hint of a fight."

"I'm not quitting."

"Sure looked like it to me. Sounded like it, too." Accusation blazed in his blue eyes.

Shannon lowered her head. "I'm preparing myself for the inevitable."

"That's what I said. Quitting. There is nothing inevitable here. Your sister chose *you* to be Ryan's guardian if something happened to her. Listen—" he tucked the envelope under his arm and took hold of her other elbow as well "—that little boy up there needs you." His voice softened. "And I think you need him, too. He's the only family you have left. Remember your first drawing? You can't let him go without a fight."

"I don't know how. And what if I lose?"

His fingers tightened their grip, and he shook her gently.

Her head snapped up and she glared at him. "Cut that out." She circled her arms up and over his, a neat little self-defense trick, disengaging his hold on her.

He grinned slowly as he held up his hands, inching backward.

"What are you smiling about?"

"There's fight in you. Just takes some provoking to bring it out."

She shook her head. "You are…exasperating."

"So I've been told." He held out the papers. "Well, Shenandoah Vanderhoff, what's it going to be? Quit or fight for Ryan?"

The memories of so many other losses—her mother, her father, Willow—taunted her. "What if I lose?" she whispered.

Greg raised her chin with one finger, making her meet his gaze. "You don't go into a fight expecting to lose. You go in with your fists high, knowing you're going to win."

"I can't afford a lawyer. Lloyd and Patty can afford great lawyers. You should see the dream team they've got defending Ryan's father."

"Leave that to me. Are you free for lunch on Sunday?"

"Lunch? On Sunday? What's that got to do with a lawyer?"

"Trust me. I'll pick you up at eleven-thirty. Let me help you. And Ryan."

If anyone could teach her how to fight, it was this man. "All right. But on one condition."

"Okay."

She propped her hands on her hips. "Don't *ever* call me Shenandoah again."

Greg chuckled. "That's the spirit. I'll see you Sunday. Fight the good fight." He offered his closed fist in the gesture she'd seen him do with his kids.

After a moment, she lightly bumped knuckles with him. "Fight the good fight," she repeated.

The phrase left a sardine taste in her mouth.

DAWN HAD JUST LIGHTENED the May sky, making it easier to navigate the parking lot as Shannon trudged toward the sidewalk. Living only a few minutes from the hotel where she worked 9:00 p.m. to 5:00 a.m. as a night auditor—at least for now, considering how annoyed her boss was over her frequent requests for time off—had its advantage.

She eased the key into the lock, creeping into the apartment just in case Mrs. Kozinski, the older neighbor woman who babysat Ryan overnight while Shannon worked, was sleeping. Most mornings she was up and raring to go when Shannon came home. The strong aroma of fresh coffee as she climbed the stairs indicated this day was no exception.

Mrs. K. met her at the top step, stainless travel mug in hand, expression way too chipper for the crack of dawn. She'd obviously had more than one cup of caffeine already. "He's awake, too, dear. Neither one of us slept much last night, I'm afraid. Which could be good for you. Maybe he'll sleep now." The woman often crashed on Shannon's bed during the night, more times than not with Ryan at her side instead of in his own bed. Shannon had gone through too much to find a reliable sitter to quibble over the fact that she let Ryan sleep in her bed.

The television played softly, illuminating the living room with flickering shadows. Mrs. K. leaned over the back of the couch to tousle Ryan's hair. "See you Tuesday night, Ry. You, too, dear." She saluted Shannon with the mug, then headed down the stairs.

On the couch in front of the TV, Ryan turned his bleary eyes toward Shannon. "You're supposed to be sleeping," she said softly, wagging a finger at him. "Come on. I have to get some rest, and so do you. Let's go."

Before Ryan, she hadn't headed directly for bed after coming home from work. She'd eaten dinner—or rather, breakfast—and unwound before hitting the sack. But she'd had to adapt, trying to grab some sleep in the early-morning hours, when the boy was usually still asleep.

It hadn't been working too well for either of them.

After tucking him into the futon in the second bedroom, Shannon stumbled into her room, pulling the shades and drawing the curtains, then peeling off her clothes. After yanking on a nightshirt and matching shorts, she slid between the cotton sheets, exhaustion quickly overtaking her.

The creak of the door and a crack of light coming in from the hallway roused her some time later. Faint footsteps scuffed across the rug, and the double mattress shifted as Ryan slipped in on the other side.

Too tired to return him to his own bed as she usually did when he snuck into hers, Shannon tugged her sleep mask on and rolled to her side, letting sleep reclaim her.

GREG RAPPED on the apartment door a third time, then checked his watch. 11:35. He'd told her eleven-thirty, right?

His mother wasn't happy when people were late for Sunday dinner.

While contemplating his next move, the door inched open, and a freckled face appeared in the space just above the doorknob. "Hey there, sport. I was starting to think you guys had stood me up. Aunt Shannon's probably still getting ready, right?"

The boy shook his head, then opened the door wider. He still wore navy pajamas. The boy's hair splayed in multiple directions, and he boasted a faint chocolate-milk mustache.

"Shannon?" Greg called as he entered the apartment. "We're still on for lunch and a lawyer, right?"

At the top of the stairs, Greg paused. On the dining-room table, a half-full glass of chocolate milk sat beside the remains of a bowl of soggy cornflakes. Drips of chocolate and stray flakes dotted the tabletop; the open cereal box lay on its side. The only noise in the apartment came from the television in the living room. "Where's your aunt?"

Gesturing for Greg to follow him, the kid went to a door and pushed it open, pointing inside the cavelike room.

Concern knotted the muscles along his neck. Shannon had her issues, but being a neglectful guardian wasn't one of them. "Shannon," he called softly. "Are you okay?"

No response. The hair on his arms stood up and he tripped over scattered clothes on the floor in his hurry to reach her bed. Using the light from the hallway as a guide, he fumbled at the nightstand before turning on the small lamp.

Shannon lay on her back, left arm sprawled out, right hooked up over her head. A comforter tangled at her waist. The gentle rise and fall of her chest reassured him—until he noticed that the thin nightshirt she wore left no need for X-ray vision. He could see the swell of her breasts and the rosy outline of her nipples quite clearly without superpowers.

And what breasts they were. His palms tingled with the urge to see if they fit his hands as perfectly as they promised.

Feeling more than a bit voyeuristic, he forced his gaze higher, to her face. A royal-blue satin mask covered her eyes, so only her nose and mouth showed, coral-pink lips slightly parted.

He wrestled with the asinine impulse to lean over and wake her with a kiss, but the realization that a six-year-old stood in the doorway quickly subdued it. This woman, with her nothing-lasts attitude, was not what he needed. She was the antithesis of that woman. Kissable lips and cuppable breasts be damned.

"Shannon, wake up. It's late."

When she still didn't stir, he grabbed her left arm and tugged. "Shannon, come on. Wake up."

Everything exploded. She bolted upright and wrenched away at the same time, ripping off the mask while shrieking at the top of her considerable lungs. Her features distorted as she shrank from him.

He held his hands out. "Easy, it's just me. Greg. Ryan let me in and—"

A sound rumbled behind him, a cross between a cry and a growl, something a wounded animal might make. The next moment, a small body leaped onto his back, hammering him with little fists. Teeth sank into his shoulder, and fiery pain radiated outward from the spot. "Ow! Whoa there, buddy. It's okay. I'm not hurting her."

Greg seized the child, dragging him around and wrapping him in a bear hug to bring him under control. "Everybody take a deep breath, here." Ryan wailed, keening his distress. He squirmed, freeing his arms, then flailed, reaching out toward his aunt, who was still wild-eyed herself.

"He thought I was hurting you," Greg explained.

Understanding dawned, and she held open her arms. Greg released the boy.

She gathered Ryan in an embrace, rocking him on the bed. "It's okay. I'm okay. I was just scared. As any woman would be if she woke from a sound sleep to find a man standing over her." Shannon narrowed her eyes at him over Ryan's head.

"The door was unlocked and Ryan let me in." A defensive note crept into his voice. "You should keep your door locked."

"It *was* locked. The babysitter must have left it open this morning."

Greg eased himself down on the edge of the bed, rubbing the spot where teeth marks undoubtedly remained. "Sport, I would never hurt your aunt. Or anyone. I'm sorry I scared you guys. Man, Ryan, that was brave. I'm proud of you." Inwardly, Greg wanted to cheer. A sure sign of progress. Progress they desperately needed.

Ryan twisted his head from Shannon's chest. His tears had stopped, and his expression was quizzical. A far cry from the daggers Shannon was now launching in Greg's direction.

"Yep," he hastily continued, "totally brave to defend your aunt like that when you thought she was in trouble. Way to go." He held out his hand, and Ryan slapped him a weak high five. "Now, why don't I help you get ready? That way Aunt Shannon can get herself together before we're late for our lunch."

Ryan scrambled from the bed and was out the door in the blink of an eye.

"Ah, the resiliency of youth. They bounce back better than RubberMan." Greg rose to follow him. "Can you be ready in fifteen minutes? The cook where we're going can be temperamental about people who don't arrive on time."

Tossing aside the covers, she swung her feet to the floor, giving him an eyeful of lean, long legs. Then she stood and raised her hands over her head, interlocking her fingers and stretching in a way that pulled the night-shirt tight against her chest.

Greg's own clothing suddenly felt snug. He dropped his gaze to his toes. *Down, boy.* No sense in starting something that wasn't going to work out, setting himself up to lose.

Still, the attraction was getting harder to ignore.

She grabbed some clothes from the closet and brushed past him. "We'll talk about this later."

"I can hardly wait," he muttered.

SHANNON LET HIM SUFFER in silence during the ride. The man was unbelievable. Praising Ryan for attacking him? What was next? Martial-arts lessons? Fights with broomsticks in her living room?

And yet…Ryan had not only cried but cried out. A tiny step in the right direction that might force her to forgive Greg for scaring the snot out of her.

Besides…she needed him. Much as it pained her to admit it. She hadn't needed anyone or anything in a long time, and the idea didn't sit well.

He swung his Tracker off the country lane onto a tree-flanked dirt driveway. "I thought we were going to lunch. Where are we?"

"Home," Greg said. "Well, not that I live here anymore. But this is where I grew up. Welcome to the Hawkins's nest."

"You're taking me home for Sunday dinner?"

Numerous vehicles edged the driveway as they drew closer to the cedar-sided house. Greg parked. "Best Sunday dinner in town. Lunch and a lawyer is what I promised, and that's what you'll get."

"Just how many people show up at your house for Sunday dinner?" Shannon asked as she got out of the car.

He shrugged. "Depends. Mom likes to gather the tribe at least once a month if she can. Not everyone's here. Alan couldn't make it, and I don't see Bethany's SUV, either."

Ryan ran past Shannon, falling in step with Greg and lifting his hand, which the man took in his as if it was the most natural thing in the world.

"So, the rest of your brothers and sisters will be here?" She did a quick mental calculation. "That still leaves eight sibs."

"Along with significant others, kids and assorted strays they might have brought along." He winked at her.

She slowed her pace. "I—I don't know about this. I wouldn't want to intrude on family time. Besides, I didn't bring anything. It's rude to show up empty-handed. You could have warned me."

"And risk you not coming? Not a chance. Don't worry about not bringing anything. There'll be plenty to eat, I promise you. My brother Derek's kids are here for Ryan to play with. They're eight, six and three. There's a trampoline out back and a pond…all sorts of great kid stuff. But the rule is you have to have an adult watching you near the pond, and on the trampoline. Okay, sport?"

Ryan beamed up at Greg, nodding enthusiastically. Shannon winced. The child was setting himself up for more pain. The poor kid would be crushed without Greg in his life. Or when Ryan left to live with Lloyd and Patty.

Ryan had already lost his mother. And, God and the justice system willing, his father. Shannon didn't want him to know the pain of losing more.

So until she learned how to fight well enough to keep Ryan with her, she was stuck with Greg Hawkins. That the idea appealed to her made her all the more nervous.

They entered the house through a massive three-car garage. Only one car was parked inside. The rest of the place was filled with bikes lying on their sides, in-line skates, scooters and scattered sporting equipment. The door opened into a laundry room–mudroom combo that boasted two washers, two driers and a long double row of hooks. "You can leave your jackets and your purse here," Greg said.

She hesitantly followed Greg into the empty kitchen, where she was immediately struck with kitchen envy. A large island with a six-burner cooktop, a double-wall oven. Of course, with a family the size of the Hawkinses', this kitchen was a necessity. It wasn't as though they were cooking for one or two. Her cheeks flushed.

The scents of roasted meat, garlic, onion and tomato sauce lingered in the air.

"Uh-oh," Greg said as laughter and conversation, punctuated by occasional shouts and high-pitched shrieks, came from the next room. "They started without us. My ass is grass now. Oops." He glanced down at Ryan and grimaced. "Sorry. Pretend I didn't say that, okay, sport?"

He leaned in to Shannon and whispered, "That's one plus of a kid who's not speaking—he won't repeat your faux pas or naughty words." Herding Ryan ahead of them, he grabbed Shannon by the elbow and pulled her into the dining room.

An overwhelming number of people sat at an enormous table filled to overflowing with dishes and food. A toddler sat in a high chair drawn up near the table, banging a spoon on her tray.

As she and Greg were noticed, the room slowly quieted down. Shannon blushed under everyone's frank and open appraisal.

Greg finally cleared his throat as he steered her toward the end of the table. "Sorry we're late—"

"It's my fault," Shannon said. "I, uh, I work nights, and I overslept this morning. I'm sorry."

A man with salt-and-pepper hair—heavier on the pepper—and the same strong jawline as Greg sat at the head of the table. He put down his fork and smiled at her as he climbed to his feet, extending his hand. "Hello there."

"Dad, this is Shannon Vanderhoff and her nephew, Ryan. Shannon, this is my dad, Michael."

"Nice to meet you, Mr. Hawkins."

"And this is my mom, Lydia."

Lydia Hawkins had beautiful short silver hair, piercing blue eyes and didn't appear old enough—or worn enough—to have birthed and raised a dozen children. "Greg's told us a little bit about you. Perfectly understandable that you might oversleep. Working nights and acting as a single parent is a tough gig."

"Not as tough as mothering a brood of twelve, I'm sure."

"I can certainly offer you some tips, if you need them."

Shannon nodded. "I do."

"Everyone, this is Shannon and Ryan. Shannon, this is everyone else. They're not as important as food right now, so you can meet them all later."

"Welcome, Shannon!" "Says you, Greg!" "Nice manners. Emily Post you're not." "I'm important, right, Dad?" A cacophony of calls overwhelmed her as Greg led her down the length of the table. He bopped one man on the head as they passed, glared at another in response to eyebrow waggling in Shannon's direction.

Ryan clung to her hand.

Soon enough, they were seated and being passed roast beef, lasagna, garlic bread and other assorted foods. Nothing gourmet, but simple, tasty fare. Ryan enthusiastically gulped down his lasagna and bread.

While they ate, Greg not only kept up three different discussions, but also pointed to each person around the table in order, giving Shannon their name and a brief tidbit of information. Her head swam. "You should provide name tags."

He chuckled. "Don't worry. There won't be a quiz."

It was easy to see where Greg had gotten his good looks. There wasn't an ugly duckling in the entire family. And all the Hawkins men had the same angular jaw, obviously inherited from their father.

So how come the grins two of his brothers were

flashing at her from the opposite end of the table didn't make her pulse quicken the way Greg's smile did?

The children pushed away from the table first, asking to be excused before carrying their plates into the kitchen. A boy a few years older than Ryan returned. "You done eating? You can play with us if you want."

Ryan turned uncertainly to Shannon, who glanced at Greg, equally unsure. "They'll just be in the family room for now."

"Okay, Ryan. Go ahead."

"Show him what to do with his plate and silverware, Jack."

Ryan slid from his chair, trudging out behind Greg's nephew, plate balanced in both hands. At the doorway, he stopped, shooting Shannon a long look.

She nodded, jerking her head toward the kitchen, and the child left somewhat reluctantly.

"Don't worry, he'll be fine," Greg said.

"I know." Shannon chased a grape tomato around her salad bowl with the tip of her fork. Some of the adults also began leaving the table.

Attempting to remember who was who just gave her a headache. There were too many people, too many names.

"Hi, I'm Elke." A young woman whose brown hair flashed honey highlights in the sun streaming through the sliding glass doors plonked down at the vacant chair on Shannon's right. "I'm Greg's favorite sister."

"No, she's not. Kara's my favorite sister," Greg said. "You are my nosiest sister. Listen, Shannon, don't let her grill you. Five minutes alone with Elke, and she'll know everything about you. Don't say I didn't warn you. Elke wanted to be an interrogator for the FBI, but even they couldn't stand her."

Elke stuck her tongue out at him, then propped her chin in her palm and turned her complete attention to Shannon. "So, tell me about yourself, Shannon. How did you find yourself in the company of my loser baby brother who still plays with crayons?"

The snort of laughter Shannon stifled made her choke. Vinegar from the salad dressing burned her nose.

"Now see what you've done." Greg whacked Shannon between the shoulder blades.

"I'm sorry," Elke said. "It's not like I meant to—"

Shannon held up her hand. "I'm fine," she managed to say between coughing fits. Her eyes watered. "Really."

She dropped her napkin on the table and pushed back her chair. "I think I'm done, though. I'm sure I can figure out what to do with my dirty dishes."

"Are you kidding me? Are you trying to get me in more trouble with my mom?" Greg jumped up, taking the plate from her and stacking it on his own.

Shannon risked a glance at Greg's mother and discovered the woman's narrowed eyes turned in their direction. "Sorry," she murmured. "You know, this family stuff is far more complicated than I remembered."

Greg's laughter drifted over his shoulder as she followed him from the dining room. "No, it's not. There's one thing to remember—If Mama ain't happy, ain't nobody happy."

"She was strict with you?"

"With twelve kids, you're either strict and structured or mowed over by absolute chaos."

In the kitchen, Greg joined the process already in motion as one woman rinsed dishes, another loaded them into the side-by-side dishwashers. One of the guys packaged the small quantities of leftovers, while

another—not a Hawkins, judging from the jaw—
scrubbed the face and hands of the protesting toddler
from the high chair.

Elke came in with an armload of serving dishes and
joined the fray. Shannon fidgeted by the island.

She straightened up as she was flanked by the two
guys from the opposite end of the table.

"So you're the Shannon we keep hearing about," one
of them said, his wide grin revealing a long, deep
dimple in his right cheek. "Nice to finally meet you."
He held out his hand.

"I'm sorry, but I don't remember your name," she
admitted as his grip enveloped her fingers.

"Finn, living inspiration for my brother's superheroes,
at your service." He brushed his lips over her knuckles
before the other brother elbowed him out of the way.

"I'm Hayden." He took her hand and picked up
where Finn had left off, placing a chivalrous kiss on the
back of her hand. "And I'm in love. Greg neglected to
mention how beautiful you are."

Shannon's cheeks warmed, and she gently disengaged her hand from his grasp. "I'm flattered, I think.
Do you always fall in love so easily?"

"He's superficial," Finn said.

"Back off, bozos." Greg wedged himself between his
two brothers and hip-checked first one, then the other,
widening the space. "She doesn't need either of you
slobbering all over her."

The other guys exchanged a look, eyebrows lifting.
"So, it's like that."

"It's not *like that*." Greg took Shannon by the elbow.
"Come on. It's time to meet with that lawyer I promised
you. Cathy," he hollered across the kitchen, "you ready?"

The woman nodded. "Just let me get my stuff. I'll meet you in Dad's office."

Shannon once again found herself following Greg through the house. The living room featured vaulted ceilings with exposed beams, a towering stone fireplace and two sets of sliding glass doors that opened out onto a wraparound deck. They went down a short flight of stairs to a slate-floored foyer that had an enormous coat closet and a suit of armor…

A suit of armor?

Greg didn't give her time to ask, just barreled down the next staircase. She scrambled to keep up.

"This is the rumpus room," he said. "We did a lot of rumpusing down here growing up." She glanced around, taking in another fireplace along with a Ping-Pong table, a Pac-Man game table, a pinball machine and a dartboard sans darts hung on the wall.

Passing an efficiency kitchen just off the rumpus room, he led her down a short hallway, then into a room with a built-in bookcase behind a large desk. Greg grabbed two padded folding chairs from behind the door and opened them in front of the desk. "Sorry about the chairs. Dad doesn't often hold meetings in here."

"What does your father do?"

"He's a lawyer, too. But he does big corporate stuff."

"So your sister followed in Dad's footsteps?"

"Yep. Along with my brother Alan. And Kyle's in law school now."

Cathy came in, laptop cradled in her arms. She had lighter hair than Greg, though the hint of darker roots suggested the chestnut with honey highlights hadn't come from the Hawkins gene pool. She radiated confidence and professionalism that immediately gave

Shannon the sense that she was in good hands. "Goodbye, Greg," Cathy said. "I'll take it from here."

"I thought I could stay."

"No. You're burning time. Don't let the door hit you on the way out. I promise not to bite your friend."

Greg paused in the doorway. "If she does bite you, you let me know, and I'll take care of it."

Shannon nodded. The family's good-natured ribbing intrigued her. Her family—back when she'd one—had never been this…comfortable…with one another.

"Let's get started," Cathy said once Greg had closed the door behind himself. "My brother tells me you have a custody fight on your hands. He's told me some of what's going on, but I want to hear it from you. Give me all the details."

Shannon launched into a summary of how Ryan came to live with her, ignoring the sympathetic glances from Greg's sister. Cathy's fingers danced over the laptop's keyboard as she took notes.

"How long have you lived in Erie?"

"About six months."

"And how long have you worked at your present employment?"

"About five months."

Cathy asked her numerous other questions, from the jobs she'd held in the past to the relationships she'd had with men in the past five years. She dug into corners of her life Shannon hadn't expected, like the status of the rest of her family, whether or not she'd ever done drugs and what skeletons would drop out of her closet if someone rattled it long enough.

"What kind of support system do you have here for Ryan?"

"Support system?" Shannon shrugged. "I have a babysitter who stays with Ryan at night while I work."

"Friends? Distant relatives?"

Shannon shook her head. "That's it."

"No, it's not. You've got Greg Hawkins, talented art therapist, on the job. You've got a social worker. You've got Ryan's other therapist, Dr. Lansing. Plus, you are now plugged into the Hawkins-family support system. When the other lawyer asks you about it, that's what you say. And you say it confidently."

"Okay."

"The first thing we do is file for a change in venue. We want this heard in Erie, not Philadelphia. Since Ryan lives here with you now, we'll try to convince the court that this is where his custody should be decided."

"Can you tell me my chances of keeping custody?"

Cathy leaned back in her chair. "There are never any guarantees in a courtroom. I fight to win, but never make promises. Now let me ask you a question. Is losing an option?"

"What?"

"Is losing an option? Can you accept your nephew living with the people who raised the man who murdered your sister?"

"No," Shannon murmured.

"I'm afraid I don't believe you. Try again."

Shannon straightened. "No."

"Better, but I think you're still holding back."

"No," Shannon ground out, "I do *not* want Ryan living with the people who raised the man who *murdered* his mother."

Cathy smiled. "Now, *that's* what I'm talking about."

Great. Another Hawkins coaching her on fighting

tactics. She'd have a few choice words with Greg when he took her and Ryan home.

And he probably wasn't going to like what she had to say.

GREG MET THEM as they came out of the office. Ryan grabbed at Shannon immediately, tugging on her arm.

She glanced from the boy to Greg.

"He wants you to go outside with him. The other kids are bouncing on the trampoline, but I wouldn't let him go on it until you said he could."

"Thanks." She turned to his sister. "And thank you."

"You're welcome."

"Ryan, why don't you show me the way to the trampoline?"

Greg started to follow them, but Cathy laid her hand on his arm, holding him back. "You guys go ahead. I'll be right there."

Shannon waved her agreement as Ryan hauled her down the hallway toward the rumpus room and the doorway that led to the backyard.

"What's up, Cat?"

Cathy clutched her laptop to her chest, shot a quick look down the corridor, then spoke softly. "I'm walking a fine line here between attorney-client privilege and big-sister privilege. So just shut up and listen to me for once in your life. I told her no men until the custody trial is over. Now I'm telling you. Not that woman, ever."

"Not that woman? What's that supposed to mean?"

Cathy scowled, her disgust rumbling in her throat. "Don't play stupid with me, Gory."

Greg rolled his eyes at the nickname she'd dumped

on him as a baby, when she'd decided that just because everyone shortened Gregory into Greg didn't mean she couldn't chop his name up another way. Gory had so much more pizzazz, she said.

"No men for her. No *her* for *you*. Got it?"

"And even if I was interested, which I'm not saying I am—"

Cathy snorted.

"But if I was, why not?"

"Her track record of revolving-door relationships. Any judge is going to hate it, and I personally don't like it for my little brother. Not for *you*, anyway. Maybe Hayden. She's the first woman you've ever brought home for Sunday dinner."

"That's just because I knew you'd be here, and—"

"Keep telling yourself that. But I'd have met her at my downtown office, like any other client, if you'd asked." Cathy hefted her laptop over her shoulder.

"Why Hayden and not me?"

"Because Hayden's methods would work perfectly for her."

"I find that hard to believe." Hayden's "methods" mandated an end date for every relationship he started. In fact, one of his exes had been known to say that a relationship with Hayden was like a gallon of milk—it came with an expiration date.

And yet, most of his exs still adored him. How he managed it, Greg would never fully understand.

"You don't work that way, Gory."

Shannon didn't know it, but she'd been damned with faint praise. As to her assertion that he didn't work that way… No, he didn't. "Can she beat the grandparents and keep custody?"

Cathy shrugged. "I'll do my best, but you know how the courts can be, Gory."

"You have to win. That kid needs her. And she needs him just as much."

And his needs…well, he'd just have to keep his needs—his *wants*—under control.

CHAPTER FIVE

"YOU DIDN'T HAVE to give my mother the bracelet off your arm," Greg told her as he drove them home. They'd lingered at his parents' far longer than he'd expected, and now the sinking sun struck him full in the face. He lowered the visor. "What would you have done if she'd admired your shirt?"

He'd been admiring the shirt—and the cleavage beneath it—ever since she'd come out of the bathroom at her apartment wearing it. A midnight-black, clingy, wraparound thing with a V-neck, it provoked all sorts of thoughts he wasn't supposed to be having at a family dinner.

He hadn't sat at the dining-room table with a quasi-boner since Thanksgiving the year he was thirteen, and Cathy, then twenty, had brought home her smokin'-hot college roommate for the holiday.

Apparently, Finn and Hayden had also appreciated the sweater, judging by their ridiculous behavior. And after Cathy's lecture, Greg still hadn't been able to keep his eyes off of Shannon. But as a bonus, thanks to his sister, he felt guilty about it.

"Would I have given her the shirt off my back, you mean?" Shannon chuckled.

Even though that was where he'd been going with the

comment, the next image to flash across his brain was Shannon, peeling off the second-skin shirt to reveal…

He cleared his throat. "Don't be silly. I just meant you really didn't have to do that. My mother certainly didn't expect it. She wasn't sure how to handle it."

"Her son gives discounted services to me. Her daughter is doing pro bono work on my behalf. So it's okay for you guys to give things away, but not me? She liked it, and I wanted her to have it."

"Pro bono and discounted work isn't the same as giving away something that belongs to you."

"The bracelet made me happy for a while, and now it will make your mom happy for as long as she has it. No big deal."

Greg eased the Tracker into a parking space near her apartment. "It was a gracious gesture. You scored points with Mom, that's for sure. Oh, and I didn't thank you for taking the heat for us being late."

"It was the least I could do, seeing as it *was* my fault." Shannon turned and glanced into the backseat, then she groaned softly. "He's sleeping. That figures."

Ryan slumped against the door, dead to the world, mouth slightly open.

"Too much trampoline, I'd wager."

"Or maybe he's worn out from fighting with your nephew." She sighed. "Scrapping, as your brothers euphemistically termed it, is precisely what I've been concerned about."

"Shannon, it was hardly a fight. It was boys being boys, and besides, Jack shouldn't have mocked Ryan for not talking. That was wrong. Don't blame Ryan for sticking up for himself."

"I don't blame Ryan. I blame you."

"Me? *Me?*" He clenched his jaw shut so he didn't gape at her.

"Yes, you, you. Who praised him this morning when he attacked you? You did. Who's been filling his head with all this superhero nonsense? Why, I believe that would be you, *Mr. Hawkins.*"

"Obviously you don't know progress when you see it, *Miss Vanderhoff.* What you're seeing now is a kid who feels more comfortable around you, around people. A kid who's starting to come out of his shell. A kid we're finally empowering." Closing the front door with a restraint he didn't feel, Greg stalked around the car, gingerly opening the back door. Once he freed the child from his seat belt, Greg hoisted the slumbering boy to his shoulder, praying Ryan would stay asleep.

Shannon brushed past him on the sidewalk to unlock the apartment door and let him in. Without a word, he carried Ryan upstairs to his room, laying the child on the futon. He removed the boy's shoes and socks, finagled him out of the pint-size windbreaker, then draped a blanket over him.

In the doorway, Shannon raised her eyebrows. He waited until he was close enough to respond in a harsh whisper, "What? You've never seen a guy put another guy to bed before? I tucked Derek in only last week after he tied one on because... Never mind. Suffice it to say I know how to pull off shoes and throw some covers over a sleeper."

He crooked a finger at her, then headed back down the stairs. In the foyer, he spoke normally again. "I'm taking you and Ryan to the zoo tomorrow. We're making progress, and we should capitalize on that.

Are you working tonight?" Greg pulled out his Treo, checked the calendar.

"No, thankfully I'm off tonight and tomorrow night."

"Good. I've got a couple of appointments in the morning, but I'll pick you up around noon, okay?" He slid the phone back into his pocket.

"Yes sir, Mr. Bossy."

"Did you see my family today? Pushovers get nowhere in that house."

"It was…interesting, that's for sure. To have that many people related to you…interesting."

A glimmer of longing flickered in her eyes, kicking Greg in the gut. How lonely must her life have been? He couldn't imagine taking on the world without his brothers at his back, having his sisters to torment and share their insights into the opposite sex—even if they were lecturing him about his love life—or without his parents there.

Shannon had only the little boy asleep upstairs, a child who also, for all intents and purposes, had lost both of his parents. And people were trying to take him away from her.

The impulsive urge to wrap her in his arms and shelter her made him step closer. The air in the foyer grew heavier, warmer, and she retreated, leaning against the wall.

"I know you don't like fighting, but do you ever at least fight yourself?" He inched forward.

"Wh-what do you mean?"

"I mean, say there's something you want that you know you shouldn't have. Say double-cheese and pepperoni pizza. You know it's all wrong for you. It's never going to work. But you want it. It looks delicious." Greg planted his hands on the wall on either side of her head, then leaned in, nuzzled her shoulder and inhaled deeply as he skimmed the graceful curve of her neck. She smelled of coconut, sunshine and summertime. He pulled back to meet her eyes. "It smells fantastic. Do you fight with yourself over tasting it? Or do you just take a bite?"

"I—" She lowered her gaze to his mouth. The tip of her tongue darted out, moistening her lips, and Greg's hormones jumped to attention like a superhero to a beacon light in the night sky. "Fighting's wrong," she murmured. "Don't fight it. Taste it."

Greg bent his elbows, easing his body weight against her, sliding his knee between hers to widen her stance so he could settle between her thighs.

Her eyes fluttered shut, and she lifted her chin, arching her neck with a sigh. "Is that your utility belt, or are you just happy to see me?"

"Shh." Once more he nuzzled her neck, this time trailing light, teasing kisses up the slope. He nipped her chin gently, just enough to surprise her eyes open, then he slowly brushed his lips over hers. A moment of testing, then he slanted his head and took full possession of her warm, lush mouth.

True to her nature, she offered no resistance, opening for him, eagerly welcoming his probing tongue, giving back just as enthusiastically.

And the inner war began in him, the voices of reason that sounded very much like his sisters'. Cathy, telling him Shannon wasn't for him and to keep his distance. Elke, pleading with him to stop before it was too late, reminding him that kissing—hell, devouring—Shannon Vanderhoff was a very, very bad idea.

Bad idea or not, she felt perfect pressed against him.

The heat index in the foyer climbed until it well surpassed an Erie summer day, headed toward Phoenix in July. The faintest flavor of hazelnut coffee and Finn's German chocolate cake made her all the sweeter.

Shannon's heart thudded faster, her pulse audible in the rush of blood in her ears. His mouth *was* as talented as his quick-sketching fingers. She tipped her hips a fraction of an inch, increasing the friction of the impressive package hidden beneath his snug jeans. Jeans she'd been admiring the fit of while he'd been bouncing on the trampoline with her nephew.

Ryan.

Who was sleeping upstairs. Who was counting on her to save him from Patty and Lloyd.

Reluctantly Shannon placed her hands on Greg's firm chest, and pushed.

He broke off the kiss, pulling back just enough so she could see his blue eyes, heavy-lidded and full of heat. "What?"

She shook her head. "We can't do this. You were right. It's all wrong. Ryan's upstairs. And I can't afford to do anything that will make me a bigger target for Lloyd and Patty's lawyers. One of the things your sister said was no men until after the custody fight. I'm pretty sure that means you, too."

Greg shifted, skimming his lower body against hers. Shannon struggled not to respond in kind, putting on her best poker face.

He stepped away from her, leaving her cold, wanting. Needing to grab him and haul him back to her.

"You learn too fast," he said. "I kinda hoped fighting yourself would take longer to master."

"Progress." She forced a smile. Under other circumstances, she'd have embraced the temporary gift Greg represented. There would have been fun times and, judging from this steam-her-socks-off encounter, incredible sex. But she had to face the new reality of her life, and that meant fighting. Even herself.

The concept still didn't sit well with her. In fact, she viewed it even less favorably now.

"Progress. Yeah, great." He cleared his throat. "I'll pick you and Ryan up at noon."

HEADING TOWARD MIDNIGHT, Greg stopped the flight of his pencil long enough to really examine the panel he was sketching, one where the hero confronted a flame-throwing villain on a city street while horrified onlookers watched. He tossed down the pencil in disgust, then pushed back from his drawing table and rose to pace the length of his third-floor studio. Again.

Two of the bystanders in the crowd bore a significant resemblance to Shannon.

A man's ego could only take so much, and his wasn't sure what to make of her late-in-the-game rejection. Up front, he could understand. But in the midst of one of the most mind-blowing kisses he'd ever experienced?

The signals she'd been sending had said she'd been just as caught up in the heat as he'd been.

The hardwood floor creaked beneath his feet as he drifted from one end of the spacious room to the other, past the shelves of comic-book memorabilia, past the superhero wall mural featuring some of his brothers. He turned at the brick fireplace in the middle of the street-facing wall and headed in the opposite direction.

At a rap on his door, he stopped and listened as footsteps climbed the short set of stairs to his refuge and workplace. Finn appeared at the top and held out a long-necked amber bottle. "Heard you pacing up here. Repeatedly. Brought an ale to chill you out."

Greg snorted. "There's beer in the minifridge. But…thanks." He took the bottle from his brother, who, along with Hayden, lived in the big old house on West Tenth Street. Greg had purchased it five years ago and renovated it, using sweat equity from all of his brothers, even their father. The girls had pitched in, too, and now the house was quite respectable, considering three bachelors lived in it. The former attic had been converted into Greg's workspace, a studio complete with a drafting table, a light table, space for his computer and scanner—every bit as much an artist's tool as his pencils and inks—a half bath…and plenty of room to pace.

Finn twisted the cap off his own brew, then wandered to the oversize chairs in the corner, slumping into one of them with his leg draped over the arm. "What's going on?"

"Nothing." Greg plopped into the chair opposite Finn, skittered the bottle cap across the short table between them. It teetered to a stop on the edge.

"And a fantastic-looking nothing she is, too."

Greg paused with the bottle to his mouth, glaring at his brother over the rim.

Finn laughed. "You couldn't take your eyes off her all during dinner. And don't think it's just Hayden and me who noticed. I think even the kids picked up on the sparks you two were throwing. And Mom was watching you watching her."

"Shit."

"Yeah. I think you stepped in it this time, little brother."

"There's nothing to step in. It's a business thing. The kid needs my help. They both need my help."

"And so superhero Greg rushes in to save the beautiful woman in distress, right?"

Greg flipped Finn a one-finger salute.

"No, thanks. You're not my type. However, if you're saying that you're really *not* interested in Shannon, I'll take her phone number."

"Like hell you will."

Finn arched a dark eyebrow at him.

"She's off-limits until the custody hearing. Cathy said so. No men. It could hurt her chance of keeping the boy."

His brother said nothing, just stared at him.

Greg slumped deeper in the chair. "Shit."

Finn leaned over and clinked his bottle against Greg's. "You're screwed." He got up and started to leave, stopping at the top of the stairs. "Let me know if it gets to the point that Hayden and I should start thinking about new digs, huh? Don't evict your own flesh and blood without notice." The stairs groaned as Finn went down.

"Finn?"

He paused, peering through the railing spindles at Greg. "Yeah?"

"I still haven't found anyplace else to host my program. I need that kid to start talking, to help me keep my program at the university. Need the PR he can bring."

"I wouldn't tell her that." The door slammed behind his blunt statement.

Greg took another pull of the beer, glanced over at the sketch with Shannon's face appearing twice in the crowd. "I am so screwed," he muttered. Why was he drawn to a woman who wouldn't keep him even if they did start something? Why hadn't he felt like this with Denise? She wanted him. She was fighting to get him back.

While Shannon, the pacifist, the Zen take-it-and-leave-it woman, held him at arm's length despite a sizzle that had damn near set fire to the coats on the hooks near where they'd kissed.

God sure had a warped sense of humor.

SHANNON WATCHED from the fence as Greg swung Ryan onto one of the horses on the Erie Zoo's merry-go-round. The man had an easy rapport with the boy she envied. He was a natural with kids.

While she was still…awkward.

The tension between her and Greg today had made her even more awkward. Neither of them had brought up the night before, but it hung heavily between them.

Greg fastened the safety belt around Ryan's waist, then the boy shoved him on the shoulder. Greg said something Shannon couldn't catch, nodding, then came off the ride to stand beside her. He leaned over, propping his elbows on the weathered wood. "He wants to ride alone. Said he's not a baby."

Shannon gaped at him. "He *said* that?"

"Not in words. But I understood him, loud and clear."

The calliope music started, and the carousel slowly chugged into motion. Shannon waved to Ryan as he circled past. Without the child to engage with, she and Greg stood there in uncomfortable silence for three or four rotations. Unable to stand it any longer and desperate to clear the air between them, she blurted, "We should probably talk about last night."

Greg jerked upright. "No, we probably shouldn't. I should have trusted my first instinct. I'm sorry. Won't happen again."

"Which is too bad. I found it rather…nice."

"Nice?" He slapped the center of his chest like she'd wounded him. "Nice? Nice is when I kiss my sister. Or my mom. What happened between us last night was smokin'. Set-off-the-fire-alarms hot."

Her skin began to tingle and her pulse kicked up a notch. "That, too. I'm still new to this idea that I have a child to worry about. Someone I have to put ahead of what I want. Scares me to death if you want to know the truth."

"I can imagine. But you're doing great. Everything's going to work out."

"Thanks." They turned back just in time to wave to Ryan as he went by again, and then the ride began to slow.

"You go get him," Greg said. "I'll wait here."

Ryan had already unfastened the seat belt by the time she reached him. She grasped him by the waist, and he threw his arms around her neck. For a moment, she just held him, warm and sticky from cotton candy. A memory surfaced of Willow, laughing as she opened her mouth wide, letting pink cotton candy dissolve on her tongue.

Willow's son was her sister's legacy. Shannon squeezed Ryan tighter, until he squirmed and struggled in her embrace. She slid him to the ground.

A mother with a baby on her hip and a toddler by the hand shook her head. "He's a big boy. Shouldn't he be in school?"

Ryan froze, then looked up at Shannon. She squeezed his shoulder. "Are you the truant officer?"

"Uh, well, no," the woman sputtered.

"Then I guess it's none of your business, right? For all you know, he's a genius who completed his high-school courses yesterday, and we're celebrating before he starts college tomorrow. Come on, Ryan, let's go see how many more of the animals you know the scientific classifications for. I've seen enough of the species *Annoyus buttinski*." She took Ryan by the hand, leaving the woman standing on the merry-go-round platform with her mouth hanging open.

Greg chuckled softly as she stormed out of the gate with Ryan in tow. "Excellent," he murmured, scrambling to keep up with her as she raced from the children's section of the zoo. "Way to tell that woman off. *Annoyus buttinski*. I love it."

Shannon tried to glare at him, but ended up dissolving into laughter herself. Ryan slipped his other hand into Greg's and, as the three of them walked around the swan pond, he jumped, lifting his feet and making them swing him. Sunlight glinted off the rippling water, and for a brief moment, all seemed right in Shannon's world. For a moment, she allowed herself the fantasy of a normal life—something she'd never even considered before. Life with a man, a child…children. A family. A big family.

For keeps.

Greg checked his watch. "Okay, sport, we've got to go now, so we have time for our art before I have to get to another appointment. Okay?"

The fantasy melted like cotton candy in the rain, like fantasies always did. Which was why Shannon didn't often indulge in daydreaming.

Or hope.

As they approached the parking lot, she heard hushed voices and scuffling, then three men in… Shannon blinked. Yes, three men in formfitting spandex costumes, one red, one green and one blue, burst out from behind a van. Two more people pointing small handheld cameras also appeared.

Greg stopped in his tracks, muttering under his breath.

"We are the ABC Men!" the guy in red said. "I am A." He pointed to the giant letter *A* on his chest, then propped his fists on his hips, striking a pose Shannon assumed was meant to be superheroish.

Ryan giggled.

"I am B Man!" B Man wore blue spandex—*B* for blue?—that emphasized his jiggling beer belly. Also *B* words. He, too, struck a pose.

"And I am C!" said the green-clad guy. They all wore small color-coordinated masks.

"We are the defenders of the preschool set," A announced. "Wherever there's a bully throwing sand in a sandbox, wherever a kid is unfairly put in timeout or wherever a little boy—" he gestured to Ryan "—won't eat his vegetables, we'll be there." A folded his arms across his chest.

Several other families in the parking lot watching the spectacle clapped, sending the ABC Men into sweeping bows. Then they all clambered into the open sliding door of the van, followed by their camera crew. As the van carefully pulled out of the zoo parking lot, the "superheroes" waved to the kids.

Greg shook his head. "How do they keep finding me? And why? Wanting a comic book signed, I can understand, but what the heck was the point of that performance?"

Shannon poked him in the back. "Is this a normal occurrence for you?"

He jingled the keys in his hand. "It started a few weeks before I met you and Ryan. Seems to happen about once a week or so. But things have been slow lately, so I thought they'd stopped."

"Hmm…interesting. Who knew we were coming to the zoo today?" Shannon helped Ryan into the backseat of the Tracker. He smiled broadly at Shannon, warming her all over. "You thought that was funny, huh?" She tapped his freckled nose as he nodded. Shannon buckled him, then did the same for herself in the passenger's seat.

"Nobody except us. They never show up at my house or work. Which is why I haven't worried about it too much. But it's getting kinda weird and tiring, even for me."

"They're probably college kids." Frat boys who'd had too many keggers, judging from B. Shannon tapped her fingers on the armrest as Greg headed down Thirty-eighth Street. "That's why you haven't had any incidents lately. They've been busy studying for finals. Maybe this was their last hurrah before they head home for summer vacation."

"Uh-huh. Erie University has a popular summer semester, plus there's all the college kids who live in Erie who come home for the summer. I don't know that I can expect a break."

"Guess you'll have to wait and see."

"Guess so." He shook his head again. "The ABC Men for preschoolers." He chuckled. "At least they're semicreative. Maybe *Sesame Street* would be interested in booking them."

Back at her apartment complex, Ryan, head held high and chest puffed out, helped Greg carry the art supplies inside. Once at the table, Greg took a large sheet of paper and folded it into fourths, then opened it. He used a black marker to trace the folds. He did the same thing for two more sheets of paper. "Comic books are just ways to tell stories with pictures. That's what we're going to do today. We're all going to draw the story of our trip to the zoo in these boxes."

The reason for the trip to the zoo became clear. Greg had been building a shared experience to use in Ryan's session. It had been an actual field trip, for educational purposes, not a fun outing.

Why did that make her feel hollow?

"So, in this panel—" he pointed to the upper left box "—we'll draw something that happened first. Then here—" the upper right box "—we'll put what came next." Greg continued demonstrating the sequence of the boxes. "So, think of something you'd like to draw first."

The phone rang. Shannon pushed back from the table. "Sorry. I'll be right back."

The wall phone over the counter was the only one she had, so Shannon was able to watch Ryan carefully choose a pencil, examine the tip as he'd seen Greg do on numerous occasions, then begin drawing.

The woman on the other end of the line identified herself as Ellen Kelaneri, with the Philadelphia D.A.'s office. Shannon's stomach tightened. "Yes? Is there something wrong?"

"No, no, Miss Vanderhoff. We just wanted to know if we could send some people up to interview Ryan now."

Shannon glanced at the boy who was happily drawing away. "Not yet. But maybe soon."

"His testimony is critical to the case against his father."

"Uh, you know, this phone connection isn't very good. Can I call you back in a minute?" Shannon gestured at Greg, motioning like she was writing. He tossed her a crayon, and she jotted down the phone number on the paper she was supposed to use for her zoo-trip comic. "Okay, I'll call you back shortly."

After hanging up, she crossed back to the table, glancing down at Ryan's drawing. "You're doing a great job." She turned to Greg. "Can I borrow your cell phone? That was an important call, and I couldn't hear anything on the connection."

Wordlessly, he passed her his cell, the slightly raised eyebrow telling her he understood.

"Uh, it's long-distance."

"Unlimited calling is a wonderful thing. No sweat."

"Okay. I'll be back in a few. Keep drawing, Ry." Shannon smoothed her nephew's wavy hair, then leaned over and impulsively pressed a kiss to the top of his head. He twisted around to scowl at her, indicating she was interrupting his work. "Sorry."

Out on the front porch, she dialed the D.A.'s office. "This is Shannon Vanderhoff. Sorry, I couldn't talk with Ryan in the same room. What do you mean, his testimony is critical? Last time we spoke, you said you thought it was a slam-dunk case against my brother-in-law, and you weren't even certain Ryan would have to testify."

"Miss Vanderhoff, we have a fairly strong case against him, but Ryan's testimony will be the nail in his coffin, so to speak. Juries can be fickle. Your brother-in-law claims he remembers nothing of that night and that there's no way he killed his wife. That an intruder must have done it."

Shannon snorted. "Ah, yes, the unknown intruder. The not-me argument."

"Exactly. There's no evidence of a break-in or

anyone else at the scene. The physical evidence points to him. But Ryan's testimony...that would make our job so much easier."

"I'm not interested in making your job easier. I *am* interested in healing my nephew, and seeing that the son of a bitch who killed my sister spends the rest of his miserable days behind bars. But Ryan still isn't speaking."

"Trevor Schaffer's defense attorney is pulling out all the stops to rush this case to trial. Please, call us as soon as Ryan starts talking."

"I'll do that." Shannon snapped the phone closed. What if Trevor got off? What would happen to Ryan then? The idea of her nephew testifying against his father made her queasy, but the idea that the man could get off and regain custody of Ryan made her downright want to vomit.

Shannon headed back inside, setting the phone on the table near Greg's elbow. "Now, where were we?" She grabbed another sheet of paper and a pencil. "Okay, drawing our trip to the zoo. This is going to be fun." Greg eyed her curiously, questions about the phone call or her sudden newfound zeal for his art therapy, or maybe both, plain to see.

The wall phone rang again. "Oh, honestly." Shannon tossed down her pencil and went back around the island.

And nearly hung up as she recognized the voice this time. But Cathy had warned her to be gracious and polite. Shannon forced a smile to add enthusiasm to her response. "Hi, Patty. What can I do for you?"

"I'd like to speak to my grandson."

"He's in the middle of something right now. How about I have him call you back later?"

"No, that won't work for me. I have things to do later. I want to talk to him now, please."

Please? Maybe their lawyer had warned them to be polite, too. "All right. But not too long."

"It's rather tedious to keep up a one-sided conversation…I assume he's not talking yet?"

"No, no, he's not."

"Oh, okay." Was that a note of relief in Patty's voice? "So I won't keep him long."

Shannon covered the mouthpiece. "Ryan? Grandma wants to talk to you."

The boy's shoulders slumped. He shook his head, pointing at his drawing and Greg.

"I know. But she promised to keep it short. Come on, buddy. She's your grandma. And—" Shannon swallowed hard and forced the words past her clenched teeth "—family is important." But not all family was created equal. Shannon felt better about using the term to apply to Mrs. K., Ryan's babysitter, than she did about using it with Patty and Lloyd. Even if they were his blood relatives.

Ryan slid from the chair and trudged over.

"Okay, here he is. I'm putting him on now." Shannon handed the receiver to the boy, who dutifully held it up to his ear. The canary-on-steroids chirping spilled out, but Shannon couldn't make out what Patty was saying.

For a minute or two, the only sound in the room was the faint scratch of Greg's pencil on the paper as he continued drawing casually keeping an eye on Shannon and Ryan.

Then the boy slammed the receiver down on the island countertop. He looked up at Shannon with wide eyes and trembling lower lip, then turned and dashed to the table, pausing only long enough to grab a black crayon and scribble across his paper before he raced from the room. The bedroom door slammed a moment later.

Torn between going after him and demanding answers from the woman on the phone, Shannon hesitated.

"I'll see to Ryan." Greg's long strides quickly covered the length of the apartment's hall.

Shannon snatched up the phone. "Patty? What did you say to him?"

"Nothing. Why?"

"Nothing my rear end. Nothing doesn't make a kid go running."

"I have no idea what would upset him. I told him we'd seen his father, and his daddy was asking about him, that's all. And that hopefully he would get to come live with us soon."

"And you don't see how either of those two things would upset him? Buy a clue, Patty." Shannon wrapped the phone cord around her finger until the tip turned red. "Goodbye." After fumbling to free her hand, she forced the hand piece into the cradle so hard the ringer jangled.

In Ryan's doorway, she pulled up short. The boy had wrapped himself like a monkey around Greg's body. The man sat on the edge of the futon, rocking gently, patting Ryan's heaving back. "It's going to be okay, sport. You know, Aunt Shannon and I could help you a lot better if you'd talk to us."

Ryan shook his head hard.

"You know we're not going to be mad at you, right? No matter what you say?"

No, she wasn't going to be mad at Ryan, but she sure as hell was mad at his grandmother. She moved to sit next to Greg, reached out toward Ryan's back, hesitated, then at Greg's nod of encouragement, she too stroked the child. "Ryan?"

In a flash, her nephew scrambled from Greg's lap to hers, wrapping his arms around her neck and his legs around her waist, squeezing so tight it became difficult to take a breath.

A blinding flash of white-hot panic froze her for a moment, the depth of the child's need overwhelming her.

He'd chosen her over Greg. He wanted her.

Nose tingling, and cold fear giving way to warmth, she enveloped Ryan in her embrace. "It's okay. I've got you."

Shannon didn't know how long they sat there, but Ryan's quivering body slowly settled, and the sniffling sounds muffled against her neck—her now moist and icky neck—eventually stopped. Greg left, returning with a handful of tissues. Shannon eased Ryan from her, taking the tissues and mopping his face, running one over the sopping-wet crease near her collarbone. "Ryan, are you upset because Grandma Patty wants you to live with her and Grandpa?"

The little boy nodded, wiping his arm over his face.

"Do you want to live with them?"

He shook his head fiercely.

"All right. We already have a lawyer. Remember Greg's sister Cathy?" At Ryan's affirmation, she continued, "Well, she's going to help us." Shannon cleared her throat, but still had to force out the words that were like a foreign language. "We're going to fight." She held up her closed fist.

Greg smiled at her over Ryan's head. "And I'm going to help, too." He held up his fist. "What do you say, Ryan?"

Ryan bumped his knuckles against both of theirs.

The team was forged.

CHAPTER SIX

PATTY STARED at the wireless phone she'd replaced on the mahogany night table. How dare that woman?

The maid, a load of freshly washed towels in her arms, bustled toward the master bath.

"Would you believe it, Rosa? That woman told me to buy a clue. *Buy a clue*. What on earth is that supposed to mean?"

Rosa shrugged. "I don't know, Ms. Patty. I'm gonna put these towels in the bathroom. You ready for me to draw your bath?"

"That will be fine. While I'm soaking, make sure the black-and-white linen dress is ready for this evening."

Trevor's call—she knew it was him by the prison's name on the caller ID—came as she was fastening the black-pearl-and-diamond earring that completed her ensemble. She'd be so stunning at the Philadelphia Art Museum's charity dinner that no one would dare look at her with pity in their eyes, or whisper things behind their hands, stopping when she drew near. Whispers that compared her son to Scott Peterson, or O. J. Simpson. *Ignorant, small-minded people*. "Hello, Trevor."

"Mom."

"I trust you're well."

"I'm in jail, Mom. What do you think?"

She sighed. "That's no excuse to speak to me that way."

There was a momentary silence. Then Trevor said, "You're right. I'm sorry. Live in a cage long enough, and eventually you're reduced to acting like an animal."

"You're *not* an animal." The comment came out more sharply than she intended.

Trevor's laugh was equally sharp. "Loyal to the end, Mom. Glad to know I can count on you to have faith in me."

"You'll be out of there before you know it. Your father got an update from Harvey Lowenstein. They're doing everything they can to speed your case to trial."

"Good. Yesterday you said you were going to call Ryan. Did you?"

Patty glanced at her thin diamond-encrusted watch. Lloyd would be home to pick her up in five minutes, and he hated to be kept waiting. "I did. Frankly, I only knew he was actually on the phone by his breathing. Unnerving, I must tell you. And he slammed the phone down in my ear. Almost ruptured something, I think. And—"

"So he's still not talking?"

"No. And that woman…"

"What about her?"

"She had the nerve to tell me to buy a clue. What does that mean?"

"It means she's not the person we want raising Ryan, Mom. Get him back before she ruins him, will you?"

"These things take time, Trevor. I'm doing the best I can."

"He's your grandson, Mom. *My* son. Make sure your best is good enough." Trevor hung up.

Once again Patty found herself staring at her wireless phone, marveling at her son's rudeness. Jail had eroded Trevor's manners.

No matter. He'd shape up again once he'd been exonerated. Why, even knowing Ryan was with them would probably help his disposition.

Family meant everything to Trevor.

As she tucked a clutch purse under her arm and hustled from her room, Patty vowed to push the lawyers harder.

"I'M SORRY TO BOTHER YOU, but I just didn't know who else to call." Memorial Day weekend behind them, the two weeks since the zoo excursion had passed with little incident—and no progress. Actually, after Patty's phone call, Ryan had regressed to the point that coaxing a smile out of him took a lot of effort. While cradling the phone against her shoulder, Shannon crumbled the last piece of feta cheese. She stirred it into the mixture already in the long casserole dish. "They want me to come in early tonight to make up some of the time I've missed, and Mrs. K. just called. She's not feeling well and can't sit with Ryan tonight. She thinks it was something she ate."

Greg didn't respond right away.

"I can't lose my job. What's a judge going to say about that?"

His quick, blown-out breath echoed through the phone. "I don't mind watching Ryan for you. It's just that I'm already watching Derek's children tonight until about eight. He's got a dinner meeting. If you're willing to drop Ryan off at my place, I can bring him back to your apartment after Derek picks up his kids, or when Hayden gets home and can take over for me, whichever comes first."

"That's fine, thanks. Give me your address and directions." Shannon jotted down the information. "I really appreciate it. I owe you one."

"Remember that." He hung up, leaving Shannon staring at the phone. There'd been an uneasy edge to his voice, one she hadn't heard from him before.

After packing up a few items, she got Ryan from his room where he'd been playing a learning game on her computer. She planned to send him back to kindergarten in the fall, so she was trying to make sure he kept up with his letters and numbers. He deserved every advantage she could give him because of the emotional blows he'd suffered—and those yet to come, if he had to testify against his father in court.

Ten minutes later, she parallel parked in front of a charming old house, complete with a wraparound porch. Narrow driveways separated the homes in the neighborhood. Kids next door drew chalk art on the sidewalk while a bored teenager sat on the stoop, cell phone glued to her ear.

Greg's front door was opened by a little girl—his six-year-old niece Katie, if Shannon remembered correctly. "Uncle Greg said let you in and he'll be right down. He's working up in his lair."

"His lair, huh? Is that like the Batcave?"

Katie giggled. "Uh-huh." She turned to Ryan. "We're watching a movie in the theater room. Come on." She took his hand and began to pull him from the foyer.

"Just a minute. Let's get your coat off first." Shannon set her armload on the seat of an oak bench, next to a slumped-over stack of newspapers. As she reached to help Ryan with his windbreaker, he scowled at her, unzipped it and thrust it at her.

"Sorry," she murmured. "Of course you can do it yourself." She crouched, meeting him square in the eye. "Listen to me. I don't care what Jack says to you today. I do *not* want you fighting with him, do you understand?"

Ryan looked down at his toes.

She lifted his chin with her finger. "Ryan? I mean it. Physical fighting is never the answer. When I told you we were going to fight, I was speaking about the legal system. The justice system. I'm not actually going to have a wrestling match with your grandparents to see who gets custody of you."

The corners of Ryan's mouth edged up.

Shannon chuckled. "I know, it's an appealing image. But that's not the way to solve problems. That's make-believe. Just like the superheroes are all make-believe. You understand the difference, right?"

The boy nodded.

"Okay then. No fighting with Jack or anyone else, no matter what they say. It's very nice of Greg to keep you, so you have to behave. Right?"

This time Ryan's nod was exaggerated. *Yes, Aunt Shannon, can I go play now?* was easy enough to read in his expression.

She tapped the tip of his nose. "Go on. Have fun."

Finally dismissed, Ryan scrambled after Greg's niece.

"Oh, hey, where's the kitchen?" Shannon called after the girl.

"Straight down this hallway." Katie's words echoed off the walls, then their small feet pounded up a wooden staircase.

She grabbed the loaded bag she'd set on the oak bench, then headed down the hallway, which was two-tone beige with some sort of painted texture.

The cozy kitchen wasn't what she'd expected. A small desk next to the refrigerator overflowed with papers, but that was the only messy thing in sight. A square wooden chopping block served as a kitchen island, and Shannon set her bag there, drawn to make a closer investigation of the backsplash over the black-and-stainless stove.

A Tuscan village perched on a hill in the distance. In the foreground, as if on a windowsill, sat assorted glass bottles, one filled with black olives, another with some spiced oil. A bunch of deep purple grapes and some other bottles occupied a shelf above the sill. A tree branch dangled across the top left portion of the frame. She reached out to touch the tiles.

"You like it?" Greg asked from the doorway, making her jump and yank back her hand.

"I do. It's beautiful."

"Thanks. Took me about a day and half with all the details."

"You did it yourself?"

"I did."

"Wow. I didn't know your art skills were so versatile."

Greg laughed. "Yes, I do more than sketches and comic-book art. But don't ever tell my kids that I paint on anything other than paper, okay? Especially not Cheryl. Not after that incident with Michael's head the day we met."

"Ah, yes. The Sistine Chapel argument."

"Right. Now, what brings you to my kitchen? This isn't exactly where I expected to find you. Can I get you a drink? Coffee? Tea? A beer?"

"No, thanks. Actually, I brought you something. I

hate imposing on you, and don't want you to have to feed Ryan, so I brought dinner. Enough for all of you. Luckily I was making a big batch to freeze." She opened the canvas bag. "Just pop it in the oven at 325 for about forty-five minutes."

"Uh-oh. Um…" He peeled back the tinfoil on the top of the glass dish and peered in while she pulled out a few more dishes. "Hey. That almost looks like mac and cheese."

"I prefer to call it five-cheese pasta."

He wrinkled his nose. "And is one of those five cheeses goat cheese?"

She laughed. He was so cute when he did that. The man had no inhibitions about appearing "funny," and she found that appealing. The view on the wall might be faux, but the man was real. "I guess you'll have to try it and find out. Ryan and I have made some culinary compromises. He eats this. That should be all you need to know."

"But, but…mac and cheese is supposed to be glow-in-the-dark orange."

"Don't you have enough color with your artwork, without needing artificial ones in your food? There's plenty of color in real food. If you look closer, you'll see that there's some cheddar in there, and it's orange."

"Well, okay. Thanks. We'll try it. I just won't tell Derek's kids about the goat cheese."

"Good idea." She dug in her purse. "Now, here's a key to my apartment—"

"Awesome. Already we're exchanging keys. I like how you think." He took the key ring from her fingers, giving her a wink that turned smoldering. Cute Guy was gone, replaced with the hot, handsome man who could actually be a superhero.

Shannon blushed, then groped for something to say. "S-smart aleck."

It was as if she'd flipped a switch, activating every nerve in his body and triggering a flood of hormones. Greg set the keys on the cutting block and stepped even closer to her. The rise of scarlet up her neck and in her cheeks clued him that she'd felt it, too. "What is it about you—" he stroked the back of his fingers over her cheek "—that makes me forget common sense, forget that we agreed not to go here for Ryan's sake, and just makes me want to kiss you senseless again?"

She grabbed his wrist and forced his hand away from her face. "I—I... I have to get to work," she stammered, backing away from him. "That's a spare key, so you can lock the door behind you when you take Ryan home. I'll—I'll see you in the morning. Thanks again."

The sway of her ass in the clingy black dress pants as she hustled out of the kitchen sent a further surge of testosterone through him. He parked himself in the archway to watch her stride the length of the hall and didn't move again until the front door closed behind her.

He wanted to see her in the morning, all right. But not exhausted after a long night's work. He wanted to see her heavy-lidded and languid, silky hair spread out across a pillow, rousing from sleep after a long night of lovemaking, to start the morning off with another round.

Damn, he had it bad.

Lust. It's just lust. Nothing that a long cold shower wouldn't cure. At least, temporarily. Unfortunately, with four kids running around the house that was out of the question right now.

So he'd have to deal with it.

The house phone rang. Greg went to the desk,

fumbling through the piles of junk mail before locating the wireless handset. Caller ID said Blocked Caller, but that would be typical of most of his brothers. "Yell-ow."

"No, blue." At the sound of familiar feminine giggling, Greg's gut lurched.

"Denise." He sighed. The phone call worked better than a cold shower, as his libido—and its physical manifestation—shrank. "What's up?"

"Not me, that's for sure. I've had a really bad day at work. So much that I'm in need of chocolate-cream pie. I thought I'd see if I could pick one up at the bakery and swing by your place. I could use someone to help me eat it. If I eat the whole thing myself, I'll just be more upset."

Chocolate-cream pie with graham cracker crust and whipped cream on top happened to be his favorite. As Denise very well knew. "Sorry, Denise. I've got plans tonight."

"Yeah, I know. Elke told me you're babysitting for Derek. That's okay, I don't mind the kids. Besides, they're not staying that late."

"Elke doesn't know everything. Actually, I've got an overnight babysitting gig. Even if I didn't, Denise, the answer would still be no."

"Overnight? Who are you babysitting overnight?"

"It doesn't matter—"

"It's for her, isn't it? The one with the kid who doesn't talk? Elke told me you had them to Sunday dinner a few weeks ago, and couldn't keep your eyes off her."

"Sorry you had a crappy day, Denise. I have to go now." Greg disconnected the call, vowing to answer no more Blocked Caller numbers, his brothers be damned. He immediately dialed another number. He felt like an ass, racing from Denise to Elke, but he had a few choice words for his sister before his ex got to her first. "Elke," he snapped, before she'd even finished saying hello, "I want you to stop discussing me with Denise. Enough already."

"What are you talking about, Greg?"

"I'm talking about the fact that Denise knew all about me babysitting for Derek tonight, and about Shannon and Ryan coming to Sunday dinner."

"So? She's my best friend. I tell her all sorts of stuff about my life."

"Discussing *your* life is fine. The parts where I come in are now off limits, got it?"

"Geez, I don't know what you're so mad about."

Greg took a deep breath and dropped his voice to a low, silky tone. "Elke? You know your wedding this summer? Unless you want me showing up in the Captain Chemo costume, I suggest you stop talking to Denise about me. Do I make myself clear?"

"You wouldn't!"

"Don't try me!"

"That's just wrong."

"Yes, it is." Overhead, an ominous thud shook the ceiling. "Gotta run, Elke. See ya on the funny pages." At the funny farm was more like it lately. He tossed the phone on the desk and headed for the stairs to investigate. By the time he hit the landing, the sounds of shushing, interspersed with childish giggling, reached him. Super Uncle instincts kicked in—they were up to trouble.

He stopped at the top of the stairs and folded his arms over his chest, as Jack hoisted his three-year-old sister, Lila, to unlatch the hook and eye on the door to Greg's studio. Ryan glanced over his shoulder, twinkling eyes going wide beneath the black mask he—like the rest of the gang—wore.

Greg shook his head, putting his finger over his mouth. "Just what do you think you're doing?"

"Ack!" Jack fumbled with the toddler, and Greg raced forward to catch her. He set Lila on the floor.

"Geez, Uncle Greg, you scared me. I almost dropped Lila!"

Greg stepped in front of his door. "You didn't answer me, Jack. What are you doing? You know this room is off limits. The lock is up here to keep short people like you out. And read this sign. What does this say?" He pointed to the red street sign bolted lower on the door, eye level to any six-year-old, Ryan and Katie included.

"Stop," Katie said.

"Stop," Lila repeated, nodding solemnly.

"Stop," Greg agreed. "But what do I find? A bunch of rugrats trying to break into my secret lair. You know better. Just for that, you're all banished from the second floor tonight as well. You're stuck watching the old television in the living room."

"Aw, Uncle Greg, we just wanted to show Ryan all the cool stuff you have in there," Jack said.

"Exactly why you're not allowed in there without me. That's *my* cool stuff." He snapped the elastic on the back of Jack's head. "What's with the masks? You're all burglars?"

"'Course not!" Katie squeaked indignantly, propping her fists on her hips. "We're superheroes!"

"Superheroes don't break and enter. They leave that for the villains. Now, downstairs, all of you. Git!"

The three older kids scrambled down the stairs. Greg

descended behind Lila, who clung to the banister and took one precise step at a time.

There were just too many people in his life these days who didn't know where the stop signs were. As he headed back to the kitchen to put the five-cheese pasta in the oven for his masked gang of sure-to-be-starving-soon superheroes, his thoughts wandered back to Shannon, and the impulse to kiss her.

Hell, even he had a hard time observing the boundaries.

The good stuff always lay just on the other side.

GREG LOOKED OVER at the boy on the sofa. Apparently an evening of racing around his house playing super-hero—the little TV hadn't held as much appeal as the wide screen in the theater room—had taken its toll. The movie they'd brought from his house when they'd returned to Shannon's apartment for the overnight portion of his babysitting gig had barely started, and already Ryan had crashed. The holes in the black mask he still wore revealed shuttered eyelids. Opting to let sleeping kids lie, Greg pulled a crocheted blanket from the back of the sofa and covered Ryan.

At the table, Greg opened his portfolio, pulling out some sheets of vellum, and tried to pass the time usefully, working on the latest issue of *Y-Men* he was sketching. But he hadn't worked outside his studio in a while, and it felt odd. Not to mention the fact that he was in her place.

An intense need to know more about her tormented him. He headed for her room. Once inside, he sat on the edge of the bed, giving the mattress an experimental bounce. The satin mask she'd worn the morning he'd scared her lay on the bedside table, along with a stack of hardcover library books. The top book was about changing your thoughts to change your life, using the wisdom of the Tao. Very Shannon. But the other two… *The Zookeeper's Wife: A War Story* and the biography of Charles Schulz, creator of the Peanuts…

Interesting. Not what he'd expected from her. Fascinating that a woman who seemed to so actively dislike comic books was reading the biography of one of the most famous comic-strip artists ever. But then she often caught him by surprise. A woman of contradictions. He'd love to know the why behind that reading choice.

And why he couldn't stop thinking about her.

He jumped from the bed to prowl the perimeter of the room, socks scuffing against the low-pile carpet. There was nothing on the top of her dresser, not a hairbrush, not a bottle of perfume or makeup, not a piece of jewelry. His sisters had always had cluttered dresser tops, overflowing with all sorts of girlie crap. But Shannon's austere lifestyle even reached her bedroom.

Greg's chest tightened.

Finn would have a field day with that reaction, but the truth was, he hurt for her. For both her and Ryan.

Enough mushy stuff. He eased open the top dresser drawer, hoping to learn more about her.

And came face-to-face with Shannon's secrets.

Or at least her lingerie.

Another surprise. Because there was nothing austere or Amish-like about the woman's taste in undergarments. He'd expected white cotton briefs. What he found was…not.

Matching bra and string-bikini sets. One was eggshell with eyelet details and a scalloped edge along the waistband. Another was midnight black with embroidered hot-pink flowers and a cream bow between the cups.

A soft pink set lay beneath the others.

It wasn't his chest that tightened this time.

He'd give his left hand—his drawing hand—to see her in the black.

"What are you doing?"

Greg jumped, slamming the drawer shut while heat flamed his face. "I'm not—nothing—" Realization dawned. "Ryan? What did you say? Did you talk? You're talking!" Heart hammering, Greg forced himself to slowly head for the boy. "That's terrific! Your aunt Shannon is going to be so happy, Ryan."

"I'm not Ryan. I'm SuperKid." The boy propped his fists on his hips, striking a pose like the ABC Men at the zoo. "You're not supposed to be opening Aunt Shannon's drawers. She doesn't like that."

Great. The kid starts talking and my ass is grass because the first thing he's going to say to Shannon is that I was pawing her underwear. That would score points with her. Scratch the possibility of ever seeing her in the sexy lingerie. "SuperKid, huh? That's cool. Should we call Aunt Shannon at work?"

Ryan shook his head. "She doesn't like it when Mrs. K. calls her at work."

Apparently Aunt Shannon had a number of dislikes, and Ryan knew all of them. "Okay. We'll wait and surprise her in the morning. Let's go watch the rest of the movie, huh, sport?"

He held out his hand, and the boy accepted it. Greg felt like celebrating with a touchdown dance. For whatever reason, the boy was speaking.

With any luck, Ryan's success story and the promo they could get out of it would be enough to save his program at the university after all. The dean loved positive press relating to the school. Not to mention it would look pretty bad to dump a program that heroically helped kids.

SHANNON TRUDGED UP the apartment stairs. The extra hours, while great for the paycheck, had taken their toll. She wanted nothing more than to crawl into bed and sleep. A pair of large, bare, masculine feet hanging over the end of her sofa brought her up short.

Ryan, the usual occupant of the couch, didn't have feet that size.

It wasn't that she'd forgotten Greg was spending the night in her apartment. But the reality of finding him on her couch at five-twenty in the morning was something else.

Did it mean she was developing a foot fetish if she admitted that those bare feet, so strong, so unabashedly male beneath the hem of his dark denim jeans, were sexy?

Shaking her head, she crept into the living room. Greg sprawled on his back, one arm dangling onto the floor. A picture-book version of *The Ransom of Red Chief* by O. Henry tented across Greg's chest. Ryan's favorite. They'd checked it out four or five times since he'd come to live with her.

Shannon gingerly plucked the book from Greg's torso, wincing at the crackling of the plastic library cover as she closed it and set it on the end table behind his head.

In sleep, without the distraction of the twinkle in his eye or the quick grin, the angles of his face—the high cheekbones, the sharp jawline—demanded exploration. She reached out.

No touching! Though her fingers yearned to caress him, she had to keep her hands to herself. A pity. Shannon fled the temptation, searching for Ryan instead.

She found him where she'd least expected to, in his own room, in his own bed. Score another point for Greg Hawkins. He knew how to get kids to sleep where they belonged. A black mask lay on the floor near the bed. Shannon picked it up, setting it on the computer desk on her way out.

She went to her own room, closed the door, and went through her morning ritual of darkening the room. It was odd to slide between the sheets knowing Greg was only a few feet away in her living room. She had no idea what time he had to head off to work, but that wasn't her problem. She had to grab what rest she could before Ryan got up.

She inhaled deeply and exhaled slowly, let her muscles relax, willing herself to sink into the mattress, into sleep.

It seemed like only minutes later that a harsh whisper woke her. "Shannon? I come in peace, okay? Let's not have a replay of our first bedroom scene, huh?"

She cracked open one eye, blinking against the light he'd turned on. "You're like Ryan."

He paused at the side of the bed. "I am?"

"Yeah. Cuter when you're asleep. Go 'way." She rolled onto her side, giving him her back. "Thanks, though," she mumbled.

"But I have amazing news. Ryan spoke."

"Wh-what?" She sat up. "He did? What did he say?"

Greg laughed. "A lot. Did you know he can recite all of *Red Chief?* Come on." He held out his hand.

She let him pull her out of bed, grabbing her bathrobe

as they passed the closet. Greg led her into Ryan's room, her heart hammering with excitement.

Greg leaned over the futon and shook the boy. "Ryan? Hey, wake up, sport. Look who's home. Aunt Shannon. Say good morning to her."

Ryan knuckled his eyes.

Shannon knelt on the floor. "Ryan? Hey, buddy."

He blinked a few times, glancing from one to the other. Then he shook his head.

"No what, Ryan?"

He tossed back the covers and bolted from the bed, then the room. The bathroom door slammed a moment later.

Shannon raised her eyebrows as she got to her feet.

Greg shrugged. "When a guy's gotta go, there's no time for words." He headed for the door. "I know what will get him talking."

She followed him as far as the bathroom, then waited there while Greg dashed to the living room. The toilet flushed, then water ran in the sink. A moment later Ryan reappeared.

"Sport, c'mere! Look, I have *Red Chief*. Let's read it to Aunt Shannon, huh?" The plastic crinkled as Greg waved the book.

Ryan turned his big eyes toward Shannon, gazing up at her. He slowly shook his head, then returned to his room.

"That's not talking." Shannon's stomach tightened. "What the hell kind of a game are you playing?"

"I swear to you, that kid was talking last night. Actually, I wasn't sure he was going to shut up once he got started. I don't get it." Greg dragged his hand over his face. "I don't get it."

"Maybe it was just a dream."

"It wasn't a dream. Dammit, that kid talked to me last night!"

"Well, he's not talking now. And I have to get some rest. Thanks for babysitting. I really appreciate it. But like Ryan, I'm going back to bed now."

"Ta-da!" Ryan, who'd obviously not gone back to bed, jumped into the hall, the black mask she'd put on the computer desk in place over his eyes.

Shannon pressed her palm against her chest, a lump swelling in her throat. So that's what he sounded like. It had been so long she'd forgotten.

"I'm SuperKid," Ryan pronounced. In a firm, *strong* voice.

Shannon wanted to sink to her knees and thank the universe. But she had to play it cool. Ryan's psychiatrist had advised her not to make a big deal of the fact that he didn't talk, so she couldn't make too much fuss that he now was. "SuperKid, huh? I wondered whose mask that was on the floor." She bent over and gave him a hug. "Now, how about I make us a special breakfast? What do you want?"

"SuperKid needs to be strong." Ryan flexed a non-existent bicep. "So he can fight the good fight. How 'bout red-and-green eggs?"

"Seems like a plan to me." Amazed at just how normal Ryan sounded, Shannon headed for the kitchen. Well, the therapist had said he'd talk when he was ready. Apparently, he was right.

"Red-and-green eggs?" Greg asked.

"Tomato-and-spinach omelet," Shannon explained. "Ryan, take that mask off and go wash your face and hands so you're ready to eat."

"SuperKid doesn't take off his mask." Ryan set his feet wide and propped his fists on his hips.

"He does if he wants to eat at my table."

"Uh, Shannon," Greg started, "I think—"

"That's enough playing around." Though thrilled at Ryan's miracle, she was tired. She went over, pulled the mask off and handed it to him. "Go on. Put this away and get ready."

Ryan's shoulders slumped as he turned away.

"You want some red-and-green eggs, too?" she asked Greg.

"I don't think you understand what's going on with Ryan."

"And you do?"

"I believe so, yes."

Shannon lit the flame under the sauté pan and flicked some butter into it. "Enlighten me, Mr. Know-it-All." She stifled a yawn with the back of her hand.

Greg folded his arms across his chest. "No. I think I'll let you figure it out for yourself."

"So you're staying for breakfast?"

"Absolutely. I wouldn't miss this for the world."

"Red-and-green eggs?"

"As long as the green isn't artichoke, I'm game."

Shannon made short work of turning out three omelets. Greg poured orange juice. Ryan slouched in his chair, chin propped on his hand. When Shannon set his plate in front of him, he nodded.

Like he had every other morning.

"Ryan?" Knowing nagging and cajoling hadn't worked to get him to talk in the first place, Shannon searched for something that would entice him to respond. "Did you have fun at Greg's house last night?"

A halfhearted nod.

"What did you do?"

A lazy shrug.

Shannon shot a worried glance at Greg, who simply raised his shoulders and one hand. Saying very clearly in the silent language she'd become adept at decoding, *Don't look at me.*

"Did you have fun with Katie and the other kids?"

Another nod.

"Did you get into a fight with Jack this time?"

Indignant head-shake.

"Ryan! Why won't you talk to me? You talked to me just a few minutes ago. I'm sorry if I hurt your feelings about the mask."

Ryan shoveled eggs into his mouth.

Shannon pushed her plate away, no longer hungry and more than a bit apprehensive that she'd done something to derail Ryan's miracle.

Greg left the table, returning with the black mask. He slipped it on Ryan's head, carefully adjusting it so the boy could see. "There you go, SuperKid."

"Thank you," Ryan said, sitting up straighter.

"Tell Aunt Shannon what we had for dessert last night."

"We made chocolate-chip cookies," he said around a mouthful of omelet.

"Don't talk with your mouth full," Shannon murmured. There was something she hadn't expected to tell him anytime soon. "Cookies, huh?"

"Yeah. Me and Katie got to scoop the dough out of the bucket. Jack took them off the tray when they were cooked."

"Impressive." Shannon's mind whirled. What did it

mean that Ryan—or rather, SuperKid—would only talk with the mask on?

The implication made her stomach queasy. "G-Greg? Can I see you in the other room? Ryan, finish your breakfast. We'll be right back."

She didn't wait to see if Greg followed her, but darted to her bedroom. When the door closed, she spun to face him. "What did you do to him? You broke him."

CHAPTER SEVEN

"WHAT DO YOU MEAN, I broke him? Don't be ridiculous. I helped fix him. He's talking, right?"

"*Ryan* is not talking. SuperKid is talking. Not only did you push my nephew into multiple personalities, but thanks to you, his other personality is a superhero."

Greg's mouth dropped open like a ventriloquist dummy with no ventriloquist. Then he started to laugh, and for a moment, Shannon wanted to forget she didn't believe in using violence to solve problems and slug him. "I don't see what's funny."

"Oh, Shannon. Ryan doesn't have multiple personalities. He's pretending. The mask and the superhero persona make him feel safe. Empowered. Trust me, this is a great first step. Eventually he won't need the mask to talk to us."

"How do you know for sure?"

"Didn't you ever pretend as a kid?"

Head reeling, Shannon perched on the side of the bed. "Doesn't mental illness tend to run in families?"

"What? Was someone in your family mentally ill? Ryan's mother?"

"Just answer the question. Does it run in families or not?"

"It can," he said. "But I'm telling you, Ryan hasn't

disassociated into multiple personalities. He's using SuperKid as a safe haven to start talking to us."

"You'll forgive me if I don't take *your* word for it. I'm calling Dr. Lansing's office this morning as soon as they open. Hopefully he can see Ryan today." Shannon opened the night-table drawer, searching for the psychiatrist's card.

"Great idea. He'll tell you the same thing I have."

"Then I guess I'll owe you an apology." But right now, she wanted firm answers. From someone with more letters after their name than Greg.

LATER THAT AFTERNOON, Greg paused as he reached the beach, shielding his eyes with his hand. Wind blew in off the lake, stirring up small waves out beyond the break wall. A golden retriever with a stick in its mouth towed its owner past him.

Shannon sat on a blanket halfway to the water while Ryan, jeans rolled up to his knees, hopped around in the damp sand at the water's edge. The boy wore the mask.

Greg resisted the urge to pump his fist in victory. If Ryan was wearing the mask—in public, no less—then the shrink must have confirmed what he'd told Shannon. He trudged across the shifting beach surface, cursing under his breath as the sand seeped into his shoes. He flopped down beside her on the blanket.

"I see you got my message."

"I did. You really should get a cell phone." Greg untied his shoe, removed it, then dumped the sand out.

"I don't need a cell phone."

"If you had a cell phone, you could have called me from here and told me what Dr. Lansing said. You could have called me from Dr. Lansing's *parking lot*. So, spill it. What *did* he say? When do I get my apology?"

She glared at him, which made him want to laugh. If Shannon were a superhero, one of her powers would be vaporizing beams shooting from her eyes.

"I'm sorry," she said. "You were right."

"That wasn't so hard, was it?"

"Remember when I said you were exasperating?"

"Yes."

"Clearly I understated things."

Greg surrendered, letting himself laugh out loud. "My sisters would agree. So, details. What exactly did Dr. Lansing tell you?"

She wrapped her arms around her knees. "Ryan's fine, just like you told me. In fact, Dr. Lansing repeated you almost word for word. This is a positive first step. That the mask and the SuperKid persona make him feel safe. Empowered. I believe that's the term you and the social worker both used to get me to try the art therapy, right?"

Greg emptied his other shoe. "It was. To prove what a terrific guy I am, I'm not going to say I told you so. Still, with your dislike of superheroes, I'm surprised you're letting him run around the beach with the mask on."

"According to the psychiatrist…and you…he won't be a superhero forever. Eventually he'll be just a boy again. But if it makes him feel safe right now, after all he's been through, who am I to take that security away?" She lowered her head, her fluttering hands smoothing the blanket.

"You didn't have a very secure childhood, did you?"

She looked back up, her expression softening. "What gives it away?"

"I'd like to take credit for seeing it in your art, but no. It's in your demeanor. Your lifestyle. Your whole just-let-it-go attitude."

"Really?"

He nodded. "Yeah. Does it have anything to do with that mentally ill family member you mentioned this morning?"

She focused on Ryan. Waves lapped at the shoreline and gulls keened overhead, filling the silence.

"Would it be easier to talk about it if you had a mask on?"

Startled, she returned her attention briefly to him before watching the boy again. "Hmm. Yeah, I guess it would." Her fingers picked at the hem of her jeans. "My father. I don't know if he was ever diagnosed, but considering his behavior, I think maybe he was mentally ill. Bipolar or obsessive-compulsive." She shrugged.

"What kind of behavior?" he asked gently, bracing himself. He'd heard all sorts of stories from the kids he'd worked with.

"He gave away everything I ever cared about. Toys. Books. Clothes. There was always someone he knew who needed it more. We didn't *need* it. He even gave away our cat.

"My mother ran interference the best she could. Mostly she supported what he did. He was teaching us to be good people. To be givers. To help others. But…" She paused. "My mother died when I was eight. Dad got worse after that."

"Damn." He wanted to ask how her mother had died but didn't dare interrupt as she opened up to him.

"Yeah. Willow split the minute she turned eighteen

and didn't look back. My father died a month before my high-school graduation. I was already eighteen, so I finished school living with a friend's family, and then I followed in my sister's footsteps and left town."

That explained her lack of attachment to things. Or people. His admiration for her rose another notch. In her childhood, she'd learned it was better to just let go before she got too attached. Yet here she was, doing her best to parent and keep Ryan.

"You're an amazing woman, Shannon Vanderhoff."

"Not so amazing. You do what you have to. Enough about me," she said. "What about you? I guess you had a secure childhood, huh?"

"What do you think?"

She averted her gaze again, intent on the swirl she was drawing in the sand with her fingertip. "I think you're a lucky guy."

"Yeah. I think so, too." He reached out and stroked her face. The soft, smooth skin made him want to know if the rest of her felt the same. He had to taste her again. "Very lucky." He shifted closer, leaned in…

"Aunt Shannon! Lookit."

Greg retreated as Ryan charged for the blanket, cupped hands held in front of him.

"Hey, Uncle Greg! Look."

Shannon raised an eyebrow. "Uncle Greg? When did you become Uncle Greg?"

"Last night. Apparently it's something he picked up from Derek's kids." He shrugged. "No biggie. I'm uncle to so many, what's one more?"

They oohed and aahed over Ryan's green beach glass. "You know," Greg told him, "some people make jewelry out of that stuff." The slivers of old glass, once part of a bottle, had been tumbled smooth by the water of Lake Erie.

"Cool! SuperKid will find more. Here, hold this." The boy dumped the pieces into Shannon's hand, then scampered back down to the waterline.

Greg shook his head.

"Amazing, isn't it? Almost like nothing had ever happened." Shannon propped her chin on her knees, drawn up to her chest.

"What's wrong? You know he's okay, so shouldn't you be happy about it?"

"I am. But now that he's talking again, I have to call the D.A.'s office and let them know. I hate the idea of them asking him questions about that night."

"I can understand that." Greg peered at her more closely. The bags—more like steamer trunks—were parked beneath her eyes again. A few thin, red lines crisscrossed the white of her eyes, making her a perfect candidate for a Visine commercial. "You're exhausted."

"I'm running on about an hour and half's sleep, and it's been quite a day. Who'd think happy events would be emotionally draining?"

"Do you have to work tonight?"

"Yes."

"And do you have a sitter?"

Shannon's shoulders lifted, then fell. "I haven't heard from Mrs. K. yet."

"Tell you what. How about you let Mrs. K. have another night to recover from whatever bug she's got. I'll take Ryan with me, and you can go home to peace and quiet and get some sleep. I'll bring him over just before you go to work so you can say good-night to him, and I'll stay with him again."

"You don't have to do that."

"No, I don't *have to*. But I want to."

"Why?"

"Why? What kind of a question is that?"

She let her legs drop down, her body slumping. "An ungrateful one. I'm sorry. I guess I just wondered what we'd done to merit your going well above and beyond the call of duty. I mean, you don't babysit for your other clients, do you?"

He shook his head. "No, not usually. You really want to know why?"

"Sure."

Greg edged closer, catching a fleeting and tempting whiff of her coconut scent as he whispered, "I like Ryan. I like *you*."

She mustered a weary smile. "Despite my better judgment, I like you, too. For a comic-book artist, you're not half-bad, Greg Hawkins. But you probably shouldn't let your sister know you're coming on to me with flattery and favors."

"I won't tell if you won't."

She pressed her lips together with her fingers.

"Okay. Let's round up SuperKid and get out of here, huh? The sooner you go home, the more sleep you can get."

Shannon called Ryan over. The boy dragged his feet through the sand on his way, as if he knew beach time was over. His initial protests while Shannon dried his legs and brushed sand off him with a towel quickly subsided when she told him he was going home with Greg again.

"What do you say we grab some pizza for dinner?"

The boy narrowed his eyes behind the mask. "Not

artichoke pizza, right? Artichoke pizza makes Super-Kid weak."

Greg laughed, ruffling the boy's hair. "No, I was thinking more like pepperoni."

"How about sausage?"

"That'll work, too."

"All right!" He wiggled impatiently as Shannon tied his sneakers.

"Wasn't that water still cold?" Greg asked. Though almost June, Lake Erie generally didn't warm up until July.

"Not for SuperKid," Ryan assured him.

"Of course. What was I thinking?" Greg extended his hand, then pulled Shannon up from the blanket. She shook out the towel and the quilt before folding them. They made their way toward the dune that led down to the parking area.

There was a rightness to their being together.

Like they were a family.

A family? What the hell was he thinking? Especially now that he knew just how deep her emotional wounds ran, how hard it would be for her to overcome her let-it-go tendencies. He stumbled, sliding down the last few feet of the dune. See what that kind of thinking got him? Off balance and shoes full of gritty, irritating sand.

A clear warning if ever there'd been one.

Shannon dumped the towel and blanket in the trunk of her battered old Taurus. The car probably didn't even have air bags. "Are you holding this thing together with duct tape and twine?" he asked.

"No, chewing gum and rubber bands. Hey, it runs fine. It gets us where we need to go. Who wants more than that?"

"As long as it's safe, I suppose."

Shannon stooped and hugged Ryan. "Behave for Greg, okay? I'll see you later, before I go to work." She straightened. "Thanks again. You're a lifesaver."

"So don't I get a hug, too?" He held open his arms.

She hesitated a moment. He'd only been joking, but she stepped into his arms and he wrapped her in an embrace. Once again the scent of coconut filled his nose and a sense of well-being centered him.

Weird. Completely opposite to how he'd felt only moments before.

Was he supposed to cave in to his attraction, or stay the hell away from her?

She patted him on the back, then pushed away, and the friendly hug was over long before he wanted. Greg held Ryan's hand and they waved as she backed out of the parking space. Then he swung the boy into his Tracker and buckled him in. "Okay, sport, let's go run some errands, then we'll get some sausage pizza and head home."

SuperKid gave him a thumbs-up.

HAYDEN MET HIM at the front door. That wasn't a good sign. Greg had barely gotten in the house, juggling two pizzas and a six-pack of dark ale, not to mention herding a mini-superhero who didn't want to be herded because he was more interested in watching the next-door kids shoot hoops, when his brother descended.

"Man, I'm sorry! I couldn't get her to leave. She was on the front porch when I got home, and just wouldn't take no for an answer. That is one determined woman, dude."

The woman in question hustled down the hallway, a

pie carefully cradled in her extended hands. "Greg! You're home. Look what I brought. I figured since you were too busy to share a chocolate-cream pie with me last night, I'd just bring one over tonight."

Ryan stepped out from behind him. "Chocolate pie? With whipped cream?"

Hayden crouched down. "Well, hey, Ryan. I didn't know you were coming over again. Gimme five."

The boy slapped palms with him.

Denise stopped short. "I didn't know *he* was coming over again, either. And I thought he didn't talk?"

"Hayden, take Ryan and dinner into the kitchen, will you?" Greg stifled the urge to throttle her. Even Hayden possessed enough instinct not to draw attention to the boy's dramatic recovery. Obviously she didn't.

"Sure." His brother collected the pizza boxes, balancing the six-pack carefully on top, then took Ryan by the hand, leading him around Denise. "Let's go, little man. You can help me find some paper plates."

Ryan stared over his shoulder at Greg, who nodded at him. "I'll be there in a minute, sport."

"Why are you babysitting that boy again? There *is* something going on between you and his aunt, isn't there?"

An upset, potentially angry female with a pie in her hands. Not a good combination.

Greg gently took the pie from Denise and set it on the bench in the foyer. "We're friends. Friends do favors for each other. Like you bringing this pie over. Thank you. But I thought I'd made myself clear. I don't know how to say it any plainer, Denise. We are *over*. A chocolate pie is not going to get us back together."

"Maybe you don't know it yet, but I do. There's something going on between the two of you, and I'm telling you now, she's not the keeping kind. That kid and his aunt will break your heart. And when they do, don't come running to me for comfort. Because I'm not waiting around for you. This is your last chance."

"Good," he murmured.

"What?"

"I said, food. I'm hungry, and my dinner's getting cold in the kitchen. Plus, Ryan doesn't know Hayden that well, so I should probably go check on how he's doing." He sidled toward the door.

Her lower lip quivered. "You always said you admired my determination. My loyalty. How I never give up."

"I did. I do. But I've discovered that there's a very fine line between persistence and stalking. You're crossing that line." He cleared his throat, shifting his feet in place.

"Really?"

"Yes. Really. I'm sorry. I don't mean to hurt you, Dee. You've been Elke's best friend since I was in kindergarten."

She tilted her chin up in defiance of the tears he could see gathering in her eyes. "You didn't hurt me. But you're not getting this." She snatched up the pie along with her purse. "And I might still be Elke's best friend, but *we* are *not* friends. Don't expect any more favors from me." Lips tightly pressed together, she looked at the pie, then at him.

He flinched, bracing himself.

She laughed, a cold, hollow sound. "You're not worth it. I'm not wasting this by tossing it in your face, no matter how tempting."

When the door clicked shut behind her, Greg heaved

a huge sigh. Hopefully she meant it this time. He headed for the kitchen, where Ryan knelt on a chair at the table, busily chowing down on a slice of pizza. Hayden raised one eyebrow in question, and Greg shrugged. "Well, guys, there's no chocolate pie for dessert. Maybe we'll just go get some ice cream instead."

"Chocolate?" Ryan asked, mouth smeared with red sauce.

"Is there any other kind?"

"Artichoke," the boy said, then giggled.

"Artichoke ice cream?" Hayden shook his head. "You have some strange taste, little man. We should hook you up with Finn."

The running joke between him and Ryan made Greg smile. And despite his protests to Denise, despite his love of chocolate, despite the conflicting signals he was getting, Greg had to admit, he'd developed a hankering for something different.

For a woman who liked artichoke pizza.

IN THE 2:00 A.M. DARKNESS of the apartment-complex parking lot, Shannon leaned her head against the steering wheel.

Breathe in, breathe out, let go.

She repeated the mantra a few more times before heading into the apartment. The light over the table shone down into the foyer, and she heard a chair shift as she climbed the stairs.

"Shannon?" Greg rose from the table, which was spread with papers and art supplies. "What's wrong? What are you doing home?"

"What are you doing *up?* I figured I'd find both of you guys sleeping."

He gestured at the comic-book pages. "I've had a bunch of business meetings lately, so I'm behind with this."

"Business meetings?"

"Yeah." His shoulders slumped.

"Try not to sound so excited. They didn't go well?"

"No, they didn't."

"Is there any way I can help?"

His wry smile was tempered with sadness. "Got a hundred thousand dollars you could lend me?"

"Absolutely. Let me just write a check. You don't mind if it bounces, do you?"

He chuckled. "Exactly my problem, too. Enough about my troubles. Now, you answer my question."

She set her purse on the kitchen island. "I got fired."

"Oh. That sucks. What happened?"

She sighed. "I fell asleep at my desk. First time that's ever happened. And I even had a nap today, thanks to you."

"I'm so sorry."

"It's just a job. I'll get another one. I was checking into doing something else anyway. A day job. Especially if Ryan's talking now. I couldn't keep this up."

"Just let it go, huh?"

"Exactly."

"I don't think Cathy's going to be happy. But I'm sure she'll spin it to your advantage. You're searching for a job that makes it easier for you to care for Ryan." Greg gathered up some of his papers, putting them into a large leather folder. He blew on another page, the ink still glistening. "The woman from the district attorney's office called."

"She did?" Shannon leaned against the counter.

"Yeah. The detectives are coming up on Saturday

to take Ryan's statement. I volunteered my workroom at the university for it, that way you can watch through the window."

"Through the window? I can't be with him?"

Greg shook his head. "She said if possible they like to talk to the kids alone. They're bringing their shrink, too."

"Great. I can hardly wait. Why Saturday?"

Greg shrugged. "The sooner the better, she said. Apparently the defense attorney is fast-tracking the trial. Probably to try to get it done before Ryan recovers and starts talking. Well, we fooled them." He punctuated the statement with a thin brush in the air. "Saturday is the soonest they can come. Eleven thirty. That's when I finish up with my second group of cancer kids on Saturday mornings."

Shannon shivered, then rubbed her arms, pacing a short circle in the kitchen. "What if he gets off, Greg? What if Ryan can't tell them what happened? What if he tells them something that doesn't fit the evidence?"

"Hey." He stopped packing his plastic supply case and came over to grip her by the shoulders. "Stop it. Take one step at a time, right?"

"Yeah. But…" The implications struck her hard. Not only could she potentially lose Ryan to his grandparents, an even worse case scenario would be losing Ryan to his father.

To the man who'd murdered her sister.

Greg pulled her into an embrace, stroking her hair. She tucked her face into the curve of his neck, inhaling deeply. The faint, clean scent of soap mingled with warm, musky man. She wished she could just lose herself in him. To forget all the problems she faced and just…enjoy. She lifted her head….

And found a hunger smoldering in his blue eyes, mirroring her own. "We're not supposed—"

"Shh. I've been wanting to do this all day." He slid his hands into her hair, cupping her head, holding her firmly.

Shannon shut her eyes as he closed the gap between them. Without hesitation, he crushed his mouth to hers, his tongue seeking entrance, which she gladly granted.

He walked her backward until she bumped into the counter. She fitted against him so perfectly. Pulling gently on her hair, he forced her head back, grazing his teeth over her neck, sending shivers of pleasure coursing over her.

She flexed her hips, and denim brushed denim as she arched into him like a demanding cat, needing more attention. He ground his erection over her sweet spot, and she gasped.

"Like that, do you?" he growled into her ear.

"Oh, yes," she panted. "More."

"I...want...you." He punctuated each word with a grind, while his nimble fingers opened the top buttons of her blouse and slid into the cup of her bra.

"No kiddi—oh." She moaned as he stroked her nipple to attention.

He changed up the rhythm, faster, slower, faster, then almost nonexistent, and her mind went blank. She clutched his back. "Don't stop!" she hissed.

His mouth fastened on hers again, his fingers, his body, all driving her closer and closer to the goal.

Almost, almost, almost...

She shuddered against him, an orgasm claiming her. After a few moments, the high was replaced with blessed languidness. She sagged weakly.

Greg supported her, pulling his lips from hers to stare at her with surprise. "Did you just..."

"Oh, yeah." Shannon blew out a long breath. "I did. And it was good."

His expression turned smug. "Cool." He waggled his eyebrows. "If you thought that was *good*, just wait. I can provide *great* if we're both naked." A slow grin lit up his face. "I think we just found your superpower. Besides vaporizing men with your laser-beam glare, I mean."

"Superpower?" Still dazed, she wasn't following.

"Oh, yeah. Remember those ABC guys? I dub thee Lady O. But I envision you with a much sexier costume than those guys." He fingered the eyelets along the edge of her bra. "Something skimpy. And I can't wait to see you in it. This was hot—" he cleared his throat "—especially for you. But I want more."

"Actual sex?"

"That's a start, yeah."

"Greg," she began, fumbling for the right words, "if you want more than that, I'm not sure we should go there."

"You just went there."

"I did." She stroked her finger over his high cheekbones, delighted to finally get the chance to touch them. "You're a terrific guy, Greg. You're great with kids, you're talented, you're compassionate…"

"Geez, why does that sound like a post-hookup kiss-off when we haven't even hooked up yet?" He slid his hands along her waist and pulled her to him again.

"I just want you to know what you're getting into. I don't generally get involved with guys like you."

"Comic-book artists?"

"No. Guys with forever in their eyes."

"And here I thought it was lust."

Shannon chuckled. "Oh, that was there, too. But tell me you're not looking for what your parents have. What you grew up with."

"I...um—"

"Precisely. I can't give you that."

The sound of Ryan's bedroom door opening made them both jump. They moved apart faster than a speeding bullet, Shannon frantically fastening the top buttons of her blouse.

The bathroom door closed.

Greg adjusted his jeans. "I think you sell yourself short. You're not the same person you were just a few months ago. And I'll bet that scares the crap out of you, doesn't it?"

Hell, yes, it scared the crap out of her, but she wasn't about to admit it.

"Precisely," he said in response to her non-answer.

For a moment, they just stared at each other across the narrow kitchen. "I'll see you Saturday morning?" Shannon asked, moving into safer territory.

He glanced away from her, but not before she'd caught a flicker of...anxiety? guilt?...on his face. What was that about?

"Yeah. Saturday morning."

CHAPTER EIGHT

SHANNON CLUTCHED Ryan's hand as they walked into the Children's Center. A dull ache throbbed in the back of her head, and a flock of gulls, like the ones in the campus parking lot, had apparently taken up residence in her stomach.

She didn't want to put him through this.

But there was no choice. Willow deserved justice, and that meant her sister's son had to tell what he'd seen and heard that horrible night.

They climbed the stairs to the second floor, and headed down the corridor that led to Greg's art therapy room. She'd arrived ten minutes ahead of schedule, wanting to show Ryan the observation room, to assure him she'd be nearby if he needed her.

Shannon came to an abrupt halt, processing the commotion outside the room. The unnaturally bright light, the crowd of people. She edged closer.

The light came from a television camera. A reporter held a microphone up to Greg, who was animatedly talking, gesturing.

The gulls wheeled and careened in her stomach.

"...not just cancer kids," Greg was saying. "My program helps many children who need empowering. Victims of child abuse, kids whose parents are going through a divorce, those who've lost a parent or sibling. This program is important."

"Have you tried to find another organization to sponsor your program?" the reporter asked.

"I have. They already have their budgets in place for this year, so they can't take on anything additional, even if they love the idea."

"Do you have any cases that stand out for you?"

"Yes." Greg caught Shannon's eye, looking straight at her. "A child who became mute because of a traumatic experience. If we're lucky, maybe his aunt will tell you about it."

The reporter followed his gaze.

With one hand, Shannon pulled the mask from Ryan's head, eliciting an indignant squawk from the boy. She shoved it into her back pocket, grabbed him by the arm and forced her way through the throng of gathered parents, some of whom she recognized from their excursion to lunch the day she'd met Greg. "Excuse me, let me through."

"Ma'am? Could we ask you some questions about your experiences with Mr. Hawkins's art therapy program?"

"Absolutely not." Shannon kept her body between Ryan and the camera. The media had hounded them in Philadelphia, going so far as to film Willow's funeral from across the street. Whisking Ryan away to Erie had the added benefit of making him anonymous again. She wasn't about to blow that by feeding the vultures for any reason. "I'm sure these other fine folks would be happy to sing Mr. Hawkins's praises."

"Please, Shannon," Greg pleaded as she barreled past.

"No!" She shoved Ryan into the observation room and slammed the door behind them.

The kids working in Greg's room all glanced up at the mirrored window as the wall rattled. Another cameraman was filming the children and their drawings.

Hands tightly clenched, Shannon paced. Greg had let her walk into an ambush.

Ryan's wide eyes stopped her. She crouched down. "I'm sorry if I scared you. I don't like reporters." She pointed to the window. "See the kids working in Greg's room? That's where the lady is going to talk to you. I'm going to be right here. So even though you can't see me, you'll know that I'm close by, right here, okay?"

The boy just stared at her.

Shannon pulled the mask from her pocket and slipped it on his head. "There you go, SuperKid."

He didn't say anything, just moved closer to the window. For the next few minutes, they watched the children clean up the art supplies and tables. Some parents wandered in, collecting their kids. Eventually the room cleared out and the commotion in the hallway died down. Shortly after that, Greg escorted a woman and two men into the room. Shannon recognized one of the men as Detective James.

The other man began setting up a video camera on a tripod, pointing it at the table. Greg rapped on the window and gestured for her to join them.

"Ryan, I'm going into Greg's room now. You stay here and watch me through the window, okay?" At his nod, she left.

"Ms. Vanderhoff." Detective James extended his hand. "Nice to see you again. This is Dr. Martin, a psychiatrist who works with us. She'll be the one questioning Ryan. And that's Detective Evans. He was assigned to the case after you left Philadelphia with the boy."

After the introductions and assurance that they had Ryan's well-being firmly in mind, Shannon returned to the observation room, her heart in her throat. Greg followed on her heels. She pretended he didn't exist.

Ryan was plastered to the window. Shannon stooped to his level. "They're ready for you, Ryan."

He shook his head and yanked off the mask, thrusting it at her. She grabbed both his hands in hers. "Ryan, remember we talked about this? These people are the good guys. They're police detectives. They're here to see that your mom gets justice. This is how we fight the good fight, remember? Through the justice system? They need you. Your mom's counting on you."

Tears welled up in the boy's eyes and Shannon fought the urge to scoop him up and run away with him. Her nose tingled and she blinked hard several times.

But she slipped the mask back on his head. "Super-heroes are all about truth and justice. Isn't that *right*, Greg?" She growled his name, annoyed that she needed him to back her up.

He cleared his throat. "Absolutely."

"You can do this," she told Ryan. "Just go in there and tell the truth. No one's going to be mad at you. You're not going to get in trouble, whatever you say. There's nothing to be afraid of."

"SuperKid isn't afraid." The faint quiver in his voice said otherwise.

"Of course not." She willed her hand steady as she extended her closed fist.

Ryan bumped his fist into hers less than enthusiastically.

"I'll be right here, watching, okay?"

He nodded.

"Okay, sport, I'm going to take you in there and get you settled," Greg said. "Then I'm going to be in here with Aunt Shannon."

Shannon got to her feet as Ryan took Greg's hand. "You told them about…" Over the top of the boy's head, she gestured to her face, mimicking the mask.

"I did. They weren't thrilled with it, but…" Greg shrugged. "It's not like they have a lot of options right now."

Greg accompanied Ryan into the other room, providing him with paper and crayons. Something familiar for him. The doctor shook Ryan's hand. The other adults did their best to fade into the background. Greg tousled Ryan's hair and left.

Shannon turned on the speaker, facing the window. Warm-up chitchat started as Greg came back into the observation booth.

"Shannon, about the reporter—"

"Don't talk to me."

"I needed the press. You know how much this program means to me. I'm in danger of losing it. The *kids* are in danger of losing it."

She snapped her head around to glare at him. "*I'm* in danger of losing it right about now. And the only kid I care about is in there. So *shut up* and let me hear what's going on."

The doctor took her time getting Ryan comfortable. She complimented his drawing, and the mask, turned the talk to superheroes, the differences between telling a lie and telling the truth…

At first, Ryan answered nonverbally. Then with one or two words. Finally he offered short sentences.

Greg grunted. "She's skilled. Ryan's in good hands."

Eventually the questions veered to the night of Willow's death.

Shannon took a deep breath, willing all the strength she could through the glass to the little boy on the other side.

"Did you hear anything that night, Ryan?"

He nodded but didn't look up from his drawing. "Ryan heard yelling. It woke Ryan up. They were fighting."

"About what?"

He shrugged.

"Did they fight a lot?"

"Sometimes." Ryan deliberated on which crayon to choose from the box, then pulled out gray. "But not so loud."

"Then what happened?"

"Ryan's mom was crying. He went to see why."

"Where?"

"To their bedroom."

In the observation room, Shannon reluctantly turned to Greg. "Why is he using the third person? He's never done that before."

"He's distancing himself as far as possible from the events of that night. It's okay. It's a coping technique."

Ryan described how he'd snuck to his parents' room and stood, unnoticed, just inside the door. How he'd seen his father strike his mother, several times, until she'd fallen. The boy went silent and stopped drawing.

"What happened next, Ryan?" the doctor asked gently.

Shannon closed her eyes and leaned her forehead

against the window. Greg placed his hand on her shoulder, giving it a squeeze.

"Daddy got on top of her." Ryan's voice was barely discernible through the speaker.

"He's switched to first person," Greg whispered. "He's lost his distance. He's in the memory now, in that night."

That made Shannon feel even worse.

"On top of her how?"

"H-he, like, sat on her."

"Where on her body? On her feet? Her knees? Can you show me?"

Shannon opened her eyes to see Ryan point to his chest. "Here."

"Did Mommy say anything?"

Ryan shook his head. "But her fingers were, like, waving around, and her feet were kicking the air. She kept kicking and kicking…"

"And then?"

"And—and then…she stopped."

Shannon covered her face with her hands, stifling the cry that threatened to escape. The image of Willow, struggling to get air, to break free from her husband while her son watched, was horrifying.

Greg tried to pull her into his arms, but she shook her head, pushing him away. "Don't touch me. I—I have to stay strong. For him." She inhaled slowly, forcing herself to watch Ryan in the next room. If he could be strong and brave, so could she. Falling apart could wait until later.

Much later.

"What did you do, Ryan?"

"I—I just stood there. I was scared. Daddy got up. He looked scared, too. And mad. Really mad. He kicked her, but she didn't move or cry anymore. He called her bad names."

"Did he see you in the room?"

"Yeah," Ryan said.

"What happened when he saw you?"

"I—I wet my pants." The child started to cry. He pulled off the mask, threw it on the floor, then put his head on the table.

Shannon bolted for the door, but Greg grabbed her by the wrist. "No, Shannon! Let them finish." He jabbed the speaker on the wall, and despite her struggles, wrapped her in a strong embrace against his chest, preventing her from seeing into the art room.

She stood rigidly in his arms for a few moments, then gently banged her head against his shoulder over and over. "I want to hurt him," she said. "If he were here, I think I could hurt him. I hope they fry him. Bastard! I hope they fry him!"

Tears streamed down her face in spite of her best efforts to stop them. She looked up at Greg. "What kind of person does that make me?"

"A human one." He wiped at her cheeks with his thumbs. "Just human." Cradling her head in his palms, he leaned down and tenderly kissed her. Short but, oh, so sweet.

"What was that for?" She ran her hand across her nose after he released her.

"Distraction. The bathroom is down the hall on the left. You might want to, uh, you know, fix your face? It's probably better that Ryan not know his story got to you."

She straightened up. "Right. Listen, when they're done with him, will you take him outside to the playground? I have a few questions for them."

"If that's what you want, you know I will."

Halfway down the corridor, she once more came to an abrupt halt. She *had* known he'd do it, even before she'd asked.

So that was what it was like, to have someone you could depend on.

But then she remembered how he'd tried to throw them under the bus with the reporter.

More proof that the only person you could ever really count on was yourself.

TWENTY-SOME MINUTES LATER, Shannon emerged from the Children's Center through the back door. She headed for the playground that served the university's day care as well as the local community. With classes not in session and most of the students gone for the summer, the campus was largely deserted. Ryan, who had the entire playground to himself, lay on his belly on the edge of the swinging bridge, drawing in the sand with a stick.

Greg sat on a nearby bench, bent over with his elbows propped on his knees. In his hands, he toyed with SuperKid's mask.

Shannon dropped onto the end of the bench.

Greg didn't look at her, just kept fiddling with the elastic band. "Get your questions answered?"

"Yes." She now knew that Ryan's account coincided with the physical evidence. An autopsy had determined Willow's death to be caused by compression asphyxiation. Trevor claimed he'd been under the influence of sleeping meds and unable to remember the events of that night. However, toxicology tests hadn't revealed the presence of any drugs. Ryan's interview, despite the superhero persona and partial third-person narration, would help the case. "They're hoping Ryan will be able to tell the story again without the mask and without slipping into third person." Ellen, the A.D.A., would want to interview Ryan herself, soon, since she hadn't been able to make the trip to Erie with the detectives this time.

"Yeah, well..." Greg sat up. "I wouldn't expect that in the next few days. Actually, I don't think Ryan plans on talking to us at all right now. Not even through SuperKid. He wants nothing to do with this." He handed her the mask.

"So, what do we do now?" Shannon reluctantly tucked the black plastic into her purse. She'd grown rather fond of her pint-size, freckle-nosed superhero.

"We go back to the drawing board. Literally. We keep doing more of the same, supporting him, strengthening him, making him feel secure. And we hope." Greg laid his hand on her knee, patting it twice before squeezing it. "How are you holding up?"

"Okay. As long as I don't think about what he said in there."

"I'm sure... Look, Shannon, about the reporter—"

"Really, Greg, I don't want to talk about that."

"Well, I do." He released her leg and shifted on the bench, turning sideways to face her. "I didn't mean any harm. I'm just trying to save my program here."

"I didn't know it was in danger."

Greg grunted. "Remember those business meetings I told you about the other night? The ones that didn't go so well? My need for a hundred thousand dollars?"

Shannon nodded.

"Well, the new dean wants to put her own stamp on the university. She has the same distaste for 'comic-book artists' as you do. Did." He grinned. "Hopefully by now I've changed your mind. But it means I'm out so *her* pet project can move in. Shannon, I love doing comic books. I get paid for having more fun than any adult should. But my true calling is art therapy. Helping these kids. Individual therapy can continue easily enough without this space. But my group sessions… I have to have a place for those. An office of some sort. That means rent or a mortgage. Utilities. Insurance. A hell of a lot of things I don't have if the university kicks me out."

"I'm sorry. It's a worthwhile program, Greg. There's no doubt about that. But to ask me to discuss Ryan on camera… Do you have any idea how much media attention surrounded Willow's murder? An upper-middle-class man, whose family owns a chain of furniture stores in the Philly area, murders his wife with his child in the house? The news ate that story like your brother's chocolate cake."

"I know. I remember."

"But you set me up to walk into that anyway?"

He shrugged. "I didn't think. I was so caught up in my own stuff that I just didn't think about how you might react. I'm sorry." He offered his hand. "Forgive me?"

She pressed her lips together and was silent for a while. "Okay," she finally said, taking his hand. The physical awkwardness between them tingled. They stared at each other for a moment, then Shannon yanked her hand back. Forgiving him—or at least giving lip service to forgiving him—was one thing, going *there* again was something else entirely.

"I don't think you should be alone today." Greg glanced at his watch. "I have someplace to be this afternoon, but

I'd love you and Ryan to come with me. It might be just the thing to keep your mind off this morning."

"Uh-oh. Where?"

"The Children's Cancer Institute is sponsoring a picnic at Waldameer this afternoon. Captain Chemo is putting in a guest appearance, and I'll be signing *Captain Chemo* comic books as well as presenting a donation check from myself and my publisher. There will be food, and you can take Ryan on the rides." He cleared his throat. "There'll be reporters there, too. The woman from this morning is meeting me to continue the story. The newspaper is also sending someone."

Shannon looked across the stretch of grass at the boy who halfheartedly dangled a stick over the edge of the bridge. Much as she hated the idea of taking him anywhere near reporters, an afternoon at the local amusement park might be just the thing to perk him up.

Not to mention keep both their minds off the picture he'd painted for the detectives.

"All right. We'll go. But no pointing us out to reporters. I don't want you talking about him, either. Not even in general terms. All I need is for Lloyd and Patty to get wind of that. They'll call it 'exploiting the child' and add it to their list of strikes against me, I'm sure."

"Deal."

GREG'S FACE ACHED as he smiled for what he hoped was the final picture by the newspaper's photographer. He, Captain Chemo and Randolf Kendal, the president of the Children's Cancer Institute, posed in front of the Waldameer train.

"Okay, great. That's it, we're done. Thanks." With a wave, the photographer trotted to the park's exit.

Mr. Kendal folded the check and tucked it into the pocket of his jeans. "Thanks again, Greg. We appreciate all the support you've given the institute. I'm sorry we haven't been able to help you out in return. I promise, we'll see about getting your program into our next budget. That doesn't mean it will fly, but I'll do my best."

As Kendal left, Captain Chemo, aka Hayden, gave Greg a slap on the shoulder that appeared friendly but left his ears ringing. Then his brother leaned in to hiss, "Next time you design a superhero you might want me to impersonate, let's go more with a Zorro instead of the traditional, huh? Maybe a contemporary hero who wears jeans and a trench coat? These damn briefs are giving me a wedgie. And the tights are hot."

"I didn't hear you bitching when those two blondes were checking out your six-pack in that spandex." No fake abs of steel for Hayden, who worked out three times a week.

"There is that. Captain Chemo has scored four numbers today. But seriously, Gory, am I done?"

"Almost. Come say goodbye to the kids still in the picnic area." As they sauntered back to the pavilion, small boys ran up to Hayden to shake his hand. Captain Chemo also posed for several pictures, including one Greg took with a cell-phone camera at the request of a group of giggling teenage girls. Captain Chemo was immortalized with his mouth gaping open as he yelped.

The girls ran off, grabbing the phone from Greg as they darted past.

"What's the world coming to?" Hayden asked. "Would you believe one of those girls reached under my cape and pinched my ass?"

Greg bit the inside of his lip. "Sorry. I've heard

costumed characters are often abused, but I didn't think anyone would disrespect Captain Chemo."

"Where's the nearest phone booth? I am so out of this gig." Hayden scratched his head with his purple glove. "Hey, where *does* a Superhero change his clothes these days? Cell phones have made phone booths extinct."

After Hayden bid goodbye to the kids still hanging out at the picnic area with their parents, Greg did the same, then walked his brother to the restroom and waited until he emerged as himself once again, Captain Chemo tucked securely into a gym bag. "Just leave that in my Tracker on your way out."

"No problem. See you at home later."

Greg scanned the passing crowds, searching for Shannon and Ryan, who'd wandered off shortly after the arrival of the reporters and had been missing ever since.

"Or maybe I won't see you at home later."

"What?"

"Greg, you might be eighteen months older than I am, but you're still way behind when it comes to women. I've never seen you so, I don't know, entranced, before. What is it about this one?"

Greg shrugged. "I wish I knew."

"Is it because she needs a hero?"

Greg laughed. "I promise you, the last thing Shannon is looking for is a hero."

"She might not be looking for one, but you're sure playing the part. Cleverly without wedgie-inducing spandex, I might add. You're babysitting for the kid, spending way more time with them than I've ever seen you with a client, you got Cathy to rep her for the legal stuff…"

"Bye, Hayden. Thanks for playing Captain Chemo

today." Greg cuffed his brother on the shoulder to repay the shot he'd taken earlier.

"Next time, make Finn or Kyle do it," Hayden called after Greg as he trotted into the thick of the park.

He waved a hand over his head without turning. If Shannon had a cell phone, he could call and meet up with them. Instead, he was reduced to searching Waldameer end to end.

He found them standing in front of the Tilt-a-Whirl, Ryan tugging on Shannon's hand while she, pasty white, shook her head.

"Hey, guys. What's going on?"

Ryan dropped Shannon's hand and grabbed his, pointing at the ride.

"That's a great idea. Greg can take you on it, and I can sit on that bench over there and watch." She turned pleading eyes on him. "If I ride that thing one more time, I swear, I'm going to puke. I don't do well with rides that go in tight circles."

"Well, we certainly don't want you puking. Ewwww, gross, right, Ryan?"

The boy nodded. Greg once again rescued the damsel in distress. Maybe Hayden had a point. But hell, what man didn't want to feel needed? Important? He was definitely making a difference for Shannon.

But he'd been riding a Tilt-a-Whirl ever since he'd met her. The episode in her kitchen had left him reeling. He'd brought her to orgasm without even touching her…and he wasn't sure what to make of that. Had it been their chemistry that night, or would any source of friction have worked for her?

In other words, had she actually needed him at all?

As they spun, Ryan gripped the safety bar, closing

his eyes. The boy didn't appear to be enjoying himself, making Greg wonder why he'd had a fascination with this particular ride.

When the cart stopped, Greg held the boy's elbow as they staggered down the steps. At the bottom, Ryan broke free and ran to the bench were Shannon waited. He threw himself down and draped his arm over his face.

Greg raised an eyebrow at her.

She shrugged. "Beats me. He's done that every time he's gotten off the thing. I think they should call it the Tilt-and-Hurl."

"Not the best marketing strategy."

"Probably not." Shannon shook Ryan's leg. "How about we go on something that doesn't spin? What about the log flume?"

Ryan sat up, cocking his head to the side. Not an enthusiastic response, but not abject uninterest, either. And considering the experience Ryan had had earlier in the day, better than what Greg dared hope for.

"That sounds like fun. Can I come?" he asked.

Ryan nodded. He slid from the bench, holding his hand out to Greg. Instead, Greg swung the boy up onto this shoulders, eliciting a gasp and squeak from him. Holding on to his wrists, Greg headed for the log flume, passing a variety of stands that tantalized the nose with the scents of French fries, funnel cakes and hand-squeezed lemonade.

Once they got in line, he put Ryan down. The late-afternoon sun slanted into the park from over the lake. As they waited, a pair of youthful voices, one male, one female, called for Greg's attention. "Mr. H.! Yo, Mr. H.!"

Cheryl and Michael waved at him. Greg returned the gesture. Then Michael leaned over to whisper in Cheryl's ear. A wide grin filled her face, and the pair darted off.

"Uh-oh," Greg said. "That can only mean trouble." The Dastardly Duo had already narrowly missed being thrown out of the park for flying paper airplanes off the skyride. Kids their age often roamed the small family-friendly park without being tethered to their parents, who were probably sitting on a bench in the shade somewhere, exhausted from trying to keep up with them. It was almost a rite of passage in Erie, the first time your parents let you wander the park without them.

He kept an anxious eye out for the pair as they moved forward in the line but didn't see them. Soon Greg stepped into the back of the boat, with Shannon in front of him, and Ryan in front of her. As the ride climbed the first hill, she settled against his chest. He tightened his thighs around her, ignoring the pang of desire the position inspired. The wind fanned her hair, making it fly in his face.

At the top of the peak, the chain released the boat and it dipped free into the trough. "Look how pretty the lake is from up here," Shannon said.

The sloshing water rushed them along the turns and drops of the ride. When they hit the top of the final drop, Ryan shrieked.

They hurtled down the plunge, landing with a big splash that only dampened them. But then two blasts of water slammed into them. Shannon took the brunt of the hit, but enough nailed Greg's arms and face. Loud shouts came from the viewing area, where quarter-fed water cannons allowed guests to drench flume riders.

"We got you!" Michael yelled. "Score! We soaked you, Mr. H.!"

"You sure did!" Greg yelled back. "Just wait!"

Michael poked Cheryl, and the pair vanished into the crowd. As their log headed back into the carousel, Shannon wrung out the bottom of her T-shirt.

Ryan was miserable when Greg helped him out. Bedraggled hair framed Shannon's face, and...

God help him.

Her cream T-shirt had gone translucent and skin-tight. Beneath it she wore a pink bra with delicate decorations on the edge and thin, pink ribbons trailing down the middle.

One of the bras he'd admired on his late-night snooping session.

The heat that flashed through him was enough to evaporate all the water in the ride.

Hell, all the water in Lake Erie.

"Sir!" one of the ride attendants hollered. "You've got to get off the platform! Please keep moving!"

Shannon grabbed him by the hand and pulled him along with Ryan off the rotating surface to the more stable platform at the base of the stairs to the exit.

The unsteady sensation when he staggered onto the nonmoving floor reinforced the point.

Attraction to Shannon made him off balance. Mostly.

To the point that he kept forgetting the boy's needs. The custody battle. Shannon's track record for revolving-door relationships.

Somehow he had to find a way to maintain an even keel.

To keep the volatile chemistry between them in check.

CHAPTER NINE

"THE END." Shannon closed *The Ransom of Red Chief* and struggled up from the futon. Ryan knuckled his eyes, then rolled over and reached under the pillow to pull out another book. "No, it's time for you to go to sleep now. We've got to get on a normal schedule."

Ryan tapped on the cover of the book *Are You My Mother?* Shannon gently took it from him and placed both library books on the small bookcase she'd bought at the local consignment store. She knelt alongside his bed and tucked the blankets firmly around him. The story about the baby bird searching for its mother had obviously struck a chord in her nephew.

Shannon brushed back his hair, leaning over to kiss his forehead. "I'm not ever going to take your mom's place, Ryan. But I'm going to do my best to do all the things for you that she would. Your mom is watching you from heaven, and she's so proud of what you did today. She knows—and so do I—how hard it was. But you told the detectives the truth, and that's what matters." Shannon lightly tapped the tip of his nose. "Being brave and telling the truth? That makes you a real hero in my book, Ry."

His exhaustion-bleary eyes didn't buy it.

"I mean it. You're a real hero." She opted to change the

subject before either of them started thinking too much about what he'd said earlier. "Did you like Waldameer?"

A slow nod.

"Me, too. We'll have to go there again."

Ryan's mouth edged upward, and he spun his index fingers in circles.

"Maybe. No promises about the Tilt-and-Hurl." She ruffled his hair. The kid had been a mess of contradictions all day. Even the things he'd seemed to enjoy had become issues afterward, when he'd slumped into a deeper funk. Getting soaked on the flume ride had been the final straw for Ryan. Greg had received a phone call that had thrown him into a foul mood as well, and he'd quickly agreed to take them home.

"Go to sleep," she told Ryan. "See you in the morning." She blew him another kiss, then stood, turning on the train night-light he'd selected during their shopping trip to the secondhand store. She pulled his door shut.

In her bedroom, she faced a confusion of scattered furniture. She'd moved her desk out of Ryan's room and into her own to make it easier to use after he'd gone to bed. She'd started work for a company that employed virtual assistants, including bookkeepers. This way she could make her own hours, and even work from home during the day while keeping an eye on Ryan.

It beat night shifts, hands down.

But now she had to put the computer pieces back together with the miles—or so it seemed—of wires that connected everything. Monitor to computer. Computer to printer. Computer to Internet connection. The project also served to keep her mind from straying to the images of Willow that had haunted her all day long.

Before that, though, she needed the furniture in a

workable layout instead of the crowded jumble she currently had going on in the bedroom.

About an hour later, finally satisfied, Shannon started reassembling the computer. A soft sound made her freeze. She tilted her head. There was another gentle knock on her apartment door.

Shannon glanced at her alarm clock, but it just blinked a red 12:00, reminding her in its not-so-subtle way that she'd forgotten to reset it. She scrambled down the stairs, praying it wasn't another ambush visit by Patty and Lloyd. After the day she and Ryan had had, that would be the proverbial last straw.

She peered through the peephole.

Greg.

She flipped the lock and undid the chain, opening the door. "Hi. This is a surprise."

He pulled his hands from his pockets. "I just wanted to check on you. Make sure you're doing okay. Mind if I come in?" He didn't wait for an answer, just brushed past her and up the stairs.

"Why no, not at all." Shannon closed the door and followed him. He paced the length of her living room as restlessly as the new polar bear at the Erie Zoo had paced the perimeter of the exhibit's pool. Coiled energy radiated from him. "What's with you?"

He stopped, but bounced lightly on the balls of his feet. "Nothing. Like I said, I just wanted to see how you were making out after today. Ryan's sleeping?"

"Yes. Amazingly enough."

"And you?"

"I'm not thinking about it."

"Is that how you do it?"

"Do what?"

He waved his hands. "What you do. That whole let-it-go thing. You just don't think about it? How does that work?"

Shannon stared at him. The edges of his eyes were red. "Have you been drinking? Or something else?"

"What? No." He shoved his hands back into his pockets and resumed stalking the small space.

"Greg." Shannon eased onto the couch, patted the leather cushion next to her. "Sit. You're making me anxious."

"Sorry." He dropped onto the end of the sofa, facing her, one leg pulled up. He drummed his fingers on his knee.

"So, are you going to tell me what's going on?"

"I need to know how you do it. Let it go."

"Why?"

He shrugged. "Why not?"

Shannon shifted closer to him, took his twitching fingers into her hand. "What happened, Greg?"

He blew out a quick breath and stared up at the ceiling. "I got a phone call today."

"While we were at the amusement park?"

"Yeah. Turns out one of my former cancer kids, one who 'graduated' from my program a few years ago and was in college now…well, she relapsed." His gaze met hers. "Captain Chemo didn't kick cancer's butt this time. Cancer kicked hers. She died this morning out in California."

"Oh, Greg. I'm sorry."

He pulled free and jumped to his feet. "So how does it work? How do you let go of people like they never even existed? 'Cause I'm not so good at that." He rubbed the center of his forehead. "It hurts, dammit, and I hate it. I don't want to feel this. Teach me how to cut off my feelings."

His words kicked her square in the chest. He thought she was cold? Unemotional? That she pretended the people who'd mattered to her never existed? "It's not like that. It's about acceptance. You accept that all things are temporary. You enjoy and embrace them while you have them. You cherish the memories you keep. Even pain is temporary."

"Thank God for small favors," he muttered, raking his hand through his hair.

"Surely you've lost one of your cancer kids before?"

"I have. And every damn time it kills a part of me." He prowled stiff-legged around the sofa, into the dining area where he stopped in front of the long double window that looked out over the parking lot. He leaned his head against the pane.

Shannon followed. She extended her hand toward his shoulder but stopped, dropping it back to her side. "Your empathy's part of what makes you so strong at what you do."

"You think?" His warm breath fogged the glass.

"Only someone who hates to lose can teach someone else how to fight for their life. Or for what they love."

"Or want?" He turned to face her, and before she could process the husky timbre to his voice, she was in his arms. His mouth crushed against hers, demanding. Mingled with desire, she could taste his need, his pain.

Her body answered with need of its own, her soul seeking to soothe its own pain. What better relief could she find than with him?

His hand trailed along her back to cup her butt. Heat from his palm radiated through the thin sweatpants she wore. The teasing caress became demanding as he pulled her flush against his body. His mouth trailed up her jaw toward her ear. "No more fighting this chemistry between us," he murmured, then nipped her lobe. "I need this. I need you. I'm going to have you tonight, Shannon."

"Not in front of this window you aren't." She reached behind and took his hand from its place on her bottom. "No more fighting. Embrace the gift." She led him from the room, flicking off the lights as they passed the switch.

She let him go ahead of her into the bedroom, then pulled the door shut, turning the lock. After switching off the overhead light, she reached for the sole remaining source of soft illumination, the bedside lamp. He grabbed her wrist. "No. I want to see you."

Before she could answer, he lifted the hem of her T-shirt, pulling it up over her head and tossing it to the floor.

Greg's mouth went dry.

She wore the black bra with the hot-pink flowers and tiny ecru bow in the center. The swell of her breasts rose over the embroidered edges, every bit as amazing as he'd imagined the night he'd pawed through her drawer. He sent a silent whisper of thanks to the Dastardly Duo and their water bombs at the park for forcing her to change her clothes, right down to her underwear.

"Beautiful," he said, reaching behind her with one hand to unclasp the bra. He slid the straps down her arms, exposing her breasts. "Even more beautiful."

The pain of the day forgotten, he bent, exhaling gently over one salmon-blush nipple. When it peaked in response and Shannon sucked in a quick breath, Greg drew the tip into his mouth.

She threaded her fingers into his hair, moaning softly. He continued to caress and tease.

Until the needy sounds she made deep in her throat spurred him onward. He shoved her sweats over her hips, sending the tiny black panties with them, letting both slide into a puddle of fabric around her feet.

Greg lifted her in his arms, carrying her to the bed where he unceremoniously deposited her in the middle.

"Hey! No fair. You still have clothes on."

"All's fair in love, war and the bedroom." A slow, predatory grin lifted the corners of his mouth. He pulled out his wallet, tossing two condoms on the bedside table.

"That's good to know." She scrambled off the bed, placing her palm square on his chest. "Since I plan to do this." She nimbly unbuttoned his shirt, then traced the exposed skin, lightly brushing the dark hair across his pecs. He shrugged out of the sleeves, adding the shirt to the growing pile on the floor.

She showered kisses along his abs while fumbling with the button and zipper of his jeans. Kneeling in front of him, she tugged them inch by painstaking inch down his legs.

Damn, he wanted her.

She paused when she had the pants just below his boxer briefs. "Hmm..."

"Hmm? That's not what a guy wants to hear when a hot, naked woman has just dropped his drawers."

"It's just not what I expected."

"Shit."

She laughed. "I expected boxers with a superhero print."

"My Y-Men briefs are in the wa—wa—" Greg lost

the ability to speak as she yanked down the underwear in question, immediately taking him into her mouth.

"Ho—holy hotness," he croaked a minute later.

Her laughter vibrated around him, through him…

Warming a spot a lot farther north than he expected.

He needed her. More than just physically.

He grabbed her by her arms and hauled her up, claiming her mouth with a fierce kiss while walking her backward until she bumped into the bed.

They tumbled down together, him settling between her legs. She arched against him, slick against his skin. He groped blindly on the night table for a condom, made quick work of getting it on.

She reached between them, taking him in hand and guiding him. She raised her hips as he eased inside, and drew a deep breath, closing her eyes.

When he'd buried himself to the hilt in her warmth, she raised a hand to his chest.

He recoiled, withdrawing. "Am I hurting you?"

"No. Come back."

He obliged, once more slowly sinking as far as possible.

"Don't move," she purred, as he prepared to withdraw again.

"Don't move?" he croaked. His erection pulsed in the silkiness of her body, *demanding* he move. His arms trembled with the effort of holding himself up, holding himself still.

And yet, it was perfect. The two of them linked as he'd never felt before. A moment, suspended in time.

One moment, one night, was never going to be enough for him. But he'd learned enough from her to try to leave tomorrow's worries for tomorrow. If he had to seduce her over and over again, well…it wouldn't exactly be a hardship.

Besides, he was used to fighting for what he wanted. Needed.

"Is this some kind of kinky Zen thing?" he finally whispered.

"Yes," she whispered back, not opening her eyes. "Kinky. Zen. Shh." She clamped her muscles around him, causing waves of pleasure that made him grit his teeth.

She caressed his chest. His heart pounded beneath her palm.

Sweat beaded across his forehead.

She rocked ever so slightly. He followed her lead, moving just enough to control the need.

"Greg." Sweet chocolate eyes stared up at him.

He wanted to melt into them, into her. "Shannon?"

"Embrace the gift. Now."

He lowered himself against her, groaning into the curve of her neck as he began the rhythm. "I thought you'd never ask."

Male ego demanded he make good on his great-if-we're-both-naked promise.

He drove her higher, faster, harder, until they were both panting and soaked with sweat. Choked-back moans rumbled deep in her throat, egged him on, made him hold tightly to control when she pulsed her pleasure around him. He slowed to a languid pace.

The second time he pushed her over the edge, she clutched his back and gasped his name, making it even harder to maintain his tenuous grip on control.

When he slowed once more, her eyes slowly fluttered opened. "You—you haven't?"

He shook his head. "Third time's the charm."

She chuckled softly. "Superheroes are *so* jealous of you."

He stilled, then bent his arms, leaning down to brush his lips over hers. "Any guy with an ounce of sense is jealous of me right now. Because I'm here with you."

She met his tentative thrust enthusiastically. "One more time, Superlover. But this time, fly with me."

He'd never been with a woman so damn responsive.

She *did* make him feel like a friggin' super man.

"Now," she said, a few minutes later, as the first ripple of her orgasm gripped him. "Now, now, now!"

Forget flying. He let go and fell with her.

Fell hard.

Shannon didn't think she'd ever move again. Every muscle in her body felt like an overcooked strand of pasta. Eyes closed, she let the afterglow run its glorious, mind-numbing, soul-soothing course, only vaguely aware of Greg's moving from the bed, returning, then pulling her to his side, settling her head onto his chest, wrapping his arms around her.

He stroked her hair. She mustered enough effort to purr, content to just be held in his warm embrace.

But the sweat evaporating from her body made her shiver. He shifted again, dragging the blankets over them.

For a few more minutes she floated, listening to the steady thud of his heart, anchored only by his arm draped around her shoulders.

Then he had to go and talk, his voice not only in her ears, but rumbling through his chest, her pillow. "I just noticed. You brought the computer and desk in here. That's terrific. You're acknowledging Ryan deserves his own space."

Ryan. Willow.

Images she didn't want, images she'd banished for most of the day, flashed through her brain. The afterglow vanished. She groaned. "Your pillow talk could use work, comic-book boy."

"Comic-book *boy?* A few minutes ago I was Superlover."

"A few minutes ago you knew when to be quiet." She sat up, the blankets falling away along with her failing grip on her emotions. "Just as well, though. I'm going to hit the shower. Do you still have my key?"

He nodded.

"Then you can lock the door behind you on your way out."

His blue eyes flickered his hurt. He quickly narrowed them. "Here's your pants. What's your hurry?"

She shrugged, heading for the closet. "I have no idea if Ryan will sleep all night or not. We're trying to get back on a 'normal' schedule. I think it would be best if he didn't find you here, naked, in my bed. Don't you?" She pulled on her satin robe, tying the belt.

"Don't hide behind the kid. If you want me to leave, I'm going." He slid out of the bed and jumped into his jeans. "My pillow talk might need work, but your kiss-off needs more."

"I'm sorry, Greg. I'm not...I can't..." Her lower lip started to tremble, and she bit it. Better he think her a bitch than to melt down in front of him. Bitches got respect. Blubbering women were just...weak. "I really need a shower." She fled, doing her best to keep quiet in the hallway. Once in the bathroom, she started the water, but waited until she heard the main door open and close before she climbed in.

Steam billowed around her. She bowed her head, the

hot water pounding her neck. The day's pain, from putting Ryan through telling his story, to the images of her sister's death, rose up. Shannon did her best to stuff it back down, to wrestle it into submission.

It didn't work. Even sleeping with Greg had only temporarily held it at bay.

So she let it come.

As though she stood behind Ryan in the doorway of Willow and Trevor's room, Shannon saw her sister, trapped beneath the bulk of her husband, feet kicking, hands twitching...

Then stopping.

The breath, the life, crushed out of her.

While her little boy watched.

"Oh, Willow." Shannon turned into the spray, allowing the water to mingle with her tears. "I'm sorry. I'm so sorry. I wish..."

I wish I'd said something about my misgivings the first time I'd met Trevor, or when I realized you'd confused material comfort with security...

I wish I'd been there for you...

I wish I'd fought to keep you closer...

Sinking to the floor of the tub, Shannon drew up her knees, resting her forehead against them. She wrapped her arms around her legs. The water cascaded over her, picking up her tears, then gurgled down the drain. She tried to envision her pain going with it.

Wishes wouldn't change anything.

CHAPTER TEN

AFTER USHERING RYAN into the entryway of the center, Shannon shook the water from her umbrella and folded it. With only a few summer classes in session, the building had a deserted air. The *squeak-squish-squeal* of their damp sneakers on the floor echoed along the hallway as they headed to Greg's workroom.

He'd canceled their session earlier in the week—something had come up involving to his sister's wedding, or so he'd said—and then he had insisted they meet at the center, not at her apartment.

She'd hurt him. She knew it. She was less sure how to go about fixing it.

Ryan stopped in the doorway, shaking his head.

"It's okay, Ryan. It's just us today. No detectives." Shannon nudged him forward, setting her purse and umbrella on the counter beside a pile of crumpled Baby Ruth wrappers. Maybe she should have brought chocolate as a peace offering.

Greg turned from the window that overlooked the playground. "My next client is here," he said into his cell phone.

His client. Ouch. She'd been seriously downgraded. She'd gone from friend to lover then back to client in two easy steps.

"Keep me in the loop. I'll talk to you later." He snapped his phone shut and tucked it in his pocket, then sank to one knee in front of Ryan. "Hey there, sport. How's it going today?"

Ryan shrugged.

"You ready to work?" Greg held out his closed fist.

Ryan rapped knuckles with him.

"All right." Greg stood, finally acknowledging her. "Shannon."

"Greg. Listen…"

He held up his hand, palm out. "Let's get right down to it, shall we?" Gathering supplies from the shelves, he spread crayons, pencils and markers on the table, motioning for them to take a seat.

Shannon sank into the small chair, accepting the sheet of paper Greg slid over to her. No matter how she tried, she couldn't get him to make eye contact.

"We're going to fold our paper in half like this, and then again like this." Greg demonstrated, then helped Ryan make the folds. "Remember how we used pictures to tell the story of our zoo trip?" That lesson had come after the one Patty had interrupted with her "good" news about Ryan living with her and Lloyd.

Ryan nodded.

Shannon felt invisible. Which made it hard to apologize, or make amends to him.

"We're going to do that again today. I'll tell you what story we're going to draw in a minute. Right now, though, let's do this." Greg used a black marker to further define the panels on the paper. Ryan watched and duplicated the process. "That's right," Greg said.

Shannon prepared her paper, fighting the urge to write

I'M SORRY in big red letters on it, fold it into an airplane and fly it at him. Pointy end right into his forehead.

Maybe that would get the message to him.

Most guys would have been thrilled to have the incredible, mind blowing sex they'd had, with no strings attached.

Her mistake for sleeping with a man who couldn't appreciate temporary gifts.

Someone who expected more.

"Ryan, the last time you were in this room, you told a story to the detectives. The story of what happened the night your mom died."

Shannon jerked her head up so fast her neck muscles seized.

"Aunt Shannon and I heard you from the observation room." Greg pointed to the mirrored window. "Today we're each going to draw that story."

Shannon shot out of her chair, knocking it over. Ryan and Greg stared at her. "Can I see you in the hallway?"

"No." Greg shifted closer to Ryan, lifted the boy's chin in his hand. "Ryan, look at me. You've already told this story. You're just telling it again in a different way. The cat's out of the bag already. Okay?"

Ryan lowered his eyes, but gave a nearly imperceptible nod.

"Attaboy." Greg offered him a box of crayons. After Ryan took it, he moved to the far end of the table with his paper.

Greg extended a pencil to her. "You, too, Aunt Shannon. Draw what Ryan told you about that night."

Stomach churning, she snatched the pencil from him, then righted the kid-size chair. She plonked herself into it and dragged her paper back from the center of the table.

Hands clammy, she adjusted her grip on the yellow wood, then set the tip to the page in the first box.

The images came unbidden to her brain. Graphic, horrifying visions. The very ones that had made her banish Greg, driven her to the shower to weep out her pain, her frustration. To try to let it all go.

Try as she might, she couldn't make the pencil move.

She glanced at Greg, whose fast-sketching fingers were already covering the paper with images. She cleared her throat.

He ignored her and kept drawing.

At the far end of the table, even Ryan was busy recreating the scene from that night.

If he could do it, she could. He was just a little boy. She was an adult, who excelled at dealing with pain.

She rolled the pencil along her fingers, then put the tip to the paper again. When she began to move it, the point snapped.

Greg handed her another one. She caught his eye as she took it. *Don't make me do this,* she mouthed to him, shaking her head.

He raised his eyebrows and glanced at Ryan, then back, as if to say what she'd already told herself.

So Shannon began, making ever-so-soft strokes that left behind almost invisible lines. The first panel wasn't so bad. She drew Ryan, in his bed, sitting up, rubbing his eyes. Hearing noises from another room.

Pins and needles tingled in her right hand as she moved on to the second panel. Shannon stretched her fingers a few times, but the sensation only got worse. The image of Ryan in the doorway began to take shape. The boy's form loomed in the foreground of the picture, taking up most of the space. In the background, she sketched a tiny version of her sister, tears streaming down Willow's face.

The tingling spread to Shannon's left fingers as well.

Ignoring it, she started the third panel. A giant hand appeared. Shannon stole a few quick peeks at Greg's hand for a model. But she couldn't imagine him ever raising a fist against a woman. Or a child.

The lines appeared darker now. Shannon's feet got into the tingling act. She curled and released her toes inside her sneakers as she sketched Willow's face—the target of the giant hand.

Shannon paused to rub her chest.

Greg got out of his chair. As he passed behind her, he leaned over to examine her paper. He grunted. "That's not bad. You might have a future in comics."

"Thanks but no thanks," she said, her voice breathy.

He stared at her for a moment, then strode to Ryan, crouching beside the boy. Greg made quiet comments Shannon couldn't catch, gesturing at the child's picture, then patting him on the shoulder.

The point of Shannon's pencil hovered over the empty fourth panel. The final box in her story strip.

There was only one image that could go here.

The pins and needles in her right hand had progressed. Or stopped. In any case, Shannon couldn't feel anything. She set the pencil down and flexed her fingers a few times, then massaged her hand.

She would finish this, damm it.

She picked up the pencil and drew furiously—until this point snapped, too.

Greg and Ryan both glanced over at her.

"I'm sorry, I'm sorry." She snatched another pencil

from the center of the table, and continued drawing Trevor's back.

A wave of dizziness made the room—and her head—spin. The pencil rolled across the paper as she pressed her fingers to her temple.

"Shannon?"

The pictures on the walls blurred. A tight band circled her ribs, and her heart pounded. Shannon tapped her fingertips on her breastbone. "I—I can't breathe."

Greg was beside her in a flash. "What's wrong?"

"Can't...can't...breathe."

"It's okay."

"Not...okay."

Through her hazy vision, she could see he'd gripped her right hand, but she couldn't feel it. "What's...happening?"

"You're breathing too fast, Shannon. Take a slow, deep breath."

"Can't. Get. Air."

Greg's own heart thudded as he planted himself on the table in front of her. Had he pushed her too far? The exercise was supposed to reassure Ryan that his story was already out. Who knew Miss Control Freak would crack like this? "Yes, you can."

Ryan ran to hover next to her, anxiously glancing from his aunt to Greg.

"You're scaring the crap out of Ryan." Greg leaned closer, putting his face next to hers. "Hell, you're scaring the crap out of me. Listen to me, Shannon. You have to slow your breathing. Just like that day out on the porch. Remember? Breathe in deep." He squeezed her fingers hard. "Do it!"

She gasped, panting.

He transferred his grip to her shoulders. "Shannon. You have to get control. Close your eyes and listen to me."

She shut her eyes.

"Breathe in. More. Good. Hold it. No, hold it. Okay, let it out slowly. Good. Again. Breathe in slowly. Hold it. Exhale. That's it." Over and over, he repeated the process until her muscles relaxed under his fingers, and her chest rose and fell in a more natural pattern.

Tears spilled from her closed eyelids, and he wiped them away with his thumbs, his anger at her easing with every tear.

"Don't cry," said a soft voice to Greg's left.

Shannon's eyes flew open, and she turned to her nephew, whose lower lip trembled as he reached out to pat her shoulder.

"Ryan?"

"Don't cry, Aunt Shannon."

Greg leaned back on the table, making room so Shannon could scoop the child into her arms. She embraced him tightly, rocking in the chair.

"It's okay," he said. "It's okay." He patted her on the back.

"Yes, my brave boy. You're right. It *is* going to be okay." After a few moments, she eased him forward on her lap so she could look at him. "I know I told you this the other night, but I mean it. You're a real hero to tell this story for your mom."

Ryan leaned into her, snuggling beneath her chin. "Don't cry," he said again. "I love you."

Shannon smoothed his hair, then kissed the top of his head. "I love you, too. We're going to get through this together." She looked at Greg. "I'm sorry," she said.

The tightness in Greg's abs loosened. "For what?"

"The other night. This is what I didn't want you to see."

Always go with the smart-ass remark when you don't want them to know how much they hurt you. "You hugging Ryan?"

"Me falling apart. I hate blubbering."

"I know. You're a control freak."

The affront in her expression faded. "I suppose I am. I didn't want you to think I was weak."

"Weak? You're one of the strongest people I've ever met, Shannon."

"And me?" piped Ryan. "I'm strong!" He made a muscle to prove it.

Greg chuckled, tweaking the boy's arm. "Yeah, you, too, sport. It must run in the blood." He hopped off the table. "What do you say we clean things up? I think we've accomplished all we needed to for today."

"But I didn't finish my picture," Ryan said.

"Trust me, sport. You did enough." Enough to make him start talking again. Of course, it had been Shannon's tears that had moved the child to finally speak again—this time as himself, not SuperKid.

God knew the tears had moved Greg. Every time he thought he had her completely figured out, she surprised him.

Like her declaration of love for the child.

Granted, it was a response to Ryan's own declaration, and she'd probably been in shock that he was speaking again.

But Shannon "keep-the-world-at-arm's-length" Vanderhoff had used the *L* word.

Only a fool would take hope from that.

Damn, damn, damn! Who was he trying to kid? Besides himself?

His heart was gone. Melted into fondue by both the woman and the boy.

At least melted things couldn't break.

The fight to convince her that she needed him as well as Ryan had only just begun.

AMAZING, THE DIFFERENCE a month could make. Shannon leaned on the railing of the Hawkinses' upper deck, watching below her as Ryan climbed the ladder of the pool's slide. He yammered away at Jack, who was right behind him.

These days her nephew was silent only when he fell asleep.

The Hawkinses' annual Fourth of July picnic was in full swing. The sliding glass doors to the kitchen were wide open, and people milled about in both directions on the deck that wrapped around three-quarters of the house.

Smoke seeped from the closed grill, where Finn, beer in one hand and spatula in the other, kept watch. Though she'd finally mastered the Hawkins-family basics, Shannon couldn't keep track of all the new folks she'd been introduced to. She turned her attention back to the pool.

Greg stood at the bottom of the slide, arms open. Water on his wide shoulders glistened in the sun. "Come on, Ryan. I'll catch you."

The boy hesitated only a split second before launching himself down the water-greased blue plastic with a shriek.

True to his word, Greg caught him as he hit the water. "Way to go, sport." He bounced up and down with the boy in his arms, making miniwaves as he carted Ryan to the edge of the pool and set him back on the wooden deck. Ryan shook like a dog, making Katie, now soaked, squeal, then he ran to get back in line at the ladder.

Greg glanced up and caught her watching him. With a broad grin, he spread his arms wide in her direction. "Come on, Shannon. Jump. I'll catch you."

She laughed. "I don't think so."

And yet, a quiet voice inside her said if ever she was going to jump, he was the one to jump to. To count on.

Greg made a face at her and slowly submerged himself, then popped up, water sluicing down his abs.

A flash of heat ignited deep in Shannon's belly.

They hadn't been intimate since the disastrous night she'd put him out of her bed and hurt his feelings, but sparks continued to arc between them anytime they got close. So they did their best to keep their distance. Neither of them mentioned that night, leading Shannon to believe Greg had truly forgiven and forgotten. She'd been promoted back to friend. He'd been there for her in every other way, from continuing his sessions with Ryan, to taking them both out for ice cream—chocolate, of course—to painting a wall mural in Ryan's bedroom at her request.

A mural that wasn't finished, but due to be unveiled soon, he assured her.

Greg had insinuated himself into her everyday existence almost as much as Ryan had. It comforted her at the same time it made her uneasy.

Waiting for the other shoe to drop, no doubt.

Shannon decided to wander. Finn had made her a gourmet burger with feta cheese and spinach and she loaded her plate with potato salad and corn on the cob.

Chatting with various Hawkinses as she ate, Shannon enjoyed the laughter, and the occasional ambush by either a child or one of the Hawkins boys—though the youngest was twenty-four, their mother insisted they were all still boys—with a water balloon or water pistol.

Even some of the grown-ups took turns on the trampoline.

When the sun set, Hayden started a bonfire, while the kids collected sticks. Shannon stuck a marshmallow on the end of Ryan's, showing him how to hold it just far enough from the fire to toast the white surface golden brown. Three marshmallows later, Ryan took off with Katie and a bunch of the other kids to catch fireflies along the edge of lawn where the woods began.

On the far side of the bonfire, Lydia Hawkins leaned back in the circle of her husband's arms, the pair laughing softly at some private joke. Michael nuzzled her cheek.

That's what forty-six years together looked like.

A sense of longing filled Shannon.

"About time I caught up with you alone," a familiar deep voice said in her ear, sending a tingle of awareness down her spine. "Can I hold you tonight? Please? I'm not asking for anything more. Just that."

She nodded, and Greg led her to a lounge chair, sinking down onto it. She settled between his legs, resting against his chest.

Overhead, stars flickered in the sky. Wood smoke mingled with the scent of the citronella torches. The fire crackled and popped; laughter and the low hum of conversation floated on the light breeze.

Shannon closed her eyes, relaxing into Greg's body, into his warmth. He held her loosely around the waist, as though afraid to grip her too tightly, skimming his fingers along her arm.

She took a deep breath and held it.

After a moment, Greg whispered, "You can't hold your breath forever, babe."

But she wanted to. It was a perfect moment. Instead of savoring it and letting it go, she wanted to hang on to it.

Forced by the laws of biology to exhale, she let the air out slowly.

The logs in the fire shifted, sending a cascade of red sparks into the air. In the distance, a child giggled.

Another perfect moment.

And that, Shannon supposed, was the problem with trying to hold on to any one moment. You'd end up missing the next one, be it better or worse.

"Time for the fireworks," someone called.

Greg nudged her from the lounge despite her protests. "Come on. We can see the university's display from the deck." The kids were gathered, and they all made their way up. Greg ushered her to the railing, where he fitted his body to her back again, wrapping his arms around her waist. Ryan, Jack and Katie appeared, slurping red-white-and-blue ice pops in various stages of melting.

Greg pressed her against the railing as the first burst of color lit up the night sky. Every nerve in her body leaped to attention, craving him. The children oohed and aahed, except for the youngest ones, who covered their ears.

By the time the display ended, Ryan was slumping in a chair, head wobbling. Shannon sighed. Much as she didn't want to leave, it was time to take him home and put him to bed.

Greg was one step ahead of her. He scooped the sleepy child into his arms. Ryan rested his head on Greg's shoulder.

"I'm taking these guys home, Mom," Greg told his mother when they passed her in the kitchen.

"Worn out, is he?" Lydia stroked Ryan's back. "I'm glad you could come."

"Thanks for having us. It was wonderful."

"You're welcome anytime. I mean it." Greg's mother folded Shannon into a warm hug.

Shannon stood stiffly for a moment, then put her arms around the woman and hugged her back. She was soft and squishy and smelled of wood smoke. More than twenty-five years had passed since Shannon had felt the warmth of a mother's embrace.

"If you need anything, you let us know," Lydia said as they disengaged. "We'll all be thinking about you next week."

Greg groaned. "Aw, Mom. You weren't supposed to mention the trial. I thought I'd been clear about that."

Shannon forced a smile. "No, it's not a problem. Really. Thank you. We can use all the good wishes we can get."

Back at her apartment, Greg carried Ryan in and laid him on the futon, which was currently in her bedroom. Ryan's room had been off limits to everyone except Greg for the past two weeks while he worked on the mural.

Shannon removed Ryan's shoes and clothes, wrestling the limp body into a pair of pajamas while Greg leaned against the door frame. When she looked up at him, he smiled.

"What?"

"That's an advanced parenting skill, in case you didn't know. The less skilled of us call it quits after taking off the shoes and socks. You've come a long way."

Shannon covered Ryan, then stooped to press a kiss against his sticky cheek, catching the faint taste of cherry. Tomorrow she'd not only have to make sure he got washed, but the bedding as well. She followed Greg into the hallway, turning out the light and closing the door behind her.

"Hey." Greg hesitated, then pulled her lightly into his arms. "Sorry about my mom."

Shannon shrugged. "I can't ignore it much longer. Trevor's trial starts next week, and I'm going to have to take Ryan down there and watch them put him on the witness stand, where he can tell the story *again*." Ryan had now told it to the A.D.A. several times as she prepped him for the case. But this time would be different. This time his father would be in the room. Along with a defense attorney who'd get to cross-examine the child. "The very idea makes me sick. But we don't have a choice."

Greg stroked her hair. "You know I'm going with you, right?"

Shannon's relief was so strong, her knees wobbled. She looked up at him. "You are?"

"Yeah. For one thing, I'm not about to let you and Ryan drive all the way to Philly in that piece of crap you call a car."

"Oh. Thanks. I think."

"And for another..." He framed her face with his hands. "I promised I'd be there for you. I know it's still a foreign concept, but we're a team."

"A team, huh?" Fear nagged at her. What happened when he decided he didn't want to be on their team anymore? Or worse, when something happened to take him out of the game completely? Well, for now, she'd embrace the help. The support. "Which one of us is the sidekick?"

"Neither. We're both equal." He lowered his head, brushing his mouth over hers, just a tease before he broke away from her, putting his hand on the doorknob to Ryan's room. "I want you to see the mural. If you don't like it, I'll paint over it and try again. You haven't peeked, have you?"

Shannon rolled her eyes. "No, I promised I wouldn't, and I haven't."

"Good. Wait a sec while I get everything ready." He opened the door just wide enough to slip through. It clicked shut behind him. Light soon trickled beneath the door, illuminating Shannon's bare feet.

A moment later Greg reappeared. "Okay, close your eyes." He radiated eagerness, like one of his kids showing a parent the latest masterpiece, but there was also a hint of uncertainty in his expression. "Close them."

She dutifully shut her eyes, extending her hand. He led her into the room. The soft squish of the carpet yielded to the stiff texture of a canvas drop cloth. He stopped her, moving behind her and placing his hands on her shoulders. "Okay. Open your eyes."

She did.

Summer had a permanent place on Ryan's wall. A large weeping willow on the bank of a river dominated the scene. Beneath the tree, propped against its trunk, a woman and boy read a book together. *The Ransom of Red Chief.*

The boy had unruly sandy-blond hair and a smattering of freckles across his nose. The woman…

It was like looking in a mirror. Only…better. He'd somehow infused her with a beauty, a glow, she knew she didn't possess.

Two thin branches dangled from the tree, one touching Ryan's shoulder, the other Shannon's, giving the impression the tree was embracing them.

The Giving Tree, another much-borrowed library book about a tree that loved a little boy, leaped to Shannon's mind. "Oh, Greg, it's wonderful."

"Look closer." He moved to the wall, pointing. "Here."

Deftly woven into the bark, hidden until he'd called her attention to it, was a delicate face.

Willow.

Right down to the freckles she'd passed on to her son.

While the symbolism of the tree hadn't escaped her, actually seeing her sister's face…

"I found her picture on the Internet. I hope you don't mind."

Shannon reached for but didn't touch the surface, letting her fingertips skim the air over the image. "It's…amazing."

"So why are you crying?" He brushed her cheeks.

"Be-because." She sniffled. "It's…my sister. It's magic."

"That means you like it?"

"Oh, yes, Greg." She tipped back her head, staring up into his soulful blue eyes. "Thank you." Her gratitude was for so much more than the artwork.

He leaned down. "You're welcome." His lips once again connected with hers, a slow, resonant kiss.

The kiss intensified, along with her hunger, her need… She struggled to push him away.

He arched an eyebrow.

"I—I don't want to hurt you again."

"Let me worry about that."

"Are you sure?"

"Someone's got to take the first leap of faith, right?"

So under the spread branches of the willow tree, on the paint-spattered drop cloth, beneath the image of her sister—and with her nephew sleeping in the next room—Shannon thanked him properly.

Without clothing.

When their bodies were joined, Greg stilled overtop of her. "You won't get rid of me so easily this time, Shannon. Fair warning. I fight for what's mine."

Mine. The note of possession rang through her head, through her heart.

"Is that forever I see in your eyes?" Greg murmured.

Shannon smiled, blinking back tears. "Maybe. At least next week anyway."

He laughed, then began to move. "Let me love you, Shannon."

"Oh, yes, Greg." She wasn't so sure about forever. Didn't know how to measure it, how to hold it, how it could possibly be that anyone or anything could stick long-term.

But right now—tonight—was as close to it as she'd ever been.

CHAPTER ELEVEN

SHANNON KNELT on the cool marble floor of the courthouse, adjusting Ryan's superhero tie—a gift from Greg to bolster the boy's courage. She smoothed his suit jacket. "Remember, who do you look at when you're sitting in the chair, telling what happened?"

"You."

"Right. We'll be there the whole time."

Greg and Shannon had been carefully instructed as to what they could and couldn't discuss with Ryan regarding his testimony. Ellen Kelaneri, the A.D.A., had practiced with Ryan, taken him into the empty courtroom and let him sit in the witness chair. They'd done everything possible to prepare him for this moment. Tammy, the victim/witness advocate, a grandmotherly woman whose sole task was to be there for Ryan, had also spent hours with him. He knew they were the ones to turn to when he had any questions. Both had a great rapport with Ryan, and Shannon trusted the women completely.

But she still wanted to grab him and run. She took Ryan's hand and placed it in Tammy's. Until he was called to the stand, he'd be waiting in the victim/witness room, a place with games and a television that had been part of their tour.

"Okay," Shannon said. "You're going to do great. Remember, your mom is watching, and she's so proud of you. And so am I."

"Me, too, sport." Greg leaned down, offered his fist.

Shannon bumped Greg's knuckles, then Ryan slowly added his hand, completing the trio.

Greg took her by the elbow, hauling her to her feet and propelling her toward the courtroom doors. "Don't turn back," he warned. "Let him be."

As Greg steered her down the aisle, Shannon caught sight of Trevor. Her whole body went cold. Wearing a navy pinstripe suit, the man who'd murdered her sister leaned forward on the table, doodling on a pad.

Almost directly behind him, in the spectator section, Patty sat with her hands folded over the designer purse that no doubt matched her shoes.

"Come on, Shannon." Greg moved her forward, then into a seat near the front of the prosecution's side of the room.

Time crawled by as a variety of witnesses were called. Shannon closed her eyes when the medical examiner displayed pictures. Pictures of Willow, pasty white in death. Pictures of bruises.

Shannon toyed with the button of her jacket.

Finally Ellen said, "The prosecution calls Ryan Lloyd Schaffer."

Trevor straightened and turned to stare at the back of the courtroom, as Tammy brought Ryan in. As they passed through the opening in the wooden railing that divided the room, Ryan stole a glance around Tammy at his father, then quickly looked down at his shiny new black dress shoes.

Shannon gripped Greg's hand. He gave it a reassuring squeeze that did nothing to calm her.

Ryan settled into the witness chair, nodding in response to the quiet questions Tammy asked him.

Trevor launched to his feet. "Not one word, Ryan! You promised me. Not *one word*."

With a hoarse cry, Ryan slid from the chair, vanishing below the waist-high panel around the witness stand.

The judge slammed his gavel. "Mr. Lowenstein, control your client."

Shannon half rose from her seat, struggling to see what was happening with Ryan. Greg gripped her forearm, restraining her.

"The prosecution calls for a recess, Your Honor."

Bang, bang. "This court will be in recess until the witness is prepared to resume." The jury filed out of the room again, after which the judge turned to the defense. "Mr. Lowenstein, there will be order when we resume, and your client will keep his mouth shut, or he will be removed. He will not make faces at the child, stare at him or do anything else to disrupt the testimony he's about to give. Understand?"

"Yes, Your Honor," Trevor's defense attorney said.

Tammy carried Ryan, wrapped around her in his clinging-monkey pose, back through the courtroom, down the aisle.

Fists clenched at her sides, Shannon got up and followed the woman out of the courtroom, Greg hot on her heels. Tammy led them to the victim/witness room down the hall. They'd barely gotten inside when Shannon peeled Ryan from her. "Ryan. It's okay. Come here."

With a sob, the boy threw himself into her arms. Shannon sank into a chair, cradling him.

"Remember, you can't discuss the case with him," Tammy said.

Shannon glared over Ryan's head at her.

"Easy there," Greg said. "She's on Ryan's side, remember?"

"Sorry," Shannon muttered, rocking back and forth as Ryan's tears gushed down her neck. She murmured soothing nonsense, assuring the little boy that everything was going to be okay.

She wanted to rip Trevor's liver out through his nose. *Not one word*. No wonder the child hadn't spoken for months. The bastard had made him promise not to say *one word*.

And Ryan had taken it literally.

Tammy extended a box of tissues to Shannon. Gratefully pulling out several, Shannon mopped at Ryan's face. "Hey, you're wrinkling your tie. You're going to make a mess of your superheroes."

Ryan shrugged.

"Oh, no, Ry. We're not going back to you not talking. No way. I will not let that happen. Look at me." Shannon forced his chin up. "You can do this. I know you can. Because you are an amazing kid. Brave. A real hero, remember?"

Ryan shook his head, then lunged forward, hiding his face in the curve of Shannon's neck again. She sighed.

"Give him to me." Greg held out his arms. "Come here, sport."

Ryan went to Greg, leaving Shannon's lap cold. She glanced down at the yellow-and-black fabric flower pinned to her lapel. The petals were crushed and drooping.

Sort of like all of them.

Greg sat in a chair and pulled a white handkerchief from the inside pocket of his suit jacket. He wiped Ryan's nose, holding the handkerchief while the boy honked. He folded it and tucked it away.

"Heroes come in all shapes and sizes, Ryan. They all have different powers. You have the power today to stand for justice. To stand for your mother. Quitters don't win, Ryan. Are you just going to quit?"

The kid shook his head.

"That's my boy. Of course you're not. You're going to fight the good fight. You're going in there, and answer all the questions the attorneys ask you. You're going to tell the truth." Greg rumpled Ryan's hair. "Then we can blow this taco joint and go get some pizza. What do you say?"

"A-artichoke."

Greg chuckled. "Anything but."

Shannon propped her hands on her hips. "Hey. I like artichoke pizza."

"We know," Greg said.

Ellen came into the room to check on her star witness. Greg slid Ryan off his lap, handing him over to the prosecutor, who took him to the sofa on the other side of the room for a private conversation. Ryan's head bobbed repeatedly, then he bumped fists with her.

Shannon and Greg headed back to the courtroom.

Hopefully the second time would be the charm.

PATTY SHIFTED to the edge of her seat as her crying grandson was carried past her. The boy's aunt and the man who'd been the child's art therapist—and then some, according to her P.I.'s research—followed right behind.

Patty hissed at her son, who turned in her direction. "Why did you do that? You made him cry."

"He'll get over it, Mom."

"But what will the jury think?"

"I'm more worried about what they'll think if Ryan doesn't keep his trap shut."

The lawyer glared at them both.

Trevor ignored him. "Who's that guy with Willow's sister? Her boyfriend? I don't like the way he looks at *my* son. You know, if you'd moved faster on the custody case, Ryan would be with you and Dad by now, and I wouldn't have to worry about it."

"They transferred the venue to Erie, Trevor, and that complicated things. Your father has no connections in Erie. Plus, her slick lawyer got the judge to postpone the hearing until your criminal case was decided." Patty opened her purse, digging for a compact and checking her makeup. The media would be waiting on the front steps as soon as court was done for the day. She could only imagine what they'd be asking after Trevor's outburst.

About ten minutes later, Willow's sister and the dark-haired art therapist came back into the courtroom. Before long, the jury was reseated, the judge had called things to order again, and Ryan once more walked down the aisle. Patty tried to wave to him, but he stared straight ahead as the court lady led him to the chair. The polyester suit he wore didn't fit quite right, and the tie was hideous. Once he was in her care, Patty would have to go shopping immediately. What had his aunt been thinking? If she dressed him like this for a court appearance, Lord only knew what his everyday clothes were like.

Ryan kept his eyes glued to Shannon as he answered the preliminary questions.

His comments didn't seem to make much of an impact. Until he mentioned seeing Trevor hit Willow.

Patty stiffened in her seat. He was lying. Trevor would never hit a woman, let alone his wife. He'd loved Willow.

Their wedding had been a fairy tale. Ryan had come along just over a year later. Lloyd had given Trevor more responsibilities at the stores then, figuring their son had settled down and was ready to take the reins.

"Daddy sat on her," Ryan said on the witness stand. "Right here." He pointed to his chest.

"What happened then?" the woman prosecutor asked.

"Mommy kicked her feet and waved her hands, but Daddy didn't get off her."

"Then what happened?"

"Then she stopped."

A low murmur passed through the courtroom. Patty pulled her jacket closed against the sudden chill. Surely Ryan was mistaken. Trevor hadn't simply crushed the breath from his son's mother.

Had he?

Patty shook her head as the prosecutor asked more questions. Trevor propped his elbows on the table, forehead in his hands.

There had to be an explanation for what her grandson described.

She tried to catch Trevor's eye, but he studiously avoided her.

Her son wouldn't look at her.

Just like when he'd been Ryan's age, and the Waterford vase in the living room had shattered. Or when he'd taken his daddy's BMW joyriding at fourteen and put it in a ditch.

Patty's shoulders slumped. On the stand, Ryan's voice trembled, a note of panic lacing his reply to a question she hadn't heard. Several of the female jury members wiped their eyes, and Patty's heart sank.

She was afraid she wasn't going to be able to get Trevor out of this one.

But as his lawyer approached the witness stand to cross-examine Ryan, Patty made a vow. No matter what happened to Trevor, she would do right by her grandson.

THE AMOUNT OF STUFF needed to take three kids to the beach for the day blew Shannon's mind. Two trips to the car transferred most of the "essentials." Now she sat on a blanket beneath the umbrella Derek had forced on her, watching as Ryan raced after Jack and Katie at the water's edge. An assortment of buckets, shovels and small trucks were scattered nearby. A cooler filled with bottled water, juice boxes and their picnic lunch served as a table to hold the bedraggled Beach Barbies, complete with Surfer Dude Ken and his board, which Katie had insisted on bringing as well.

Only a few other intrepid beachgoers had already staked out their beach real estate, but then, it wasn't quite ten in the morning. Ryan had been up at 6:02 a.m., swim trunks already on when he'd bounced into her bedroom and peeled her sleep mask off.

Muffled ringing sent Shannon digging through the quilted beach bag, beneath the bottles of suntan lotion, towels and clothing the kids had shed immediately upon arrival. She flipped open the cell phone she'd finally succumbed to purchasing to keep in touch with the attorneys. "Hello?"

"Just a heads-up," Ellen said. "The case is in the

jury's hands now. It could be hours, it could be days, but I'll call you as soon as they deliver the verdict."

Despite the summer heat, Shannon shivered. Ryan's fate lay in the hands of those twelve strangers. "Okay. Thanks, Ellen."

"I just wanted to tell you again how much I admire your attitude. It's a refreshing change. Most victim's family members hang on every word of the trial and have to be here in person when the verdict's read."

With a shriek of laughter, Ryan kicked water at Jack, then turned to run from the older boy.

"Ryan deserves as much normalcy as possible. If I'm in Philadelphia, holed up in your courtroom, how's he going to get that?" Six days ago, they'd left the city as soon as Ryan had been allowed, and Shannon had no intention of returning. It wasn't going to make any difference to Trevor if she sat in the front row and stared imaginary holes in his head. It wouldn't influence the jury's decision.

And it certainly wouldn't make her sister happy to know Trevor had messed with Ryan's life once again.

"Besides, if I want to see Trevor in handcuffs, I'll just turn on the news tonight."

"Excellent point. I'll call you when I know something."

After disconnecting from the A.D.A., Shannon hesitated a moment, then punched Greg's number. If he was with a client, she'd leave a message.

"You're calling me from the beach?" he said by way of greeting. "Ain't technology grand?"

"Yeah, great."

"Everything okay?"

"The A.D.A. just called. The jury's got the case."

"Oh. She have any clue how long it might take them to decide?"

"No."

"So now we wait?"

"Now we wait." Shannon talked to Greg for another minute or two, then returned the phone to the quilted bag. Then she pulled it out again and set it on the blanket next to her.

Then she tucked it into the pocket of her denim shorts and got up to meander to the water. She spent some time splashing around with the kids in the small waves, before heading back to their blanket, Katie in tow. The girl chattered as she dug a hole in the sand. The hole became the ocean, and she stuck Ken's surfboard into it, perching the figure on the board.

Shannon pulled out the phone, opened it. Nothing.

She snapped at Ryan when the boy squeezed his juice box, squirting sticky apple juice down her leg. Mortified at his crestfallen expression, she quickly apologized.

Just as quickly, he wrapped his arms around her neck in a hug, then scampered off with Jack to find sticks for a sand fort.

Damn, her nerves were shot. How long could it take for twelve people to agree Trevor was guilty?

"Excuse me, miss, but is this spot taken?"

Shannon shaded her eyes, glancing up at Greg. "What are you doing here?"

"Thanks, I'd love to join you." He flopped down on the blanket, stretching out on his side and propping his head on his palm. "I was in the neighborhood. Thought you could use some company. No word yet?"

She shook her head. "Not yet."

"Where's your phone? You did remember to charge it last night, right?"

"Yes, I charged it. I'm not a complete idiot, you know."

"Just a partial one?" His broad grin took any sting from the words.

"Yes. Just a partial one."

"No, you're not an idiot at all. And look at you, taking care of three kids at the beach. Three. When I first met you, I wasn't sure Ryan was going to survive, what with you pushing artichoke pizza on the poor boy. And here you are today, taking care of three kids. Though I did notice you didn't bring Lila."

Shannon laughed. "I'm not ready for a toddler."

A few minutes later, Greg's brother Derek showed up, and Katie and Jack came running to launch themselves into his arms.

Ryan hung back, sad eyes following every move Derek made with his kids. Finally Greg peeled off his shoes and socks, rolled up his jeans and took off down the beach with the boy on his shoulders.

Shannon watched wistfully. The man had the father thing all over Trevor. Had Trevor ever played with Ryan on the beach? Somehow Shannon doubted it.

Had he ever been in tune with someone else's feelings enough to know what they needed, the way Greg seemed to know what Ryan needed? What she needed?

Also doubtful. Trevor was as self-centered as they came.

Derek sat on the edge of the blanket to help work on the sand fort and a new castle for the Barbies.

"What brought you out here?" Shannon asked.

"Just wanted to check on you. Single parenting is hard enough. Takes a while to master dealing with multiple kids."

"Daddy, did you take the afternoon off? Can you stay and play, or is it just lunchtime?" Katie danced a sand-encrusted doll over her father's leg.

"We'll see, honey. I might be able to sneak away for the rest of the afternoon." The bond between Derek's children and Ryan had grown tighter when they'd discovered they'd all lost their mothers.

"Hey, did somebody here order sandwiches?"

Shannon turned to find Hayden strolling toward them with a large plastic bag in his hand. Greg trotted back, swinging Ryan down from his perch on his shoulders. "All right, you brought lunch. Smart thinking."

Before she could say *What's going on?*, the three Hawkins brothers had the cooler opened and were feeding not only themselves but the kids as well.

Busy with her own sandwich—turkey with alfalfa sprouts on whole-grain bread that she'd packed at home—Shannon's mouth was full when the next Hawkins arrived.

Greg's mother, Lydia, carried a bag of homemade brownies, which her sons quickly appropriated. She was followed by Judy and her toddler and baby, Bethany and her nine-year-old son, and Elke, who popped by with the excuse that she needed her mother's input on the final seating arrangement for the wedding.

The beach was literally crawling with Hawkinses. "We're going to need a way bigger blanket," Shannon muttered. She pulled out her cell phone yet again, setting it to vibrate before she tucked it back in her pocket. With all the commotion of the impromptu family reunion, she wasn't sure she'd hear it ring.

She scanned the crowd for Greg, and fixed him with an evil eye. Eventually he looked over at her, and she crooked a finger at him. He handed a blue Frisbee to Ryan and slunk to her.

"You beckoned, m'lady?"

"Greg, what's going on? Surely your entire family didn't show up just to make sure I didn't lose one of Derek's kids. Did they?"

Greg shrugged. "I don't think so."

"So why are they here?"

Greg glanced down at the blanket, pulling off a speck of lint and tossing it aside. "I, uh, well… I might have called Hayden and told him that the jury has the case. And he probably called Derek, who called Elke, who… Well, let's just say that the Hawkins-family grapevine runs fast and furious. We *all* have cell phones."

"They all came because I'm waiting to hear the verdict?"

Greg nodded. "We thought you might need some company. Support. That's how families work, Shannon. In a pinch, you've got people you can count on." He started to tick off on his fingers. "Finn couldn't get away from the restaurant right now, but said his money's on guilty. Dad's taking depositions out of town this afternoon and Cathy's in court herself. But they both sent text messages to keep the faith. The twins are God only knows where, and they're the only ones who didn't send a message." He ran another quick count. "Wait, I forgot Alan. He said he hopes they fry Trevor's sorry ass."

Shannon scanned the beach. The laughter, the camaraderie, the knowledge that they would always be there for one another.

She got to her feet quickly and took off, headed away from the group.

"Shannon! Hey, wait." Greg caught her as she skidded down the dune toward the parking lot. "What's wrong?"

She turned to him, wiping at her eyes. "I—I got sand in my eyes. I was going to the bathroom."

"Liar." He pulled her into his arms.

She let him hold her, drawing solace from his embrace. Until her phone vibrated. Then she shoved him away, scrambling to get to the thing. "Hello?"

"Jury's back. I'm on my way into court right now. I'll call you as soon as I can." Ellen hung up, leaving Shannon gaping at the phone in her hand.

"Well?" Greg asked.

"She's just going into court now to hear what they decided. Crap." Shannon trudged back up the dune. At the top, she paced a short circuit.

"Not much longer," Greg said, following her. "Don't lose your cool now."

"My cool?" She stopped, hands clenched. "I lost my cool months ago. He murdered my sister, and I want him to pay. I don't want him to be able to get anywhere near his son ever again."

Unable to contain her nervous energy, Shannon trotted down the beach. As she passed, various Hawkinses fell silent, staring at her. "Soon," Greg called out to them. "The jury's back. We'll know soon."

She headed along the tide line. The cool water lapped at her toes. After she'd put enough distance behind her, she turned toward the trees, planting herself on one of the weathered picnic tables that dotted Presque Isle.

Greg sat next to her, taking her hand.

The comfort in his touch coursed through her. Mr. Reliable. In the four months she'd known him, he'd become a constant in her life.

Ryan didn't need his services anymore. But she counted Greg as one of the most fortunate things to come out of the horror Ryan had faced.

The idea of letting Greg go didn't fill her with the peace she normally associated with letting go.

It filled her with dread.

They waited, together, the sound of the rolling waves and the distant laughter of children carrying on the breeze.

Shannon set the phone on the table and stared at it, willing it to ring.

Instead, it chattered against the wood, rattling along the surface. She snatched it up. "Well?"

"Guilty." Triumph laced the A.D.A.'s voice. "We nailed the bastard."

Shannon slumped over, head resting on the table, her shoulders shaking. "Thank you," she said softly.

Greg gripped the top of her arm, and Shannon sat up again. Worry etched lines in his face, and his hands flew in the air. She stuck her thumb up, and he pumped his fist in victory.

"It was my pleasure," the A.D.A. said. "I'll let you know the details of the sentencing hearings when I have them. You should consider making a victim-impact statement. For yourself, and for Ryan."

"I'll think about it. Thanks again." Shannon closed the phone and put it away.

Greg yanked her from the bench and spun her around. "Woo-hoo! How's it feel to win?" he asked when he'd set her down again.

"I could get used to it," she said.

She could get used to a lot of things, it seemed. Not the least of which was the presence of this man.

And his huge family.

Maybe a lifetime really was within her grasp.

But first…one more court case. Ryan was safe from his father.

Now she had one more fight to win. She rolled her neck, and danced in the sand on the balls of her feet, smacking one fist into her palm. "Bring on the next loser."

Greg laughed. "I've created a monster."

No, the monster was safely headed to prison, where he belonged.

One victory down, one to go….

CHAPTER TWELVE

GREG ADVANCED TOWARD CATHY on the steps of the Erie County Courthouse with his hands palm out. "You talking to me today?"

"No."

"I said I was sorry."

"Sorry doesn't cover stupidity of that magnitude."

He scanned the pedestrian traffic on the far side of the street, watching for Shannon. "It looked worse than it really was."

"What it looked like, Gory, was you making out with my client in front of an open window. At night. With the lights on in the apartment. I don't appreciate being blindsided like that." Cathy sighed. "I told you specifically to stay away from her. And I've watched you grow closer and closer, despite my warning. I'd been planning to spin your relationship with her as a positive thing, a stable influence on her and Ryan. Positive male role model, and all that. But I didn't think you'd be so idiotic as to get photographed, in her apartment, with Ryan just feet away, with your hands on her ass."

"Do you think it hurt her case?"

"Who knows? The Schaffers have a lot of cards in their favor, money being a big one."

Across the street, Greg spotted Shannon in the laser

lemon jacket and black skirt she'd worn for the criminal trial. The colors attracted the attention of more than a few men, who gave her long legs and great rear appreciative stares as she passed. He waved to her, getting a charge out of the envious glares he got from her sidewalk admirers when she waved back. *That's right, suckers, she's with me.*

"Rumor has it you bought a ring."

Greg's hand froze midwave. He slowly lowered it, turning to face his sister. "Who narced?"

She shook her head. "Two rules if you want to keep something private. Don't make out in front of lit windows at night, and don't tell Hayden."

He cursed under his breath. "When I get my hands on him…"

"He's worried. Seems to think you've totally lost it over her. When are you planning to pop the question?"

"Tonight. I figured to ask her when she's riding the victory."

"And if she says no?"

"Then I plan to ask her every day for the rest of my life until she changes her mind."

"In this state, that's considered stalking." Cathy checked her watch, then glanced at the opposite sidewalk, tracking Shannon's approach.

"I love her, Cathy."

His sister's well-groomed eyebrows inched upward.

"And I love Ryan, too," he added quickly as Shannon drew nearer. "I can't bear the idea of being without either of them. Why is that such a problem with the family?"

"It's not a problem with the family. Geez, don't be so defensive. Her track record isn't outstanding when it comes to stability and commitment, but I think she's changed a lot since Ryan—and you—came into her life."

"Does everyone feel that way?"

"Almost everyone showed up to wait with her for the criminal verdict, right? That should tell you all you need to know, Gory. Even Hayden was there, and he's afraid he's losing his best friend to a woman. You'll have to cut him some slack."

Slightly breathless, Shannon bounded the final few yards to their side. "Sorry. I meant to be here sooner, but Mrs. K. was running late."

"No problem. We've got time. Shall we?" Cathy gestured toward the courthouse entrance.

The blast of air-conditioning was a welcome relief from the summer heat. The women's purses and Cathy's briefcase rode the X-ray machine while they passed through the metal detectors. Outside the courtroom, Greg stopped. Family court proceedings were closed except to participants, and he'd already done his part by testifying about Ryan's progress and Shannon's ability as a guardian.

Of course, he'd come across biased as hell when the Schaffer's lawyer produced the picture of them together in her window, him feasting on her neck like some sort of vampire wannabe.

"You ready for this?" he asked Shannon.

With a broad smile, she held out her fist. "I'm ready, Coach."

"You've fought well, my Padawan." Instead of bumping knuckles, he took her hand, unclenching it and raising it to his lips. "I'm proud of you. Now get in there and show them that the good guys win with grace. No making faces at Patty, okay?"

She laughed. "I'll try to resist the temptation to gloat."

Cathy had the door open. "Shannon?"

"See you in a bit." Greg leaned in to give Shannon a quick kiss.

Amazing how such a friendly little public display of affection from him could zap right through her. Shannon turned and, head held high, she followed Cathy into the small courtroom.

Lloyd and Patty were already seated behind their table, their Ivy League lawyer at their side.

But all the high-priced attorneys in the world couldn't beat a single Hawkins, and Shannon had one at her side, one waiting outside the door and the rest of them pulling for her.

The judge kept them waiting a few minutes, but soon enough, the proceedings were under way.

Judge Victoria Otis leaned forward, propping her arms along the edge of the desk. "I want to say up front that this has been a difficult decision. As you all know, I've waded through reams of reports from various professionals, and listened to several days' worth of testimony.

"Ms. Vanderhoff, you've done an exemplary job of taking a child so severely traumatized that he was mute, and helping him recover to the point that he appears to be functioning very well."

Shannon fought the urge to peek at Patty, to see how the woman was taking that. She smiled at the judge, dipping her head slightly.

"However, I also have to consider your past pattern of behavior. Anyone can find themselves in a crisis situation in a new place. But when I examine your record, it is indeed a pattern. New living places every few years. New jobs even more frequently. Relationships that don't last. You never stay in one place long enough to put down roots.

"Stability is absolutely essential for a child."

Uneasily, Shannon tucked her hands into her lap to hide their trembling.

"Your financial situation is another source of concern for me. Ryan's grandparents, on the other hand, have lived in the same house for decades. They run a highly successful chain of stores and can provide for their grandson's every need. Though they're older, they're reasonably healthy." The judge folded her hands. "This decision has kept me awake for the past two nights. I'm charged with determining what's in Ryan's best long-term interests.

"Therefore, it is my decision that custody of the minor child, Ryan Schaffer, shall be awarded to his paternal grandparents, Lloyd and Patty Schaffer."

Cathy quickly reached over and grabbed Shannon's hand.

Her whole body went numb.

"In the interest of not prolonging the pain for either Ryan or Ms. Vanderhoff, transfer of physical custody shall take place no later than 9:00 a.m. tomorrow morning. I highly recommend that the parties work together to arrange visitation between the boy and his aunt. The bond they've forged should be honored, and both of them will benefit from continued contact in the future." The judge banged her gavel.

Lloyd and Patty rose from their seats, pumping hands with their lawyer.

Shannon sat and stared blankly, heart hammering against her chest wall so hard she could feel it.

Lloyd paused in front of the table. "We'll be by your apartment tomorrow morning to pick him up."

Shannon glanced up at him, nodding once. Trevor's father had the grace to appear apologetic.

Sympathetic.

"Don't bother sending any of his things," Patty said. "He and I will go shopping tomorrow afternoon."

"Patty," Lloyd said sharply. "Don't rub salt. I'll meet you outside." When his wife hesitated, he jerked his head in the direction of the door. "Go on."

Shannon wanted to bowl Patty over and bolt for the door herself, but couldn't make her muscles cooperate.

"I'll make sure you get to see him, Ms. Vanderhoff," Lloyd said softly.

Cathy tapped Shannon's leg, urging a response.

"Thank you," she replied woodenly.

Lloyd's shoes clipped a hasty retreat.

She felt as if someone had autopsied her without waiting for her to be dead, scooping out all her insides.

A huge, hollow shell was all that was left.

"I'm so sorry," Cathy said.

Shannon shook her head. "You did your best. I didn't give you good material to work with." *Breathe in, hold it, breathe out.*

Let go.

She fisted her clammy hands in her lap and blinked hard. Her chair scraped against the floor as she pushed back from the table and abruptly headed for the door.

"Shannon," Greg cried as she stepped out of the courtroom.

"I don't want to see you right now." She hurried down the hallway as fast as she could in the pumps she rarely wore.

"Let her go, Greg," she heard Cathy say behind her. "She needs some time to process this."

"Shannon, wait."

Shannon whirled on him. When he got close enough, she poked him in the chest. "Fight, you said." Poke. "The good guys win, you said." Poke. "But I was right all along. Letting go hurts less." Her voice shook. "Just stay away from me. I'm going home to try to teach a little boy who trusted me—who trusted *you* and the legal system—another lesson in losing and letting go. I don't want to see you again. Got it?"

"Shannon, please..."

She turned her back on him.

Somehow she would get through the next twenty-four hours.

After that...she'd figure out how to get through the rest of her life with pain she suspected wasn't temporary.

"BUT I DON'T WANNA GO live with Grandma Patty," Ryan said as Shannon crouched in the foyer to retie his sneaker.

"I know." He'd only told her about twenty thousand times since she broke the news to him yesterday afternoon.

"She smells funny. And she looks at me all pinchy, like *I* smell. Like this." Ryan scrunched up his face, eyebrows drawn together, freckled nose thrust up in the air, and proceeded to look down at her.

The impression was so totally Patty, she'd have laughed if her heart wasn't breaking. "I know, pal, but we have to do what the judge said."

"That judge is stupid! Let's ask another judge."

"I wish we could, buddy. But we can't. It doesn't work that way."

"Don't make me go, Aunt Shannon." Ryan threw himself against her, wrapping his arms around her neck.

She fell back against the wall, hugging the boy who'd come to be her world. "I have to, Ry. Otherwise the police will put me in jail. And you'd go live with Grandma Patty anyway."

"We could run away. We'll take Uncle Greg with us, too."

Tears spilled over her cheeks. "We don't fight physically, and we don't run away. Those aren't ways to solve problems." But it was tempting.

"Don't you want me?"

Shannon sniffled. "Of course I do. I fought for you." She pushed the boy from her arms so he could see her. "I love you, Ryan. Don't *ever* doubt it. No matter what happens when you leave here, you're my boy. I'm going to miss you terribly."

Ryan framed her face with his hands. "Don't cry, Aunt Shannon."

Which made her blubber like a damn fool. She dragged him back into her embrace, her tears falling into the curve of his neck.

He patted her on the shoulder, and for a split second she considered taking him and running, just as he'd suggested.

But Patty and Lloyd were already waiting outside.

Shannon climbed to her feet. "Wait here, Ry. Just a minute." She ran back up the stairs and dashed into the bathroom, blowing her nose and splashing cold water on her face. No way in hell she'd give Patty the satisfaction of seeing her like this.

Back in the foyer, she cleared her throat and took Ryan's hand. She squeezed it. "We've been through worse," she assured him—or maybe herself. "We can get through this. Grab your backpack." The backpack held a few items. His night-light. A box of crayons and some paper. A picture he'd drawn of them at the beach.

They stepped out onto the porch—and found Greg leaning against the metal railing. She glared at him.

"I wanted to say goodbye to Ryan, too."

Ryan launched himself at Greg, who swung the boy up, holding him tight against his chest. After a moment, he set Ryan on his feet, then went to one knee in front of him. "I'll miss you, sport. Hey, I brought you a present." Greg reached for the book sitting on the top step.

"The Ransom of Red Chief!" Ryan exclaimed, hugging it.

"Yep. Your very own copy."

"Thanks, Uncle Greg."

Greg cleared his throat, his voice suspiciously unsteady when he said, "You're welcome." He put out his fist. "Fight on, SuperKid."

"I'm not SuperKid anymore. I'm just Ryan."

"Well, I think you're a super kid, no matter what."

Ryan bumped fists with him, and Shannon had to look away.

A car door shut in the parking lot, and Lloyd sauntered down the sidewalk. "Time to go, Ryan."

"I don't wanna."

"We've been through that, Ryan," Shannon said.

"I'm not going." Ryan stomped his foot.

Lloyd gently took Ryan by the wrist and picked him up, ignoring the boy's struggle. He took the backpack in his other hand. "He'll call you." Lloyd turned and headed back to the car.

"Aunt Shannon! Uncle Greg! I don't want to go—please!"

Shannon could no longer see for her tears. A huge fist squeezed her chest, and she found it difficult to breathe.

Another car door slammed, muting Ryan's gut-wrenching cries. Then a second door closed.

The car started, and gravel popped as they backed out of the parking space.

Shannon stood waving, even though she didn't know if Ryan could see her, until the car vanished around the corner.

Then her knees buckled, and she crumpled into a heap on the top step, sobbing.

Greg rushed to hold her.

She wanted to let him. To take refuge in his embrace and have him kiss the pain away. But if it hurt this much to lose Ryan, she wasn't about to let herself love Greg. *'Tis better to have loved and lost than never to have loved at all.*

Bullshit.

Loving and losing hurt like hell. Letting go had never hurt like this.

"Get…away." She flailed at him the way Ryan had flailed at Lloyd. "Don't touch me."

"Shannon, please—"

She scrambled to her feet. "This is all your fault. I feel like I'm dying. Bond with him. Fight for him, you said. That sure worked out, didn't it?"

Greg extended his hands to her. "I'm sorry, Shannon—"

"Sorry doesn't help." She dashed into her apartment, locking the door behind her. She ran up the stairs and threw herself down on the leather sofa, pulling the blanket over her head. In the dim light that filtered through, she tried to take a deep breath.

A key scraped in the lock, and footsteps pounded up the stairs. The warmth of a body settled beside her. She sniffled. "I want my key back. Don't think I'll be needing a babysitter anytime soon."

Greg dragged the blanket away. His chest tightened at the sight of her splotchy face and Rudolph-neon nose. "I didn't think we'd lose him."

"We?"

"Yes, we. I love you, Shannon. And I love Ryan, too. I didn't think it would end this way."

"Love?" She narrowed her eyes.

"I love you," he repeated. "Why is that so hard to believe?"

"Love is apparently highly overrated, comic-book boy. Love sucks. Love hurts." She thumped her chest. "I've got nothing to give you. Not when it comes to love. I'm empty."

"I know it hurts, Shannon, but—"

"No buts. You've got a whole huge family. Ryan was all I had left. Now he's gone. And I want you gone, too. I'm letting you go, Greg. Time's up." She turned her face toward the back of the couch.

"Let me help you through this."

She struggled off the sofa, feet tangled in the afghan. She kicked it away. "What part of 'it's over' don't you get? Do I have to draw you a picture?"

He rose slowly to his feet. She needed time. In a few days, the worst of it would have passed, and they could take this up again. He wasn't about to give up on her. The near-violent reaction to losing Ryan only meant she had a far greater capacity to love than either of them had suspected. "I'm going."

But I'm not quitting on you.

"Leave the key."

Greg dug in his pocket, setting the key on top of her television. "If you need anything, call me."

She turned away from him again, giving him her back.

"Okay." He descended the stairs deliberately, gripping the banister, feet heavier with each step. Out on the porch, he shielded his eyes, looking up at her dining-area window. The glare of the morning sun prevented him from seeing anything. "I'll be back," he vowed. "This isn't over."

SHANNON'S APARTMENT was too damn quiet.

Too empty.

Just like her.

The second merlot of the night had blunted the edge of the pain, but didn't make it go away. After three days, she'd expected things to be easier. That's how long it had taken her to let go of Willow. For the most part, anyway.

Shannon leaned against the doorway to Ryan's room, long-stemmed glass in hand. Several sealed boxes lined the floor, near the closet.

She'd tried to take them to the Salvation Army because someone out there needed all those little shirts and shorts and such. But she just hadn't been able to do it. She set the glass of wine on the bookcase and hefted the first box, tucking it into the corner of the closet. She piled the other two on top and shut the door. Out of sight, out of mind.

Too bad she couldn't put the mural out of sight as easily.

Shannon went to the wall Greg had spent weeks

painting. She touched Ryan's face, then skimmed her finger over the tree trunk to trace the same freckled nose on her sister. "I'm sorry, Willow," she whispered.

She turned away from the mural, picking up her glass and slamming back the rest of the dark red wine.

Inspiration struck. Where were her keys? She plucked them from the kitchen island.

Barreling down the stairs, she bolted from her apartment. Somewhere in the dusky summer, kids were shouting and laughing, pounding a basketball. She ran down the sidewalk, then took the steps to the basement laundry room two at a time. On the far side of the washing machines, she opened the door to the maintenance closet using the key provided to all tenants. Mostly so they could access things like a plunger in the event of a bathroom-plumbing emergency.

She'd had one of those when Ryan had overdone it with the toilet paper. Or maybe it was the toothbrush that had fallen in the bowl and gone unreported.

Shannon gathered what she needed and lugged her booty back to her apartment, dropping everything in Ryan's room. She pushed the futon against the closet doors, then spread the tarp. After a quick trip to the kitchen to refill her glass, she went to work, prying the lid off the paint can with a screwdriver. The boring beige used to neutralize and refresh the apartments between tenants suited perfectly. She poured some into a tray and picked up the roller.

She started on the outside edges, obscuring the river first, then the upper branches and leaves of the tree.

Erase it.

The field grew smaller. Flecks of paint rained onto her as she covered the mural.

Let it go.

She closed her eyes when she got to the magical portrait of Willow, deftly hidden in the bark. God only knew how long it had taken Greg to create the incredible image. It took her all of five seconds to coat over it.

Only the woman and the boy remained.

She set the roller in the tray and slugged back another shot of merlot.

For a long moment, she stood in front of the wall, dripping paint onto the drop cloth. Images came back to her. Ryan as SuperKid. Searching for beach glass on the shores of Lake Erie. Riding the Tilt-a-Hurl. Cuddling up with him on the sofa and reading *The Ransom of Red Chief.*

She raised the roller.

Her lower lip trembled. Tears welled in her eyes. "No more crying. Let *him* go."

She took a deep breath, held it for a moment, then let it out.

The content boy and woman vanished.

Leaving a blank wall in their wake.

CHAPTER THIRTEEN

GREG CAREFULLY REMOVED the last picture—one Ryan had made—from the wall and added it to the pile on the top of the shelving unit.

Several cardboard boxes, overflowing with colored pencils, markers and boxes of chocolate pudding, cluttered the tabletops. The room was forlorn and barren: naked walls, empty storage units, everything shades of brown and beige despite the late-afternoon sunshine filtering in the windows.

It reminded him of an elementary-school classroom the day before summer vacation started.

Only today, there was no presummer excitement.

No, in his case, summer was just about over, and the fall term loomed ever closer. He'd gone past his deadline to clear out of the room at Erie University—July 31—by one day.

He, who never missed a deadline. At least, not a comic-book deadline.

He crouched to get a broken crayon from under the edge of the shelves. Cadet blue, a color that couldn't make up its mind if it was more blue or gray.

He could relate.

Hayden bounded into the room. "These the last boxes?"

"Yeah."

"Okay." His brother scooped up two, balancing one in each arm. "You ready then?"

"I suppose."

"Don't be such a mope. There are no endings, only beginnings."

Greg snorted. "Don't quote your code at me. I've got nowhere for my groups to meet. Individual therapy isn't always as helpful as group." His cancer kids, for example, benefited from the group experience, the support and camaraderie.

The insurance premiums alone were killing him, never mind rent and all the other stuff he needed for his group practice. He'd been forced to start charging more and, as a result had lost a couple of his kids whose parents just couldn't afford the higher fees. He'd felt horrible, but he had to pay his own bills as well.

The paperwork for his nonprofit organization—the Erie Foundation for Art Therapy—had finally been approved, but funding it was a whole different matter.

"Something's going to break. Keep the faith, huh?"

"I'm trying. Head on down," he told Hayden. "I'll meet you at the car."

"It's your call." His brother paused on his way out. "Seriously, Gory, it's the university's loss. *Anybody* who cuts you loose is crazy."

Greg understood who Hayden meant by *anybody*. He nodded.

"Don't be long, man. We've got places to be and beers to drink." Hayden headed out.

Greg laid the pile of drawings on top of the final box and hefted it. He hesitated in the doorway.

So many memories here. So many kids, so many drawings...

He took a deep breath, held it for a moment, then exhaled. *Let it go.* Just like Shannon had taught him.

He might be able to let go of the room, the university. But letting go of the freckle-faced boy he'd said goodbye to a week ago wasn't as easy.

Neither was letting go of the woman who'd stood behind the observation glass and watched him, like a fish in a bowl.

A woman who'd learned to stand up for herself. To love. And let herself be loved.

And who'd lost so much more than he'd ever imagined possible.

The enormity of it made him feel even more like a chump. This was a room. A place. A small component of his program. Plenty of therapists ran their own practices. This was just a setback. He'd overcome it.

He flipped the lights off.

In the parking lot, he set the final box on the backseat of his Tracker. He peeled the Erie University Staff parking sticker off the back window, then tossed it to the floor.

"That's the spirit," Hayden said from the passenger seat.

As they pulled out from the parking lot, a cape-and-costumed figure seemed to materialize on the sidewalk. The superhero wannabe snapped to attention and raised his hand in salute.

No cameras. No crowd. No gawkers.

Just a comic-book geek giving him a send-off.

Greg saluted back, then stuck his hand out the window to wave as they drove away.

"You figured out how they know where to find you yet?" Hayden asked.

"Nope." And for the moment, he didn't care. His "stalkers" had become part of his routine, which was an odd comfort. After all, he must've still "had it" to be worthy of so much attention.

Hopefully Shannon felt the same way. He didn't relish the idea of her actually taking out a restraining order against him.

But he couldn't give up on her.

He turned toward her apartment complex.

Hayden groaned. "No. No way. We're supposed to be meeting all the guys at the Marina for beer. Elke and Jeremy are getting married next Saturday. We have to finalize the bachelor-party plans. Time lines, the route for the bar crawl."

"Just a quick stop. To check on her. It's been a week today."

"Dude, you remember how much you hated that Denise wouldn't get it through her thick head it was over? You're doing the same thing she did."

"I am not."

"You're suffocating her. Man, if there's ever a chance, you've gotta back off. Give her a chance to miss you. She can hardly miss you if she's busy dodging your calls and slamming her door in your face."

Greg sighed. She'd been doing exactly that for the past week. She'd made it abundantly clear she wanted him out of her life.

Just as he'd done with Denise.

"Don't be pathetic. She knows where to find you if she changes her mind. Man up."

Stomach churning, Greg turned down a side street

before they reached her complex, making a giant U-turn around the block.

Maybe sometimes you had to call it quits.

SHANNON MADE A FINAL correction on the newsletter she'd crafted for a client, then attached it to an e-mail and sent it winging off through cyberspace. She composed an official e-mail for another client, sent that off as well.

Then she clicked open the Internet. "Just the news," she promised herself. But the news was boring. And before she realized it, she was on YouTube, typing in Greg's name.

The red, green and blue ABC Men appeared, flexing and posing. Shannon paused the video when it cut to Greg's face.

She missed that face. And the man it belonged to.

After a moment of studying the high cheekbones, the angular jawline, she put the action into motion again, stopping next on the shot of Ryan giggling at the ABC Men's antics.

She missed *that* face, too.

Somehow, she'd lost her ability to put them behind her. Greg hadn't broken Ryan, but the two of them had broken her.

The two weeks since losing Ryan to Patty and Lloyd had been more like years.

Like a junkie in desperate need of a fix, she played several more videos, including one featuring a villain called Trash Man, then surfed to another Web site, one she'd discovered after compulsively Googling Greg and visiting page after page in the early morning hours. Her fingers flew over the keyboard, typing in the password.

A map of the area appeared, with a stationary blip.

College kids with a love of comic books had created a new game with Greg in the unwitting starring role. It had an element of geocaching, a game where a treasure is buried with a GPS unit, combined with an element of homemade reality TV. Someone had planted a hidden GPS unit on Greg's Tracker one day when he'd been signing comics at a local store.

Ironic. They were tracking his Tracker.

And she'd joined the online geeks' group with the name Mysterious Lady O in order to weasel the password to the Web site that displayed Greg's movements and location. Pathetic? Maybe. But there was comfort in knowing where he was, in watching the blip move around Erie.

At the moment, the blip wasn't even in Erie. Greg was somewhere south, almost in Crawford County. Which made her even lonelier.

She should have told him about the GPS unit, but he'd quit calling her a week ago.

Mr. Fight-the-Good-Fight had given up more easily than she'd expected. And she wasn't about to call him. She'd seen his exasperation at Denise's attempts to rekindle a romance. Besides, she didn't *want* Greg's attention.

At least, that's what she kept telling herself. *Liar!*

With a sigh, she closed the Internet and resumed working. She'd returned the computer to the extra room, positioning it so she had her back to the wall behind the futon. Despite painting over the mural, she could see it every time she looked at the space.

Shannon moved on to some bookkeeping entries. A while later, the doorbell rang repeatedly, followed by rapping on the door. In the foyer, Shannon peered through the peephole, seeing nothing.

The banging started again.

She opened the door, confused. "Yes?"

"Surprise! I'm home!" Ryan barreled over the threshold and threw himself at her, knocking her backwards.

She squatted, bracing herself with one hand while wrapping the boy in an embrace with the other. "Ryan! Ohmygosh. Ohmygosh." The warmth of the small form fitted against her was the return of sunshine after a long winter. Shannon basked in that glow until Ryan started to squirm.

"I flew in a airplane and rode in a yellow taxi cab. Did you know cars look like ants from the sky?" He wiggled out of her embrace.

She wanted to haul him back and never let him go again. "Do they?"

"Yep. I was like a superhero, way up in the clouds."

The sounds of scraping brought Shannon's attention to the man dragging an oversize suitcase up the porch steps. In the other hand, Lloyd carried the backpack Ryan had left with.

"Are you surprised?" The boy jiggled in place like an eager puppy.

"Very," Shannon said. "I didn't expect a visit quite this soon." There'd been no time to get over the first loss. Like a barely healed wound suddenly deprived of its scab, she was going to bleed again when he had to go back. But for now, he was here. With her. That would have to be enough.

She got to her feet, stroking Ryan's unruly hair. "But it's the best surprise I've ever had." She peered over

Lloyd's shoulder to a cab parked at the end of the sidewalk. "Where's Patty?"

"Patty's home with the mother of all migraines, having realized what I told her all along." He offered Shannon a weary smile as he heaved the luggage inside her foyer.

"Oh? What's that?" Uneasiness stirred Shannon's stomach. Why was Ryan here? Why hadn't Lloyd called ahead?

"I gotta go to the bafroom," Ryan announced. "Bye, Grandpa Lloyd. Thanks for bringing me home!" He scrambled up the stairs, and the bathroom door slammed a moment later.

"That boy is pure energy," his grandfather said, running a hand through his white hair.

The back of her neck prickled. "Why don't you come upstairs? Tell me what's going on."

"I can't stay. A friend of mine flew us out here. He's at the airport, refueling his plane and filing the paperwork for our return flight. I have an important business meeting tomorrow, and need to get back." He unzipped a compartment on the front of the black suitcase, pulling out a manila envelope.

"What's this?" She took it hesitantly, her hand quivering.

"Paperwork. Have your lawyer go over it, sign it, notarize it and send back our copies."

"What's going on, Lloyd?" Shannon's heart thudded against her ribs. *No, don't hope. Don't care. It'll just hurt more later.*

"My wife has realized there's a reason folks our age don't have kids. We're too old. Especially for a ball of fire like that one." He grabbed the suitcase. "Let me just take this up the stairs for you. It's heavy. Wheels aren't any help at all on stairs."

Shannon followed, envelope clutched to her chest, Ryan's backpack over her arm, the lump in her throat making it hard to speak. "So, that means what?"

"That means, we made a mistake in trying to take Ryan from you in the first place."

Shock stopped her dead in her tracks. She tried twice before she managed to choke out, "You're giving me custody?"

"Where do you want this?" Lloyd gestured to the suitcase.

"I…uh…in Ryan's room, please."

He popped out the handle and wheeled it down the hallway.

Shannon climbed the remaining stairs, then waited for him to reappear. When he did, she fired off her question again, resisting the urge to scream. "You didn't answer me. You're giving me custody? After all the lawyers, that whole big legal fight, just like that?"

"We'd like to visit, of course."

Words finally failed her. She tried to process it. Ryan was staying. With her. Her knees trembled, and she sniffed to quell the tingling in her nose.

"Um…are you okay? You do still want custody, right?"

"Oh, yes. Hell yes."

"Visitation terms are spelled out in the documents. I think you'll find it fair."

"I—I'm sure I will."

"All right." He strode back to the top of the stairs, then paused. "I'm sorry our son…I'm sorry about your sister."

Shannon swallowed hard, managing a wobbly nod.

Lloyd descended to the landing, then turned and slowly climbed back up, stopping on the first step. "I almost forgot." He hauled his wallet from the back pocket of his pants. "This is to help with Ryan's expenses. School will be starting soon, and we know that little boys grow like weeds. Or in case you need to buy a big container of migraine medicine." He smiled.

She almost refused. But something in Lloyd's eyes—something she'd seen in her own father's eyes, a need to help—made her take the blue check.

He held out a second check. "And this one is for Mr. Hawkins. Patty found out about his new art therapy foundation, and she plans to make him her new pet project. The difference he made in Ryan really impressed us both. Here's Patty's card. She'd like Mr. Hawkins to call her so they can discuss potential fund-raising events." He smiled wryly. "One thing my wife knows besides spending money is how to raise it for charity."

Fingers still trembling, Shannon accepted the second check, too. "I—I know Greg will be very appreciative. As am I."

Lloyd shook his head. "We're the ones who appreciate everything you've done—everything you're doing—for our grandson. I can't imagine what kind of shape he'd be in if not for you and Greg Hawkins. You know, you're all that boy talked about. Aunt Shannon this, Uncle Greg that..." He flipped his wrist and checked his watch, then swore softly. "I have to run. You call if you need anything, okay?"

"Okay." Shannon stood at the top of the steps, manila envelope and checks still in her hands when the apartment door closed.

She ran to the window overlooking the parking lot to confirm it really had been Lloyd Schaffer in her apartment. Not some impostor toying with her emotions.

A shriek from Ryan's room shook her out of her trance. "My painting! What happened to my painting?"

He met her in the doorway, planting his fists on his hips. "Who ruined the picture Uncle Greg made me?"

Dropping the backpack on the floor in front of his closet, right next to the suitcase, she set the envelope and checks beside the computer. Sinking onto the futon, she held her hand out to Ryan.

He crossed the room in starts and stops, dragging his sneakers on the rug. When he stood before her, she lifted him to her knee. "I'm sorry about the painting. It made me sad to see it."

"Really?"

"Yes." She cleared her throat. "Looking at the painting just reminded me of everything I'd lost. Your mom, you…"

"I'm not lost now. I'm back."

Shannon smiled, blinking back tears. "You sure are. I'm going to call Cathy to check those papers, though. We need to make sure everything is in perfect order. We don't want to count our chickens before they're hatched." She wouldn't survive losing him again.

Once had been enough.

Ryan crinkled his freckled nose. "Huh?"

"I just want to make sure they can't change their minds again, Ryan. I want to make sure all the t's are crossed, and everything is legal."

"So we don't have to see a judge again?"

"Exactly." She narrowed her eyes. "Now, you want

to tell me what happened to change Grandma Patty's mind about keeping you?"

Her nephew shrugged. "I dunno. She said I was a handful."

"A handful, huh? Sounds like there's a lot more to the story than that."

Ryan slid from her knee to the floor, digging in the backpack. "Well, she was mad when the police came."

Shannon pressed her lips together, waiting a beat before asking, "Why did the police come?"

"I called 911, like you showed me."

"Ryan, I told you, that's only for emergencies."

"It *was* a 'mergency. I wanted to come home."

Home. Her apartment was home. What a beautiful word.

"Okay. What else?"

He shrugged again, tugging a yellow truck from the bag. "I had a few accidents."

"What kind of accidents?"

"It wasn't my fault. Grandpa Lloyd even said so."

"What wasn't your fault?"

"At dinner in this special place where I had to wear a tie—it wasn't nice like the one Uncle Greg gave me, it was a boring tie—I tried to do what Grandma Patty said. I put my napkin on my lap. But then I had to go potty, and the white thing on the table got stuck on my belt, so when I got off my chair to hold Grandpa Lloyd's hand so we could go to the bafroom, *smash!*" He gestured wildly. "Everything fell on the floor and everybody looked at us. Grandma Patty's face got all red."

I'd have given a million dollars to see that. Shannon battled a laugh. *Smash, kablam, kerpow!* "That sounds like an accident to me."

"Right. Just like when I broke the TV."

She leaned forward. "What happened to the TV?"

"Me and Grandpa were playing a video game. I tried to make the ball go down the little thing and knock the pins down, and *whoops*. The thing flew outta my hand, and crashed into the giant TV set. It made sparks! Grandpa Lloyd said bad words."

"I'm sure he did." She bit the inside of her lower lip.

"The video-game thing is in here." Ryan patted the suitcase. "Grandpa said to take it with me."

Shannon made a mental note to make sure the "thing" didn't go flying out of Ryan's hand in her apartment. She couldn't afford a new TV. "That was very nice of him."

"Yep. It was." He dug into the backpack again, pulling out the book Greg had given him as a going-away present.

The puzzle pieces clicked into place. "Ryan?"

He glanced up at her. "What?"

"Are you sure those were all accidents?"

His eyes widened, and Shannon could all but see a tarnished, crooked halo appear over his head. "Uh... yeah. Well...the police weren't."

"When you called them so you could come home?"

"Yeah, and when I called them 'cause I saw a stranger in the garden. I didn't know Grandma Patty *wanted* him there. A whole bunch of cop cars came that time. They let me turn on the lights."

"Grandma Patty had a lot of headaches while you were there?" Squad cars screaming up to her house might have contributed to at least one or two migraines.

The boy wrinkled his nose. "She *always* had a headache. You can't play trucks and not make noise, you know."

"Oh, I know." The child had fought the only way he could. In a *Ransom of Red Chief*-inspired way.

And the little imp had won.

He'd accomplished what she hadn't been able to. Fine role model she'd turned out to be. The kid had rescued both of them. Her from an empty, lonely life, and he'd saved himself from Grandma Patty, who'd meant well. Or so Shannon now chose to believe.

Torn between praising him for his courage and ingenuity, and scolding him for being mischievous, she took the book from him and returned it to his bookcase, propped open on the top shelf in a place of honor.

"Can we go see Uncle Greg now? I want him to know I'm home. Maybe we can go to Paula's Parlors. You can have artichoke pizza, and me and Uncle Greg will have pepperoni."

"We can go to Paula's. We should have a celebration. This is the best day I've had in two whole weeks." And it would be even better once she'd gotten Cathy to read the papers and assure her that they really said what Lloyd had promised.

"Cool! A party. Can we invite Jack and Katie, too?"

"Oh, sweetie. I don't think so."

Ryan's shoulders drooped. "Why not?"

"Because." Shannon couldn't figure out how to explain to a six-year-old that she'd dumped the family that had welcomed them into their midst. Dumped the man he'd claimed as an uncle.

The man she'd fallen in love with.

In a preemptive strike.

Ryan once again propped his fists on his hips. "You made him mad, didn't you? Because you wrecked the painting."

"Greg doesn't know I wrecked his painting."

Ryan's mouth gaped. "Oooo, he's going to be really mad when he finds out."

More likely, he'd be hurt. Again. His hard work, his thoughtful gift, gone. "All the more reason not to call him."

Ryan shook his head. "You need to tell him you're sorry. I miss him."

Out of the mouths of babes.

"I don't know if a simple 'I'm sorry' is going to be enough to fix this."

Fate—and a six-year-old's ingenuity—had returned Ryan to her. Returned her hope and her faith.

Was it too much to ask for Greg as well?

If she didn't try, she'd never know.

"We need a plan."

SEVERAL HOURS LATER, Shannon chewed her thumbnail as Cathy read the paperwork at Shannon's table. Ryan played his new video game in the living room—with the controller securely fastened to his wrist.

Finally Greg's sister flipped the packet closed. "I'll want to go over it again, but on first read-through, this is solid. Bring it by my office Monday, we'll make a few minor changes, and you can sign. We'll have one of the staff witness and notarize it."

"Thank God." Shannon exhaled slowly, and it had nothing to do with letting go, and everything to do with the biggest sense of relief she'd ever known. And the greatest joy she'd ever known.

Ryan was well and truly hers.

To keep.

The magnitude staggered her. She leaned against

the kitchen counter. From here on out, she and Ryan were a team.

The only thing that tempered her joy was Greg's absence. The man who'd taught her—and Ryan, apparently—to stand up for what she wanted should be here with them.

Celebrating.

But she'd destroyed her chances with Greg, just as she'd destroyed his mural.

All because she'd been too scared of losing him to hold on.

How stupid was that? So stupid, in a horror movie, she'd have been one of the idiot women who went, unarmed and in her underwear, into the dark basement after several other people had gone missing.

Cathy pushed back her chair. "Congratulations, Shannon, it's a boy. And he's all yours."

"Woo-hoo!" Ryan called from the living room. "No more stupid judges."

The two women laughed.

"I don't know how to ever thank you," Shannon said.

"Don't thank me for this one. Thank Ryan. Or should I say Red Chief?" Cathy checked her watch. "I have to run. Tomorrow's Elke's wedding, so tonight is not only the bachelor party, but the kidnapping of the groom *from* the bachelor party."

Elke's wedding. The whole Hawkins family gathered together. Shannon had eagerly anticipated going with Greg. "Kidnapping of the groom?"

"Family tradition. Basically the women stop the party dead in its tracks so the groom isn't too hungover for the wedding. But because the men know we'll be coming, the challenge is to find them. They don't tell us where the party is, and they keep it moving from place to place."

"Really?" Wheels turned in Shannon's head. A plan began to take shape. She needed the rest of the Hawkinses, especially the women, back on her side if she'd ever stand a chance with Greg. "So you have to be able to locate them?"

"Exactly."

"Do you know if Greg's using his Tracker tonight?"

"They rented a Hummer limo, but believe it or not, they can't all fit in it. So, yes, I think Greg is a designated driver. Why?"

Shannon pointed at Cathy's laptop on the table. "Does that thing have wireless Internet?"

"Yes. I use a wireless phone card. I can get Internet anywhere over the cell-phone network."

"Perfect." Shannon resisted the temptation to rub her hands together like a plotting supervillain. "If I help you with your mission, can I get the Hawkins women to help me with mine?"

Cathy's eyes narrowed. "I guess that depends on exactly what you have in mind. You're persona non grata with the Hawkinses right now. I'm here because of professional obligation." Her expression softened. "Okay, and because of my brother. I'm trying to get the lay of the land here. He's been miserable."

"Cathy, I know I've hurt Greg." Not that she'd intended to. But the reality was, she had. She'd seen it in his eyes when she'd told him to leave. Heard it in his voice when he'd called to check on her, or pounded on her door, begging her to let him in. Her stomach sank. This was going to be a long shot.

"I'm *really* sorry for that. I can only claim temporary insanity over losing Ryan, and throw myself on your mercy. The truth is—" Shannon swallowed hard "—I've realized how empty my life is without him. Without all of you. A smart kid and an even wiser man taught me I have to fight for what I want. I want your brother to give me another chance."

"Do you love him?"

She wiped her palms on her jeans. Nodded. "Yes. I do."

Cathy studied her for a moment, examining her with the strip-her-down-to-the-bare-essentials gaze of a lawyer. She jerked her head downward. "All right then. Let's go to my parents' house, and you can fill in the details on the way."

CHAPTER FOURTEEN

GREG TOOK OUT his cell phone, flipped it open, then stopped. Disgusted with himself, he snapped it shut and put it away. He leaned his elbows on the scarred wood of the bar's edge, toying with the once-frosted mug that had thawed long ago. He swirled the dregs in the bottom.

A roar erupted from the men gathered in the corner, shooting darts at a life-size cardboard centerfold covered with balloons.

"You're a freakin' downer," Hayden said, dropping onto the stool next to him, a bottle of ale in his hand. "Sitting over here, crying in your root beer."

Greg snorted. "Get the hell out of here. I'm not crying."

Hayden leaned over and sniffed Greg's mug. "But you are drinking root beer."

"Hello, designated driver, remember? Besides, it looks like ale if you don't get too close. Even kicks up a head."

"What's got your boxers in a bunch tonight, Gory? No, wait, let me take a wild guess. Shannon?"

Greg lifted one shoulder. "Cathy called earlier. Ryan's back with Shannon, where he belongs. Apparently the kid drove his grandmother insane until she returned him. Kudos to him." He lifted his glass in salute, then slugged back the last mouthful of soda.

At least someone had fought for what they wanted, and won.

This giving-her-space crap was for the birds.

Greg slid off the bar stool. "I'm going over there."

Hayden grabbed him by the arm. "Oh no you're not. Not tonight, anyway. You're my designated driver, Root Beer Boy."

"I'm sure if you, Derek and Finn tried, you could squeeze into the Hummer."

"I'm not sitting on anybody's lap. Especially when they've been drinking all night."

"Call a taxi."

"You are *not* ditching us tonight." Hayden released his grip. "Look, Gory, tonight and tomorrow are for family. Besides, maybe now that she's got the boy again, she'll come crawling back to you."

"You think?"

Hayden shrugged. "Maybe. You won't know if you don't give it a chance. She dumped *you*, bro. It's only fair that she does the crawling."

Greg didn't care about fair. He just wanted her back. Still, he was obligated tonight.

And tomorrow.

"Fine. But if I don't hear from her by Sunday afternoon, I'm going after her. I'm not going to wait around and lose her because I'm too proud."

Hayden's bushy eyebrows climbed his forehead. He groaned, shaking his head in disgust. "You are so whipped."

"Someday, Hayden, you'll meet a woman, and immediately there'll be this connection. It might be vague and hard to pin down at first, but you'll feel it. And then we'll see who's whipped."

Their father sauntered over and dropped an arm around each of their shoulders. "You boys about ready to mount up? Time to move this party and keep a jump on the women. You've outdone yourself this time, Hayden. I think Jeremy may just become the first groom in recent family history to outsmart the ladies. Love the loophole. You should have been a lawyer."

"Thanks, Dad," Hayden said, puffing out his chest.

Greg slapped him across the breastbone, forcing him to deflate. "Don't get too excited yet. It's still early. Besides, if we do outwit them, just think how pissed Elke's going to be at you tomorrow."

"True," their dad said. "I wouldn't want to be you, son, if we do win this one. You know what will happen." He stepped into the center of the room, cupping his hands around his mouth. "Mount up, gentlemen. Time to take this party on the road."

"Aw, we didn't get the centerfold naked yet," someone yelled from the corner.

"Bring her with us," Hayden shouted. He'd designed the "lady" and commissioned Greg to create her.

The group left the bar with a partially balloon-clad cardboard centerfold tucked under Derek's arm. He stashed her in the far back of the Tracker.

"Push that down so I don't get a ticket," Greg ordered, after looking in the rearview mirror and discovering a wardrobe malfunction had uncovered one breast. The last thing he needed was some sort of obscenity violation.

That would go over well for a guy who worked with kids.

A guy whose new nonprofit needed funding.

As they pulled out of the bar's parking lot, Greg glanced in the direction that would take him to Shannon's.

Hayden twisted in the passenger seat and slugged him in the arm. "Knock it off. No pining until Sunday. Tomorrow, we sell Jeremy into bondage to our big sister. Tonight, we party and mourn the loss of another bachelor."

From the backseat, Derek and Finn added their agreement.

Greg rubbed his shoulder, where a knot was undoubtedly forming. He wasn't in the mood to party.

And he was mourning that tomorrow he'd attend Elke's wedding stag, when he'd anticipated being there with Shannon.

With a ring on her finger, and him the next Hawkins in line to try to avoid a groom-napping by the women.

"I FEEL SILLY," Shannon admitted to the kitchen full of women. They'd spent the early evening gathering the pieces for her costume, and now that she had it on, she wasn't so sure this was a good plan.

Mysterious Lady O—she'd refused to tell them what the *O* stood for—wore a black corset with white lacing and tiny, off-the-shoulder gauzy sleeves, a short black skirt slit up the side, fishnet stockings, thigh-high boots, a flat-top black hat and a short black cape.

Along with a mask, of course. All superheroes wore masks. Shannon had borrowed SuperKid's mask from her dresser for the final piece of the costume.

"You don't look silly, honey. You look sexy as hell," Lydia said.

"Mom." Bethany, the oldest daughter, rolled her eyes.

"Well, she does. When a woman is trying to entice a man back, she needs to use every weapon in her arsenal. And sex is a powerful weapon. Your brother would have to be blind and castrated to ignore her in that outfit."

Shannon's face heated while everyone else burst out laughing.

Lydia patted her cheek. "Don't be embarrassed. I've had twelve children, and contrary to what they sometimes like to believe, not one of them came from a cabbage patch."

"They're on the move," Cathy announced from the table, where she had her laptop open. "They're leaving the second bar now."

Everyone clustered around her, watching the blip on the screen. "This is great," Elke said. "We don't have to run all over Erie trying to find them. We've got to remember this GPS thing in the future."

"I don't think this will work again." Bethany shook her head. "Next time they'll be checking all the vehicles for planted bugs."

"Not if we don't tell them," Shannon said slyly. "Mysterious Lady O has superpowers—or at least really great superhero toys—that let her track the man she loves. Right?"

Lydia chuckled. "I like how you think."

"It's only a few minutes after nine." Kara, the youngest of the Hawkins clan and one-half of the twin set, pointed at the clock hanging over the doorway. "Elke, he's your groom. Do we intercept now, or let them party longer?"

"I think we can let them go a little longer. Jeremy promised me he wasn't going to drink that much anyway."

Lydia snorted. "That's what they all say. That's what your father said, and he got shitfaced. Believe me, he paid for it."

"And thus gave rise to a family tradition," Elke intoned. "The kidnapping of the groom from the bachelor party."

"Wait a minute." Cathy leaned closer to the screen. "They're heading out of town on Route 19."

"What? Oh, that's so against the rules." Lydia grabbed a pair of glasses from beside the napkin holder in the center of the table, and perched them on the end of her nose so she could see the computer.

"Those cheaters," Elke said. "I'll bet I know where they're headed. Jeremy's family has a cabin down toward Canadohta Lake."

Judy, focused on nursing her two-month-old son, piped up. "We'd have never found them there, seeing as they're not supposed to leave Erie. Good thing you're here, Shannon. They're in for a big surprise. I'm sure they think they're in the clear."

"Elke, you're staying here on babysitting duty—it's bad luck for the groom to see the bride. Judy, you get to stay and help her since you're sort of tied up at the moment," Lydia instructed.

Ryan, along with Derek's kids and Judy's three-year-old, was watching a DVD in the family room. When Shannon had peeked in before donning her costume, Katie had been snuggled up alongside Ryan, whose eyelids had been drooping.

It had been a long and emotionally taxing day for both boy and aunt.

And she still had to convince Greg she deserved another chance.

She shivered. What if it didn't work? What if she'd already lost him? What if he'd learned as much from her as she'd learned from him, and had already let her go?

No more thinking that way. You will fight until he sur-renders. Life couldn't be so cruel as to only give her back half of the Super Duo who'd come to mean every-thing to her.

"The rest of you, let's roll," Lydia ordered. "We've got men to surprise and a groom to kidnap."

RUSTIC WASN'T THE WORD to describe Jeremy's family cabin. Though made of exposed logs with chinked walls, rustic ended there. Besides electricity and running water, the huge place had a fully furnished kitchen, satellite TV, and best of all, with the steamy heat outside—why Elke wanted to get married in the be-ginning of August was beyond Greg—central air.

This was Greg's idea of a cabin in the woods.

Finn pulled a glass dish of seven-layer dip from the oven and set it on the counter serving as their buffet. Several containers of wings—one garlic and butter, the other a mild version of Finn's hot wings—were already picked over.

Coolers with various beverages formed the lower buffet, lined up against the base of the counter penin-sula.

The French doors that led out to the deck opened and closed on a regular basis, letting in a blast of sticky air each time.

In the living room, a bunch of guys who wouldn't have passed a Breathalyzer test were trying their skill at driving a virtual race car, with results that evoked howls of laughter from those watching.

Jeremy's brother poked Greg in the shoulder with the tip of a beer bottle. "Greg. There's a pair of masked, caped chicks at the front door, asking for you."

"Masked, caped chicks?" Greg groaned. "My stalker fans. I've got to figure out how they find me. Usually they only show up in public places."

"If these are stalkers, I gotta get me some."

Greg headed for the front door, Jeremy's brother, as well as two of his own—Finn and Hayden—on his heels.

"Ladies, come in. Don't stand out there on the porch," boomed another male voice as they approached the foyer. Jeremy's dad escorted the women in.

The cars on the screen slowed and smashed into each other as the men turned their attention to the two women in the house.

The quality of his stalkers had greatly improved, from beer-bellied frat boys to a woman who exuded sensuality.

The woman who hung back wore black jeans beneath her cape. She had a small video camera in her hand. Both of them wore masks.

But the one headed in his direction...

Thigh-high boots under a slit skirt and short cape...fishnet stockings. She kept her head down, a broad-brimmed hat hiding her face except for the tip of her chin.

She tossed her cape over her shoulders, and the testosterone level in the cabin shot through the roof. Hums of male appreciation filled the room.

Above the skirt, she wore a formfitting black corset, creating rounded swells of creamy breasts that made Greg's fingers twitch. Part of him swelled in response, triggering a wave of guilt.

But dammit, she was hot.

He was in love with Shannon, not dead. Only a dead man wouldn't respond to this woman.

Jeremy sidled up to him. "Elke's going to kill me if

she finds out we had a stripper," he whispered harshly, eyes glued on the woman's form. "And you know someone will blab. Get rid of her!"

"I didn't hire a stripper. Talk to Hayden," Greg murmured out of the side of his mouth.

"Don't blame me," Hayden said from behind him. "It's not my doing. I might bend some of the rules, but not the no-strippers rule. I like my nuts right where they are."

The woman's head snapped up, and her eyes flashed behind the mask. She propped her hands on her hips, which only drew more attention to her curves.

There was something about her...

"Oh, for crying out loud. I'm not deaf, and I'm not a stripper!"

That voice... "Shannon?" Stunned, Greg took a step toward her.

She nodded. Which made her breasts jiggle. The central air couldn't keep up with the rising temperature in the room. He wanted to tuck the cape around her, sheltering her from the predatory stares of every man in the room.

"Yes, it's me. I have something I need to tell you."

Hayden chuckled behind him. He nudged Greg. "Here comes the groveling," he said so softly Greg barely heard him. "Told you. Still, she's so hot, I might have suspended my code and gone crawling back. Way to go, Gory."

Greg swiveled to glare at his younger brother.

Shannon cleared her throat. "I stand before you a changed woman. I was wrong."

"Somebody alert the media! A woman admits she was wrong," hollered one of Jeremy's friends who'd just come in from the deck.

Someone—it might have been Derek, but Greg couldn't be sure—elbowed the guy in the stomach.

"Sorry about that," Greg said. "You were saying?"

She twisted the edge of the cape around her finger. "Without you, everything is black and white. There's no color. No joy. No surprises, no fun. No one to share my good news with. I wanted to call you today so bad when Ryan came home."

"I heard about that. Congratulations. I'm really happy for both of you." Greg's pulse pounded, and his hands grew clammy. Shannon was *here*. She'd come back to him.

"I pushed you away because I was too afraid of losing you, which was stupid. But I'd been doing it for years. And I was already hurting over Ryan.

"I guess what I'm trying to say is, I'm sorry. I'll do whatever it takes to prove that to you. I'm not going to let go, either. If I have to stalk you, hound you, dress as a superhero to get you back, I'll do it."

A lump settled deep in Greg's throat. He didn't think he could speak if he tried.

Shannon took another step in his direction. "I love you, Greg Hawkins. Will you let me be your sidekick?"

He quickly closed the gap between them. He slid the clasp down the string and removed the hat, then the mask, letting both items drop to the floor. He framed her face with his hands, holding her tight. He stared into her eyes, saw tears make the dark brown shimmer. "Is that forever I see?"

She nodded. "Yes."

He lowered his head, pressing his lips to hers. She'd never tasted sweeter.

Hoots and hollers erupted around them. "Mine," he murmured in her ear. "Mine."

"Yes," she said through laughter and tears.

Greg let her go, wrapping the edges of the cape around her and holding it shut. "Sidekick, no. But I just might be in the market for a partner."

"Awww." "Oh, that's so sweet." "Awww." A cluster of women crowded in the front door.

Greg looked over Shannon's head. The blonde with the camera stopped recording, pulling off her wig and mask to reveal his baby sister, Kara. Behind her stood his mother and two more sisters.

"Busted, gentlemen," his mom said. "This bachelor party is officially over. Cathy, Bethany, gather up the unopened booze and put it in the trunk. We'll use the leftovers for the post-reception party tomorrow night. Dump the open bottles. Shannon, since my crystal ball tells me you may eventually become a member of this family, I'm assigning you to round up the groom. Consider it your initiation. And you—" she shook her finger at Hayden "—come here."

Hayden held up his hands, backing away as their mother advanced on him. But she reached out to grab him by the ear and tug.

Hayden bent over. "Ow, ow, Mom, come on. That hurts."

"You were in charge of the locations, am I right?"

"Y-yes, ma'am."

"So you broke the rules."

"No, there's a loophole... Erie County. We didn't leave Erie *County!* We wanted to win this time." Hayden's petulant voice faded as their mother dragged him out the front door, for a lecture on cheating, no doubt.

Greg knew who'd won this time.

He had. Hands down.

Cathy and Bethany started closing the coolers, and

the men, grumbling good-naturedly, tossed empties into a blue recycling can. The bottles clanked as they landed. Finn covered up the food with aluminum foil.

"How *did* you find us?" Greg asked Shannon, who hadn't been able to attend to her assigned task because he still gripped her cape.

She smiled. "Superhero secret. We have the most amazing toys, you know."

"Forget the toys," he said softly. "I just want to know if you'll wear this costume for me one night after Ryan goes to bed." He waggled his eyebrows at her. "I'm surprised you haven't caused a forest fire out here."

She laughed. "I think we might be able to arrange a costume…party. So, I'm forgiven?"

"Absolutely. I've missed you."

"I've missed you, too. I was afraid—" her voice trembled "—afraid I'd really lost you."

"You never lost me in the first place, sweetie. Not even for a minute. I was just giving you space."

"Don't give me space ever again, okay?"

"Okay." Greg offered her his arm. The last thing he needed was her wandering unescorted through so many males who'd gotten an eyeful of her assets. "Hey, you wanna go to a wedding with me tomorrow?"

"I'd love to."

"Great. Let's go kidnap the groom. It's family tradition, you know."

"Family tradition. I like the sound of that."

EPILOGUE

Twenty-six months later

"THIS IS THE LAST ONE, right?" Ryan asked. "No more after this?"

Though the October morning had been crisp, bright sunlight streamed through the hallway windows in the Erie County Courthouse. Just outside their designated courtroom, Shannon paused. She didn't have to look as far down to meet the eight-year-old's glance. He'd grown several inches in the past two years. "Last one. After today, it's really final."

Greg held out his fist. "Final victory. Not only have we won the battle, we've won the war."

The three of them butted knuckles, then headed into the courtroom, which was already overflowing with Hawkinses, from the old to the new. Elke and Jeremy's year-old boy was being passed from person to person, everyone smooching or pinching the baby's chubby cheeks. The family, big to start with, was growing by leaps and bounds. Today they would officially add another member.

Shannon awkwardly eased herself into a chair behind the table at the front of the room, then rubbed a palm over her ribs where her own soon-to-debut Hawkins kicked her. "Settle down in there," she said. "Let's have proper courtroom decorum, if you please."

Ryan giggled as he and Greg sat beside her. "Is the baby wearing a tie, like me?" To illustrate his lame joke, he flapped the end of the new superhero tie Greg had presented him at breakfast. The old one, packed away in a memory box on the top shelf of Shannon and Greg's closet, wasn't long enough anymore. The tie tack Lloyd and Patty had sent him in honor of the day, gold, with his new initials—all *four* of them—sparkled.

"No, the baby is wearing his birthday suit." Greg leaned over to caress Shannon's distended belly. Beneath his father's hand, the baby shifted, and Greg's blue eyes lit up.

Ryan covered his mouth and giggled again.

Cathy hustled into the room, slapping her briefcase on the table. "Sorry. I got held up with another case."

"You're here now," Greg said.

And just in time, too. They were told to rise as the judge entered the courtroom. Shannon heaved herself to her feet, then sighed in relief when she was allowed to sit again.

Judge Victoria Otis, the very judge who'd awarded Ryan's custody to Lloyd and Patty oh so long ago, beamed at them from her position on the bench. "We are here today to finalize the adoption of Ryan Schaffer by Gregory and Shenandoah Hawkins."

Ryan snickered. She glared at him. He cleared his throat and straightened in his chair, and the tarnished, crooked halo she'd grown to love blinked over his head.

Greg winked at her.

It had taken several rounds of legal battles, but the State had finally terminated Trevor's parental rights.

Since he'd been sentenced to life without parole for Willow's murder, his ability to care for Ryan wasn't even a question. And it had been decided in the child's best interest to allow Shannon and Greg to adopt him.

"Both parents understand that this is permanent? Once done, Ryan will legally be your son from this day forward."

Greg took Shannon's hand. She squeezed his fingers.

"We do, Your Honor," they said in unison.

And with the signing of a few documents, and the bang of the gavel, the judge declared it so.

With everything in her, Shannon knew Willow approved.

Ryan Lloyd Schaffer Hawkins—a big name for a still-not-that-big boy—leaped from his chair to wrap his arms around Shannon's neck. She held him tightly like she'd never let go, and the baby inside her squirmed. Greg joined them in a family hug while camera flashes lit the room.

"I'm never going to let you guys go," she told them, tears spilling down her face. "Damn hormones," she muttered, struggling to wipe her tears without releasing her husband and *son*.

"Picture time!" Cathy declared. "Go on."

The three of them posed with the judge, Ryan holding the adoption certificate.

"Let's take a family picture." Lydia, camera in hand, waved people into position. By the time everyone had been wrangled into place, Shannon's feet throbbed. Lydia passed the camera to the judge, who backed against the doors of the courtroom to get the whole crew in the frame.

"Everybody smile," Judge Otis ordered. "Say family!"

Greg's arm tightened around Shannon's pregnancy-distorted waist. She leaned her head on his shoulder, filled with a sense of contentment.

"Family!" sang a chorus of voices.

They'd need a *really* big sheet of paper to sketch this group. A picture-perfect family—okay, so maybe not *quite* perfect. But warts, foibles and quirks...

They were all hers.

*Harlequin is 60 years old, and Harlequin Blaze
is celebrating!
After all, a lot can happen in 60 years,
or 60 minutes…or 60 seconds!
Find out what's going down in Blaze's
heart-stopping new miniseries,
FROM 0 TO 60!
Getting from "Hello" to "How was it?"
can happen fast….*

*Here's a sneak peek of the first book,
A LONG, HARD RIDE
by Alison Kent.
Available March 2009.*

"IS THAT FOR ME?" Trey asked.

Cardin Worth cocked her head to the side and considered how much better the day already seemed. "Good morning to you, too."

When she didn't hold out the second cup of coffee for him to take, he came closer. She sipped from her heavy white mug, hiding her grin and her giddy rush of nerves behind it.

But when he stopped in front of her, she made the mistake of lowering her gaze from his face to the exposed strip of his chest. It was either give him his cup of coffee or bury her nose against him and breathe in. She remembered so clearly how he smelled. How he tasted.

She gave him his coffee.

After taking a quick gulp, he smiled and said, "Good morning, Cardin. I hope the floor wasn't too hard for you."

The hardness of the floor hadn't been the problem. She shook her head. "Are you kidding? I slept like a baby, swaddled in my sleeping bag."

"In my sleeping bag, you mean."

If he wanted to get technical, yeah. "Thanks for the loaner. It made sleeping on the floor almost bearable."

As had the warmth of his spooned body, she thought, then quickly changed the subject. "I saw you have a loaf of bread and some eggs. Would you like me to cook breakfast?"

He lowered his coffee mug slowly, his gaze as warm as the sun on her shoulders, as the ceramic heating her hands. "I didn't bring you out here to wait on me."

"You didn't bring me out here at all. I volunteered to come."

"To help me get ready for the race. Not to serve me."

"It's just breakfast, Trey. And coffee." Even if last night it had been more. Even if the way he was looking at her made her want to climb back into that sleeping bag. "I work much better when my stomach's not growling. I thought it might be the same for you."

"It is, but I'll cook. You made the coffee."

"That's because I can't work at all without caffeine."

"If I'd known that, I would've put on a pot as soon as I got up."

"What time *did* you get up?" Judging by the sun's position, she swore it couldn't be any later than seven now. And, yeah, they'd agreed to start working at six.

"Maybe four?" he guessed, giving her a lazy smile.

"But it was almost two..." She let the sentence dangle, finishing the thought privately. She was quite sure he knew exactly what time they'd finally fallen asleep after he'd made love to her.

The question facing her now was where did this relationship—if you could even call it *that*—go from here?

* * * * *

Cardin and Trey are about to find out that
great sex is only the beginning….
Don't miss the fireworks!
Get ready for
A LONG, HARD RIDE
by Alison Kent.
Available March 2009,
wherever Blaze books are sold.

REQUEST YOUR FREE BOOKS!

2 FREE NOVELS PLUS 2 FREE GIFTS!

HARLEQUIN®
Super Romance®

Exciting, emotional, unexpected!

YES! Please send me 2 FREE Harlequin Superromance® novels and my 2 FREE gifts (gifts are worth about $10). After receiving them, if I don't wish to receive any more books, I can return the shipping statement marked "cancel." If I don't cancel, I will receive 6 brand-new novels every month and be billed just $4.69 per book in the U.S. or $5.24 per book in Canada, plus 25¢ shipping and handling per book and applicable taxes, if any*. That's a savings of close to 15% off the cover price! I understand that accepting the 2 free books and gifts places me under no obligation to buy anything. I can always return a shipment and cancel at any time. Even if I never buy another book from Harlequin, the two free books and gifts are mine to keep forever.

135 HDN EEX7 336 HDN EEYK

Name	(PLEASE PRINT)

Address	Apt. #

City	State/Prov.	Zip/Postal Code

Signature (if under 18, a parent or guardian must sign)

Mail to the **Harlequin Reader Service**:
IN U.S.A.: P.O. Box 1867, Buffalo, NY 14240-1867
IN CANADA: P.O. Box 609, Fort Erie, Ontario L2A 5X3

Not valid to current subscribers of Harlequin Superromance books.

Want to try two free books from another line?
Call 1-800-873-8635 or visit www.morefreebooks.com.

* Terms and prices subject to change without notice. N.Y. residents add applicable sales tax. Canadian residents will be charged applicable provincial taxes and GST. Offer not valid in Quebec. This offer is limited to one order per household. All orders subject to approval. Credit or debit balances in a customer's account(s) may be offset by any other outstanding balance owed by or to the customer. Please allow 4 to 6 weeks for delivery. Offer available while quantities last.

Your Privacy: Harlequin is committed to protecting your privacy. Our Privacy Policy is available online at www.eHarlequin.com or upon request from the Reader Service. From time to time we make our lists of customers available to reputable third parties who may have a product or service of interest to you. If you would prefer we not share your name and address, please check here. ☐

HSR08R

Silhouette

SPECIAL EDITION

TRAVIS'S APPEAL

by *USA TODAY* bestselling author

MARIE FERRARELLA

Shana O'Reilly couldn't deny it—family lawyer
Travis Marlowe had some kind of appeal. But
as Travis handled her father's tricky estate
planning, he discovered things weren't what
they seemed in the O'Reilly clan. Would
an explosive secret leave Travis and Shana's
budding relationship in tatters?

Available March 2009
wherever books are sold.

The Inside Romance newsletter has a NEW look for the new year!

Same great content, brand-new look!

The Inside Romance newsletter is a FREE quarterly newsletter highlighting our upcoming series releases and promotions!

Click on the Inside Romance link on the front page of **www.eHarlequin.com** or e-mail us at insideromance@harlequin.ca to sign up to receive your FREE newsletter today!

You can also subscribe by writing to us at: HARLEQUIN BOOKS Attention: Customer Service Department P.O. Box 9057, Buffalo, NY 14269-9057

Please allow 4-6 weeks for delivery of the first issue by mail.

IRNNEW09

BRENDA JACKSON

TALL, DARK... WESTMORELAND!

Olivia Jeffries got a taste of the wild and reckless when she met a handsome stranger at a masquerade ball. In the morning she discovered her new lover was Reginald Westmoreland, her father's most-hated rival. Now Reggie will stop at nothing to get Olivia back in his bed.

Available March 2009 wherever books are sold.

Always Powerful, Passionate and Provocative.

HARLEQUIN *Super Romance*

COMING NEXT MONTH

Available March 10, 2009

BUNDLES of JOY

#1548 MOTHER TO BE • Tanya Michaels
9 Months Later

With a sizzling career in commercial real estate and an even hotter younger boyfriend, Delia Carlisle can't believe those two pink lines of a pregnancy test are real. She's forty-three, for Pete's sake! Suddenly Delia's not just giving birth to a baby—*everything* in her life is about to change....

#1549 CHILD'S PLAY • Cindi Myers
You, Me & the Kids

Designer Diana Shelton is not what principal Jason Benton expects when he commissions a playscape for his school. Even though he falls instantly for her—pregnancy and all—getting involved complicates this single dad's life...until he discovers love can be as simple as child's play.

#1550 SOPHIE'S SECRET • Tara Taylor Quinn
Shelter Valley Stories

For years Duane Konch and Sophie Curtis have had a secret affair. That works for them—given their difference in ages and his social status. Then Sophie gets pregnant. And now she must choose between the man she loves and the child they've created.

#1551 A NATURAL FATHER • Sarah Mayberry

Single, pregnant and in need of a business partner is not what Lucy Basso had planned. Still, things look up when hottie Dominic Bianco invests in her company. It's just too bad she can't keep her mind *on* business and *off* thoughts of how great a father he might be.

#1552 HER BEST FRIEND'S BROTHER • Kay Stockham
The Tulanes of Tennessee

Pregnant by her best friend's brother? No, this isn't happening to Shelby Brookes. That crazy—unforgettable—night with Luke Tulane was their little secret. But no way can it remain a secret now. Not with Luke insisting they meet at the altar in front of everyone!

#1553 BABY IN HER ARMS • Stella MacLean
Everlasting Love

Widow Emily Martin loves having a newborn in her arms—her own babies in the past and now her grandchild. It's all about new life...although that's a phrase she's been hearing far too often from her children, who say *she* needs to start living again. And then she finds eleven love letters from her husband....

HSRCNMBPA0209